P9-DDB-673

River Forest Public Library
735 Lathrop Avenue
River Forest, IL 60305
708-366-5205
July 2023

I'M NOT HERE
TO MAKE
FRIENDS

ANDREW YANG

Quill Tree Books
An Imprint of HarperCollinsPublishers

Quill Tree Books is an imprint of HarperCollins Publishers.

Copyright © 2023 by Andrew Yang
All rights reserved. Printed in the United States of America.
No part of this book may be used or reproduced in any manner
whatsoever without written permission except in the case of
brief quotations embodied in critical articles and reviews. For
information, address HarperCollins Publishers,
195 Broadway, New York, NY 10007.
www.epicreads.com

Library of Congress Control Number: 2022948403
ISBN 978-0-06-322327-1

Typography by Kathy H. Lam
23 24 25 26 27 LBC 5 4 3 2 1

First Edition

FOR MS. CROWELL.
MY JOURNEY TO WRITING THIS BOOK
BEGAN IN YOUR CLASSROOM.

SABINE

AT THE TOP OF THE HILL, I PAUSE TO ENJOY MY LAST MOMENTS OF unobserved existence. In front of me stands the house that I saw in the pictures—slate walkways, gleaming white walls, palm trees shooting out of the yard like fireworks. The sight fills me with both excitement and dread.

Every year, thousands of high schoolers apply for a spot on *Hotel California*. Out of all of them, only six are chosen. Out of all of them, the showrunners have chosen *me*—little old Sabine Zhang, straight outta Moline, Illinois; Quad Cities, rep till I die. I spent all spring in nervous anticipation for the show, and I even took my finals early so I could fly out to Southern California in time for the start of shooting. Now that I'm really here, I can't help but wonder if I've bitten off more than I can chew. But it's too late to turn back.

Once I'm inside, the cameras will be recording my every move. Every moment, waking or sleeping, could make it into the final cut. I have to be on my A game.

I cross the yard, push open the front door, and check into the Hotel California.

I never thought I'd end up on reality TV. At least, not on the kind of wine-fueled, sun-soaked, *Love Island*–meets–*The Bachelorette*–meets–*Survivor* reality shows that most people know about. I'm not used to that level of attention—most of the people at my school don't know that I exist. Or if they do know me, they'll think of the eye shape, the AP classes, and the last name at the back of the alphabet, and that's it.

But *Hotel California* is different. For one thing, it's not on ABC or Disney+ or Netflix, where everyone can watch it. At my house, we get it from the fifteen-dollar cable package that you sign up for at the Vietnamese supermarket. It plays after the syndicated anime from the nineties, and before the budget K-dramas from the early two thousands.

For another thing, it's not really about dating and drama and voting people off the island. Actually, it's pretty relaxing to watch. Six high schoolers spend four weeks living in a beautiful house somewhere in California. And sure, two of them might go on a date, or even make out in the basement, and sure, there'll be a couple of fights over dirty dishes. But mostly they just hang around the house, talking about their lives, what they're afraid of, what their hometowns are like.

The thing about the show is, all of the contestants are Asian.

They don't make a big deal out of it in the show intro or on the website, but the show is on an *ethnic* network, after all—they know who their target audience is. Because of the casting, watching the show is like getting a window into a miniature utopia, where being Asian is about more than just not being white.

Most of the people on the show seem to be used to it: they're from LA, or New York, or the Bay Area, places where you're barely even a minority. But when you come from a town like Moline, in the cornfields-and-tractors part of Illinois, that kind of thing means a lot.

Enough that in the spring of my junior year of high school, the unthinkable occurred: I applied to be on the show. My friend Em helped me shoot my audition videos, which mostly featured the two of us goofing off at the mall. And yes, I told her that I was applying as a joke, but after I sent off my application, I couldn't stop imagining myself getting picked, getting on a plane to California, being a part of that place. I wanted it. I dreamed about it.

And then those dreams came true.

In the foyer, I take off my shoes. Mine are the only ones there, which means I'm the first to arrive. The season premiere always features the same opening: new cast members showing up to the house one by one, awkwardly introducing themselves, until the group is complete.

I wasn't expecting to be first. But maybe it's a good thing, seeing as I'm still a little sweaty from lugging my suitcase up the hill. I figure I've got about five minutes to dry off before the next person comes.

I shuffle into the living room, and it's eerily quiet. I feel like the audience is watching me already, even though the show won't air for months. As expected, the house is stunning. The ceilings are high, the interior is flooded with natural light, and little decorative touches—a mirror in the shape of a starburst, a pair of fragrant houseplants, a Georgia O'Keeffe lily painting—make it feel classy and elegant. Whoever actually lives here probably spends a lot of time sipping wine and musing on the meaning of art in the age of meme-able reproduction.

In the living room, I'm forced to choose a spot on the empty L-shaped couch, which feels vaguely like a personality quiz: extroverts in the middle, introverts on the ends. I go with the end cushion on the short part of the L and try not to think too hard about what that says about me. For optimal sweat elimination, I close my eyes and try to move as little as possible, hoping that my metabolism will slow down and my body temperature will drop.

After what feels like an eternity, I hear the sound of the front door opening again. Instantly, my heart rate spikes back up, and a blast of heat radiates from my chest. So much for not sweating. I give myself a final once-over to make sure I'm not, I don't know, somehow not wearing pants or something. Then I sit up straight, paste a smile onto my face, and wait for my first housemate to come in.

"Hi! I'm Chris."

Chris, it turns out, is an almost unreasonably handsome guy. He flashes me a thousand-megawatt smile that I could swear I've seen before—in my dreams (*ba-dum-tss*). Also, he's wearing one of those skintight sports-material T-shirts, which shows off his honestly *very* nice arms.

"I'm Sabine," I croak out. "I'm from Illinois."

My throat has unexpectedly clogged up since I first sat down on the couch, so my voice sounds all phlegmy. Gross.

"That's a cool name," Chris replies, as he sits on the couch. He takes a seat two cushions away from me. Polite, but still friendly.

"Thanks. My mom used to watch *Sabrina the Teenage Witch* to learn English. But she picked 'Sabine' to make it easier for my relatives in China to pronounce."

"Nice," Chris says. There's an awkward silence as we both search for conversation topics.

"So, are you a big fan of the show?" I ask.

He shrugs. "Never watched it before. I don't really watch reality shows."

"So why'd you decide to do it, then?"

"My agent booked it for me. This is my first time doing TV."

Huh. It never even occurred to me that people might be doing this show so they could actually get into Hollywood. I had always assumed that the participants were people like me, fans living out their little dreams.

Chris explains that he wants to be an actor. Given how small

Hotel California is, I feel like he's taking the long route to success. But what do I know?

He pulls out his phone to show me clips from his past gigs: he was an extra in a commercial for laundry detergent, he did a magazine ad for chewing gum, and he's in some stock images of a high school class, smiling as his hand hovers over his notebook.

"So what's your ideal role?" I ask. Based on his muscles and his suntanned skin, I could see him as the hunky jock type who's the first to die in a horror movie, or maybe the bad guy in the next installment of *Fast & Furious*.

"I do have this idea for a movie in my head," Chris says, scratching his chin. "It'd be me and my little sister, living as thieves in a postapocalyptic New York. Not my real little sister, obviously. But, um, yeah, we'd probably, like, steal from the rich and make getaways on our motorcycle. And I'm, like, trying to make her believe in the better version of the world that I knew as a kid, the one she never got to experience, because she was born after the revolution, or the pandemic, or whatever. And also I die at the end, which makes the audience cry, but not before I leave her with hope. Something like that."

He finishes his synopsis with a shrug and a sheepish chuckle, like he's embarrassed to be oversharing. For a hot guy, he seems surprisingly self-conscious. In a weird way, this gives me confidence. It'd be no fair to show up to a lo-fi show like this with zero anxiety. If we're all nervous, then maybe I'll be okay.

"I think that's cool," I say. "I'll watch it."

Chris smiles, and I breathe an internal sigh of relief. Despite my choppy introduction, I'm pretty sure I just knocked out a good fifteen seconds of screen time without vomiting or crying. It's a start.

The front door opens again. The third housemate to arrive is a cute girl wearing patterned socks and oversize, wire-frame glasses. Based on her clothes, I get a distinctly artsy vibe.

"Oh my gosh!" she says, when she walks into the living room. She fans herself, and for a second I think she's about to tear up. But instead, she comes over and gives us each a hug.

"Sorry, I'm really overwhelmed," she says. "You both look radiant. I'm so grateful to be here with you!"

She slots herself into the crook of the L, right between me and Chris. I make a mental note—classic extrovert.

"I'm Mari, by the way," she says. "I'm from LA. Not too far from here, actually. But this is my first time in Palm Springs."

Chris and I both introduce ourselves. Chris mentions that he's from San Jose, and Mari's eyes light up.

"Aha, I knew it! You look like a NorCal Asian. I have a question for you. Do you guys really say 'hella' a lot?"

Chris shrugs. "We say it. Maybe not a lot."

"And what about the drink with the chewy stuff at the bottom? What do you call that?"

"Boba?"

"Oh. Really? My friend told me you call it 'PMT.' Like, pearl milk tea? Guess that one is fake, though."

Because of our seating arrangement, Mari and Chris are practically facing each other, while I'm leaning in awkwardly, trying to interpret their bewildering terminology. I've never met a NorCal Asian, or any type of non-Moline Asian, for that matter. I'm a little jealous of their instant West Coast affinity. When Mari asks where I'm from, I feel like her eyes glaze over at my answer. She nods politely, but she doesn't ask me about any Midwest Asian slang.

The next housemate to show up is another boy, and once again, he's weirdly way too hot to be on this show. Compared to Chris, he has more of a brooding pretty-boy vibe, with sultry eyes, a long, lean frame, and chiseled cheekbones. His name is Grant, and I'm pretty sure that he's—

"You're half, right?" Mari asks.

As Grant settles onto the couch next to Chris, he has a bemused grin on his face that says, *I've heard that one before.*

"Half what?" he asks, raising an eyebrow.

Mari frowns and shifts uncomfortably in her seat. "You know, half Asian."

Grant pauses for a moment, as if deciding whether or not he'll deign to answer. Our first moment of tension. I feel bad for Mari, who seems to have a lot of feelings but not much of a filter. It's normal for the first episode to feature some questions about ethnicity, but it usually isn't this blunt. Mari is dangerously close to *But where are you from?* territory.

But then Grant grins. "Yeah, I know, I'm just messing with

you," he says. "My mom's Taiwanese, and my dad's Nigerian." He pauses to let that sink in before adding, "Which makes me a future doctor, if I know what's good for me."

That gets a laugh out of all of us. I notice that Grant has a touch of British in his accent, which comes out in the way he says "few-chuh doc-tuh." Once again, why is everyone so hot? Not to get too shallow about it, but past seasons of this show featured your ordinary sixes and sevens, maybe the occasional eight. Grant is, like, a twelve. It seems like a total one-eighty to suddenly turn the new season of this show into a Uniqlo photo shoot.

The doorbell rings, and we all go quiet. So far, we've all been walking right in, but this new housemate must not have gotten the memo. I feel a sudden prickle of dread, a premonition that someone monumental is about to join us. Just as Grant points to the foyer and mouths, *Should one of us . . . ?*, we hear the door open. I sit stone still, waiting for the new person to come into the living room. And when she does, I'm not disappointed.

Into my life walks the most stunning girl I have ever seen. Perfect hair, pearly skin, absurdly symmetrical facial features that reach straight into my soul and snatch away every ounce of my self-esteem. Instinctively, my eyes snap onto the guys. Yup, they're staring. Grant's mouth is even hanging slightly open, as if he's spotted a rare species of jungle cat.

The new girl doesn't wait for an invitation to drop onto the couch. Even though there's hardly any room, she squeezes into the crook of the L, between Mari and Chris, which I suppose makes her an *Inception*-style extrovert-within-an-extrovert. She puts her head on Mari's shoulder and unleashes a dramatic sigh.

"The traffic was so. Frickin'. Bad. I swear I was in the cab for two hours, and the driver would *not* stop talking."

"There, there," Mari says, patting the girl's head. I'm confused. Do these girls already know each other?

"It took two hours?" I ask. The cab from the Palm Springs bus station to the house should have been twenty minutes at most.

"From LAX," the girl murmurs, without lifting up her head. "And my flight was delayed. Not that that's a surprise, coming out of LaGuardia."

I recognize the name of the airport: the new girl is from New York. Maybe that explains the instant affection with Mari. The two of them have already identified each other as members of the same upper class of coastal Asian female elite.

The new girl's name is Yoona. She lives in Manhattan, and she wants to be a doctor. When she says this, Grant's eyes light up. I don't blame him, either. It's like Yoona was created in a lab to be the total package.

"We're going to have to commiserate at some point," Grant says. "I have to tell you about the time my mom took me for an MRI, just so I could ask the radiologist for advice on med school."

"No way, you too?" Yoona puts a hand over her mouth in mock surprise.

"That's what siblings are for," Mari adds. "My older sister got into Johns Hopkins, and now all the pressure's off. Liberal arts degree, here I come!"

"Doesn't work if you're the oldest," Chris says, shaking his head. "Then if you fail, you're an extra-big disappointment."

It's like the queen bee showed up, and the whole hive is suddenly buzzing. Yoona, Grant, and Mari are dropping quips in rapid fire, and even Chris is talking more. I seem to be the only one who doesn't have much to say.

At one point, Yoona looks at me with an eyebrow raised, as if challenging me to show her what I've got. Gulp. I already feel like I'm under her thumb.

Finally, the last house member arrives. His name is Danny, and like the other boys, he's tall and looks like he plays sports. When he sits down next to me and shakes my hand, I can see that he's really good-looking, but at this point I barely notice. Call it sensory overload.

Suddenly, the coffee table that we're sitting around comes to life. Out of the table pops a speaker shaped like a lava lamp, with a band of neon-blue light ringing the top.

"Welcome to *Hotel California*," the lava lamp says. It (she?) has a deep, husky drawl that I find oddly menacing. The blue light flickers along with the rise and fall of its voice. We all go dead silent.

"This summer, we're taking our show to the next level. This season will be nothing like what you've seen before."

Next level? Nothing like what I've seen before? The whole

reason I came on this show is because I thought it would be *exactly* like what I've seen before.

"In previous seasons, show participants were free to spend their time at the Hotel California however they wished. This season, there will be two new requirements. One, weekly outings. Once per week, you may invite one other guest for an exciting activity outside of the house. A film crew will accompany you."

Aka mandatory dates. A chill runs down my spine. I'm not too sure about this dating angle. So far in my life, I have exactly zero experience with going on dates. Especially not with cameras rolling.

"You will also leave the house once per week to participate in a weekly challenge," the speaker continues. "These weekly challenges will have you forming teams and competing for ten-thousand-dollar cash prizes."

Hold up. This is totally new. The whole point of *Hotel California* was that it didn't run its cast members through some high-concept social experiment, but rather depicted their actual, daily struggles. Except now, it's been turned into a dating contest–slash–game show, populated with obscenely attractive boy candy to boot. I mean, yes, the prize money is cool and could help me pay for college, but I can't help but feel that this is going against the spirit of the thing.

"The first challenge will take place at the end of the week. Before that, you will all be required to go on an outing, to build team chemistry."

Well, at least the boys are practically required to ask us on outings. I don't have to worry about not being asked.

"That's all," the speaker finishes. "Let the third season of *Hotel California* begin."

The speaker drops back into the coffee table, and my housemates start to applaud. They're exchanging excited looks, like this lava lamp just delivered the best news they've gotten all summer. None of them seems at all put off by the new rules.

This show suddenly doesn't feel anything like the *Hotel California* that I know. In fact, it feels a lot like an Asian version of your standard, big-time network reality TV show. The only thing that seems familiar to me about it is . . . me. Chris said that he hadn't even watched this show before. Could it be that the network people behind the show did some national survey of Asian grocery stores and found that what the people there want is no different from what the viewership of any other TV channel wants? It feels like I'm the victim of an extraordinarily elaborate prank, or I got off the plane at the wrong part of the multiverse. I don't know what's going on.

But I do know one thing.

This is not what I signed up for.

YOONA

OF COURSE MY MOM WASN'T GOING TO LET ME HAVE A PEACEFUL
last morning at home. I already had to get up early for the
eight a.m. flight, so it's not like I was expecting to feel my best.
But I thought that maybe since her only daughter was leaving for
the summer, she might be able to hold the lectures in. I forgot
about Murphy's Law. I should have known that if I was leaving
New York on June 17, shit was bound to go down the night
before. While I was sleeping, the New York Korean grapevine
was lighting up with hot gossip about Jessica Um, last year's "it"
girl, she of the ten AP classes and 1600 SATs. She dropped out of
Harvard, and not the good kind of dropping out, where you start
the next Facebook or whatever. Rumor has it that she got kicked
out for plagiarizing an essay. And there's nothing my mom loves
more than a scandal.

"I knew it. I just knew it!" my mom tells me, as I brush my
teeth in front of the mirror. "That girl always had a bad side. She

thought she was better than everyone. People like that have no respect for the rules."

There's no use reminding my mom that last year, she was practically frothing at the mouth to congratulate Jessica at church; she ambushed her in the back pew, shoved a gift into her hands (a watch from Anthropologie, because she insisted on spending over one hundred dollars), and begged her to share her admissions secrets.

"Don't be like her," my mom continued. "It's better to go to a state school with your head held high than be a cheater. That shows you what kind of family they are. If you want to know where she got it from, that's no secret. Her mom, Mrs. Um? Always smiling, but such a nasty woman in her heart!"

I want to laugh at the way my mom goes all out over gossip. But she doesn't like it when I do that. I clear my throat and nod so she'll see how seriously I'm taking her advice.

"Remember when you get to your television show, you're representing the family. Don't be too loud, or too rude. Don't be a show-off. But also, take a cab from the airport, not the bus, and make sure everyone knows about it."

"Okay, okay."

"Give me a call when you get to the house. Just so I know you arrived safely. After that, twice a week is fine. No need to talk every day."

"We'll be hanging out when I first get there. I'll call you in the morning. And once a week should be plenty. I'm not even going to be gone for that long."

She lets out a sigh, like I'm being difficult. Then her eyes widen, as if she's suddenly seeing me for the first time. "That's what you're wearing? Sweatpants? Go change!"

I'm wearing my comfy clothes, like I always do for long flights. It's definitely no big deal, but with my dear umma, it's always one thing or another.

"I'll change after I land. What do you want me to do, wear a dress on the plane?"

"Go change now. Don't be so careless! It's important. Especially if you're going to be on TV."

"Give it a rest, Mom!" I snap. Not that that's going to get me anywhere. My mom always has to have the last word.

"You have such a bad temper. Like your father. You better control it, otherwise your housemates won't like you."

So yeah. Now I'm irritated. I'd like to tell my mom that this is exactly why I decided to ditch New York for the summer—so that I wouldn't have to get lectured every five minutes. When I'm at home, every little thing I do wrong gets pointed out, corrected, from the way I chew my food, to the way I hang up my clothes, to the tiny drops of water that I leave on the bathroom mirror after washing my face.

Yeah, sure, table manners and being clean are important and all that. But it's the implication. It's the way my mom slips in those little digs about my temper, or my attitude, like these tiny little slips in discipline are evidence of my essential badness coming through.

The flight to the West Coast is unbearably long, and when we touch down at LAX, I'm cranky and slightly nauseous.

I step out of the terminal and get blasted by the dry heat. Whoa. This is new. I feel like the air is actively sucking the moisture out of my pores. My skin is not going to do well here.

It's still cool to be in LA, though. The land of enchantment. The palm trees looming over arrival pickups feel almost kitschy, like going to Hawaii and immediately putting on a lei and drinking out of a coconut.

I call a cab, toss my suitcase into the trunk, and collapse into the back seat. The driver asks where to, and I tell him Palm Springs. We pull out of LAX and onto the highway.

I keep my eye out for familiar scenery—the Hollywood sign, maybe, or at least some skyscrapers. But there's nothing outside of the window but squat office buildings and concrete. I get bored and start picking at a nub of dried toothpaste stuck to my sweatpants.

Wait a second: I'm still wearing my sweatpants. I forgot to change.

"Hey, would you mind stopping at a hotel or something?"

He raises an eyebrow. "Here? I thought you wanted Palm Springs."

"I want to stop for a couple minutes. I need to change outfits before I get there."

"Nothing around here but motels. If you want a big hotel, with a bathroom in the lobby, I can take you downtown."

It feels a little silly to make a detour just to change clothes. For a moment, I consider showing up to the house as I am, no matter what my mom says about looking careless. But she has a point. Anyways, if I wear sweatpants to meet my housemates, I'm going to be thinking about how much shit she'd be giving me. In the end, I'm still my mother's daughter.

Thirty minutes later, we pull up to a fancy hotel. Inside, I make a dash for the bathroom, studiously avoiding eye contact with any staff. I change as quickly as I can, fearing that at any moment, one of the receptionists will barge in and demand to see my room key. But no one asks me any questions, even when I emerge from the bathroom wearing my dress.

On the drive out of downtown, we get stuck in traffic. The six-lane highway turns into a gigantic parking lot, and the driver's GPS map shows a solid line of red all the way out of the city. I guess this stereotype about LA is true.

"Better get comfortable. We'll be here for a while," he says. He lights up a cigarette and rolls down the window.

About a half hour into the ride, I make the mistake of sharing that I'm on my way to shoot a TV show. Suddenly, the driver is interested. He starts talking about his own acting career, how he almost got on an episode of *Law & Order*, how Hollywood did him wrong. And yes, he may have flopped, and yes, he may be driving cabs now, but he's getting into stocks and cryptocurrency, and he's going to run this town someday soon. Meanwhile, the smell of cigarette smoke and exhaust is making me feel ill.

When we finally get to the house I'm about ready to claw my own eyes out. I still tip generously, though—my mom has taught me well. When he's finally gone, I take a deep breath. What a long morning it's been. And we're just getting started.

The house is *really* nice inside. Good thing, because I'm planning to spend plenty of time indoors, hiding from the sun.

Honeeey, I'm hooome, my dad's voice sounds out in my head. Every time he comes from Korea to visit, he yells out this phrase in his choppy English. He totally thinks that a cute greeting will make up for all the months of parenting he skips out on for his job.

In the living room, there they are, four of my fellow castmates. When I come in, they all stare at me. Guess it makes sense, because I'm wearing this dress, like it's picture day or something. Meanwhile, everyone else is wearing jeans. I probably come off as a try-hard. *Told you so, Mom.*

I plop myself down next to the cute girl in the glasses, and as I sink down, my body suddenly remembers how tired it is. Before I know it, my head is leaned against her shoulder, and I let out a sigh.

Out of the corner of my eye, I see the other girl staring at us, eyes narrowing. I glance at her, but she quickly looks away.

As we all start to converse, this girl, Sabine, is the only one who stays quiet. She looks distracted, maybe even annoyed. I make a joke about art history majors (that it's my mom's least-preferred major applied to her second least favorite), and Sabine is the only one who doesn't laugh, not even out of politeness. I wonder if she was put off by the entrance I made. I guess I can be overdramatic sometimes.

Last but not least, a third boy shows up to complete the cast. He comes into the living room wearing sunglasses and a backward hat. A closer look reveals that he has an earring, only in his right ear.

We quickly introduce ourselves, and he nods coolly. Only when Sabine makes room for him on the couch, and he sits down next to her, does he stick out a hand for her to shake.

"You can call me Danny," he says. With his other hand, he takes his hat off and runs a hand through his hair. There's a practiced nonchalance to these motions, like he cares very much about looking like he doesn't care.

Sabine flashes a smile, but then quickly goes back to looking distracted. I guess it's not just me that she's put off by—even with this cute, slightly douchey boy right in front of her face, she seems out of it. There must be something on her mind.

After the coffee table gives us a rundown of the show format, the six of us get up to check out the rest of the house. In the basement, there's a cozy playroom with a massive TV and multiple video game consoles. The couch down here is like an ocean, wide enough to roll around in, plush enough to sink into. If I know anything about reality shows, there will probably be more than one dramatic first kiss on this couch. For singles, there's also a cute papasan in the corner, suitable for solitary video gaming and/or crying.

We split up, boys and girls, to check out our rooms. The girls' room is decidedly cuter than the rest of the house. There's an abundance of round, fuzzy pillows, the perfect size for hugging into your chest. Opposite the door is a bay window overlooking the backyard, which I now notice has a swimming pool.

There's one thing that's noticeably absent from the room. Here, as in the rest of the house, there aren't any visible cameras. They must be here, somewhere, but even when I scan more carefully, I can't spot any. Maybe they're hidden inside the walls.

We pick our beds. Mari takes a bed by the window while Sabine and I take the top and bottom of a bunk bed, respectively. It's going to be interesting, sharing a room like this—something that I've never experienced before, being an only child.

"Hey, does something seem off?" Sabine asks. "All of these new rules about dating, and weekly challenges. Aren't they over-doing it?"

"What did you expect?" I ask.

"Nothing. That's the whole point of this show, that it's about ordinary life at a house. Have you seen the past seasons?"

Mari and I exchange puzzled looks. "Nope," Mari says. "I signed up for it at the mall. My parents sent me there to find a summer job. We're getting paid to be on the show, so technically I did what they asked."

I share the story of how I ended up here: I was in SoHo, shopping for clothes with my mom, when a woman stopped us in the street. She said that she was a talent scout, and that I'd be a perfect fit for a show that she was working on. My mom tried to shoo her away, but I chased her down and gave her my number. It felt like fate was gifting me a way out of the house.

Sabine looks horrified by our stories.

"So you guys had never even heard of *Hotel California* before signing up?" There's disapproval in her voice, like Mari and I haven't earned our right to be in the cast. It's not like this show is famous or anything—as I understand it, hardly anyone watches it. I wonder if *this* is what was bothering Sabine. She's seen the show before, and apparently the rest of us don't live up to her idea of a good cast.

I feel a little offended.

"I think it's weird that they'd make such a big change all of a sudden," she continues. "It's like they're trying to crank up the stereotypical reality show drama. And the boys. They're all so— like . . . like, weirdly . . ."

"Yummy?" Mari suggests. Sabine giggles nervously.

"Speaking of which, what do we think about *the men*?" I ask, smirking.

"Well, first of all, we need to talk about Chris," Mari says. "The one with the arms."

Sounds like Mari is the type of girl who likes to eat dessert before dinner. "He did seem sweet," I admit. "Kind of quiet, but in a good way."

"I think that's my type. I always go for the quiet ones."

"What about you, Sabine?" I ask.

Sabine looks flustered. She shakes her head and says, "I don't know, we'll see." She seems to have a slight mental block about commenting on the boys' appearance.

"It's okay to be disappointed, if you were attached to the old way of doing things," Mari says. "But maybe the changes will be fun."

"Sounds like an improvement to me," I say. "No point moping around about it."

"I'm not *moping*."

She definitely is, though, and the sooner she snaps out of it, the sooner we can all start leaning into the silliness, the indulgence of being on a reality show. Still, maybe I shouldn't have said it so directly. My mom would probably tell me off for being too blunt, if she were here. But luckily, she isn't—that's the whole point. I don't have to analyze every little thing that I do and figure out what it says about me.

I stayed home last summer, and that was a huge mistake. Spending every night cooped up in our hot, hot apartment, getting nitpicked for not putting the dishes away correctly, or walking with my toes pointed in too much—it was suffocating.

For once, it's nice to be with new people, to have no history to deal with, no reputation to overcome, no assumptions attached to the name "Yoona Bae." What happens in LA stays in LA. These few weeks are a blank canvas, and whatever silly fights, laughs, or drama we paint them with, once they're over we'll call it even and go home.

SABINE

IT'S NOT THAT MY HIGH SCHOOL HAS NO ASIANS. IN MY YEAR, there are ten of us; in the year below me, eleven; and in the year below that, a whopping fourteen. Enough for us to feel that we are not alone, but not enough for us to form groups, or have a presence in the school social scene. Instead, we are scattered throughout the student body—a few band kids, a few high achievers, a few athletes. Separate, and yet invisibly linked to each other by our eyes, our skin, and the vast continent inhabited by our ancestors.

And every so often, something happens to remind you, just in case you forgot, that you're different.

Take junior prom. My friend Em and I joked about it, but we weren't really planning on going. We had crushes, but no realistic leads on dates. Still, I held out a secret hope. Since middle school, I'd nurtured a couple of crushes on various boys, and in junior year one of them, Brock Fernandez, got seated next to me in Honors English. It was fate. With prom a couple of weeks away, I tried to flirt as best I could. Once, I even worked up the courage to tap him on the arm. For one glorious moment, crackling electricity rushed from his bicep into my hand. To my relief, he didn't pull away.

One day, I passed by Brock's locker and heard his friend talking. About me.

"What about that Asian chick who sits next to you?"

I stopped in my tracks. There was enough of a crowd in the hallway that they didn't notice me. I couldn't help but listen in.

"Sabine?" Brock said. I allowed myself to hear in his voice that he might be into it. My heart fluttered.

"Yeah, dude. She's totally into you. Trust me, I'm good at reading these things."

"I don't think so. She doesn't really talk to me."

"Dude, she is! You're not about it? She's kind of cute, for an Asian girl. You better get there before Ricky does."

Brock snickered, and my hopes were shattered into a million pieces. I slinked away before they could spot me.

The worst part was the joke about Ricky Lee. He was the only other Asian in our English class. The two of us weren't particularly close, but to Brock and his friend, we would always be lumped together by default, no matter how different we were. Not to mention that I'd been secretly dreaming of taking prom photos with Brock Fernandez, getting hundreds of likes. After that day, those dreams were just embarrassing.

So yeah, it's not like Moline is unbearable. I don't dream of dismantling the cheerleaders, or papering the walls with the photocopied pages of my Burn Book. But living there kind of feels like being a lion in a zoo. People have ideas about you from books or TV; they expect you to do one or two lion things—roar, show your teeth, tear up your hunk of meat—and that's it. If you try to do something else, no one sees it. It's like it doesn't count.

When I got picked to be on the show, I thought I'd finally gotten my chance to try out something different. Never mind my dreary origin story, I thought to myself. Going to a high school with a student body that was 2 percent Asian had stifled some of my shine, but it wouldn't hold me down forever. In the Hotel California, I would finally break free.

At least, that's what I thought.

Yoona, Mari, and I emerge from the girls' room together. In the living room, the boys are high-fiving and doing that handshake-into-one-arm-hug thing that boys do to express affection while still upholding the laws of masculinity.

"What are you guys so excited about?" Mari asks.

"The Pack Pact," Chris explains, grinning like he's announcing a scientific breakthrough. "We're going to meet in the mornings to do ab workouts. The girls are welcome, too."

"No thanks. I hate exercising," Yoona says.

"You know that's, like, the douchiest thing ever, right?" Mari asks.

Chris shrugs.

Mari raises an eyebrow, but the corners of her lips are twitching into a smile. She's clearly into Chris. I have to admit, I respect it. It takes a certain confidence to meet a guy as viscerally hot as he is and think, *I'm into him*, as opposed to, *I know he's out of my league, so, um, yeah, he's not my type.*

"All right, that's the last time we leave the boys alone," Yoona says. "Clearly, they're in need of adult supervision."

In the afternoon, we start to settle into the house. We play a few rounds of *Super Smash Bros.* in the playroom, then lounge by the pool under the afternoon sun. In the evening, we sit in the dining room to eat dinner together. There's at least one perk of the new changes to the show: the speaker announces that we can order whatever takeout we want. We get sushi, even the eel rolls and the overpriced sea urchin. Bon appétit.

"So why did you all decide to come on *Hotel California*?" Grant asks.

"Asking the big questions," Yoona says, raising an eyebrow.

I know my answer to Grant's question. But it would be pointless to keep bringing up the old version of the show. Yoona already said that I was moping; if I keep bringing it up, my housemates might start to realize that I'm the odd one out, the one person who got cast by the old rules.

"We have to make the most out of our time here, right?" Grant adds. "I want to know what you guys are about. Danny, you first."

"What am I about?" Danny rubs his chin. "I'm just about that life, I guess."

He sounds so earnest that I let out a chuckle. Grant, too, is looking at him with an expression like, *Seriously, dude?*

"That life? Anything in particular?" he asks.

"You know. That life. Being great. Doing me," Danny says, as if it's perfectly clear. His eyes snap onto mine, and for a brief second we're making eye contact. Boy, does he have nice eyes. I realize that I might have a thing for eyes. I feel my face warming up, and I quickly look away.

"It could be about working out, or school, or whatever. It's a mindset," Danny continues.

Grant looks slightly bemused, as if he's realizing this is the wrong audience for this question.

"I'm about those moments of transcendent humanity," Mari says. "There's this emotion that I get sometimes, where I suddenly feel so full, and so *human*. Like this one time, I was at the National Museum in Tokyo. I was looking at an ancient vase from prehistoric times. The placard said that the vase was used to store water, so it was purely functional. But on the surface of the vase were these patterns of lines and triangles. Just for decoration. And I thought, *This is what humans do*. Ever since we showed up on this earth, we've had this instinct to create beauty."

Yeah, I was totally right about the artsy thing.

There's a moment of silence as we all take in this verbose

answer. It's a hard one to follow up. Danny nods and says, "Damn, that's deep."

"What about you, Chris?" Mari asks. She takes the opportunity to gently tap him on the arm.

Chris scratches his chin. "I'm not sure. To be honest, it feels like there's a lot of pressure on me. This is the first time I've ever been able to book a TV role. A lot of people only ever get one shot at that. I have to find a way to prove myself, or I might not get another one. So I really want this to work out for me. I guess I'm not supposed to admit that, though."

He sounds unsure of himself, just like he did during that moment of self-consciousness that he had after telling me about his movie. I make a note to remember this about him, even though it's causing me serious cognitive dissonance.

"That's what I'm talking about," Grant says, nodding his approval. "Everyone has their thing. Even being 'about that life' is a thing. The question is, what's going to happen when you put those things together?"

"I want to hear Sabine's answer," Danny says.

Everyone looks at me. The room suddenly falls silent as they wait for my response.

"Well, I actually watch this show," I begin. "There aren't many Asians in my hometown, so I've never been around a group of just Asians before. Or no, I guess I have, when we sit alphabetically for assemblies, and I'm with the other Xs and Ys and Zs. Point is, there's not that many of us in Moline. So anyways, I thought it would be nice to, like . . . well . . . People at my school are—I mean, it's not like I have a problem with anyone at school, but . . ."

"Spit it out; you're among friends," Yoona says.

"I wanted to stand out more," I say quickly. "Not just for being Asian, which I already do. But for other stuff, too. I sometimes feel like people don't really see me."

I feel flustered, like I've been pushed into exposing a secret that I wasn't quite ready to share. Grant nods politely, like he's taking my answer and filing it away with the others: Mari, the floofy dreamer; Chris, the oldest child under pressure; and me, the girl from the Midwest with a boatload of insecurities.

After dinner, we clean up the table and start to wind down for the evening. I'm in the kitchen by myself, loading up the dishwasher, stewing a little bit over the way Yoona told me to "spit it out." She didn't make fun of Mari's answer, even though it was way more extra than mine. I would have been able to come up with something more eloquent if I hadn't been put on the spot. I know I'm being oversensitive, but a part of me still resents being called out.

"Hey."

The voice startles me, and I flinch. It's Danny. He chuckles at my reaction.

"Oh. Hi," I reply.

Danny comes into the kitchen to help me with the dishwasher.

"That was a cool answer you gave to Grant's question."

"Thanks," I say. I liked it when he said that he wanted to hear my answer. Between that and the handshake, at least there's one person who makes me feel comfortable. "Why did you want to hear what I had to say?"

He smiles. It's a cocky smile, the kind where the eyes look sly, like he's up to something. "You said you were from Illinois, right? I've never met an Asian person from the Midwest."

He's close enough that I can smell him. His scent is unexpectedly sweet, angelic: peaches and vanilla. I pour the dishwasher fluid into the dishwasher, and I have to focus hard not to accidentally spill any.

"My high school is like yours," he continues. "I go to a boarding school in New Hampshire. Two centuries of tradition, super Waspy."

"Sounds fun."

He laughs. "It's not that bad. I like the people. But there aren't many other brown dudes. So that thing you said, about standing out but not standing out? I felt that."

I'm tongue-tied, so I just nod and smile.

I turn on the dishwasher, and we go back out to the living room to rejoin our other housemates. Even though Danny and I were only together for about thirty seconds, I feel like he saw me the way I wanted to be seen. A halo of triumph ignites around my head. Finally, something at this house has gone right.

YOONA

I'M UPSTAIRS, ABOUT TO GO BRUSH MY TEETH, WHEN MY MOM
calls. I silence the ring and let her go to voice mail: I told her that
I didn't want to call her on my first night in the house. But then
she calls again, and I can practically picture her on the other end
of the line, gripping the phone, tapping her fingers on the table.
I pick up.

"Hang on a second, let me find a quiet place to take this," I say.

"Bae Yoona, do you know what you did? You threw your apple
core away in the bathroom! When I went in to wash my face: fruit
flies, everywhere! I don't think you're ready to live with room-
mates if you can't be clean."

Not even a *How's it going?* I rush out of the girls' room and
search around the second floor for some privacy.

"I am clean! And I'm a very good roommate!"

"You didn't even make your bed before you left. You call that
clean? And what about your dirty clothes? Are you throwing them
on the floor?"

"That's different! I do that stuff at home because it's my own room. Here, we have little laundry hampers that we can use. And I help with the dishes. I even wiped down the sink this evening after everyone else had already gone upstairs."

I finally end up in the supply closet at the end of the hall. I turn the light on, shut the door, and smoosh myself onto the floor next to the vacuum.

"Well, you better keep doing it," my mom says. "How is everything in the house? Do they have healthy food? You better not eat those Inside Out burgers every meal. You remember the Hwangs, the ones who moved from California? Their son always talked about that place."

I give my mom a terse update about the house, including the weekly challenges. I conveniently leave out the part about dating. No need to share everything.

After I hang up, I linger in the closet for a few moments to gather myself, let my heart rate settle back down. My mom always does this—acts like I need to watch myself, like I'm a burden on others.

One time, when I was eight, I got in trouble at church. Winnie Jung was making fun of me for speaking English with an accent, so I poured Coca-Cola in her hair. She started crying and went to her mom, begging her to get me punished somehow. Luckily, I got off easy, because I was two years younger than she was, but I still remember what she said to my mom: *Yoona is so* mean; *you can't keep letting her get away with it.* My mom was really mad. She said that by being bad, I made her look like a bad parent.

Everyone at church liked Winnie. They all thought she was smart because whenever the pastor asked us kids questions about Korean history, she would know the answer, even if it was a hard question about the Goryeo or Joseon kingdom that we didn't learn in school. My mom always talked about how sure she was that Winnie was going to get into a good college (which she did; she got into Wellesley and Cornell).

And yes, I overreacted—Winnie wasn't trying to be mean, she just couldn't stop laughing at the way I pronounced "Moses"— and yes, that wasn't the only time I got in trouble, but I feel like I'm paying for it with a lifetime of suspicion. Whenever things like this happen, especially with church darlings like Winnie, I'm always guilty until proven innocent.

On my way back to the bathroom, I pass by the boys' room.

"I don't know, that feels too fast," says a voice from within— I'm pretty sure it's Chris.

"This is the jungle, my brother. You run or you die." That's Danny.

I shouldn't eavesdrop, but they're being so loud that I can hardly avoid it. I linger at the door, scrolling through my phone as cover.

"All right, then, what are you planning to do?" Chris asks.

"I'll probably go for Sabine. She seems very innocent," Danny says. "Girls like her tend to like me. But, I mean, they're all smoke-shows. And with the way the show is set up, they kind of have to go out with us."

Gross. Anyone who willingly uses the term "smokeshow" shouldn't be allowed to go on dates. It's like I got a glimpse into how the boys really think, when the testosterone is flowing and there's no one to moderate their apelike tendencies.

I hurry out of there before I hear any more.

The house is cold in the morning. When I get downstairs, every-one else is already up, eating cereal or hanging out in the living room. When Grant sees me, he stands up from the couch.

"Hey, Yoona, can I talk to you?" he asks.

"Sure, what's up?" I reply.

"It's for the first outing. I want to go with you."

I bite back a laugh. This is definitely happening because of that conversation last night—the boys are getting antsy. It takes a lot of discipline for me not to respond, *You run or you die, my brother*.

"Okay, sure," I say. "Props to you for throwing down the gauntlet."

"Someone's gotta start things off, right?" Grant smirks.

Afterward, I can feel that the mood in the group has changed. The boys are working very hard to act chill, which makes it all too clear that they are not chill. Chris and Danny set up a game of chess in the living room, but when I watch them on the sly, I can see that they're deep in discussion, and they're not talking about the pieces on the board. Everyone else goes outside, but after last night, I'm feeling nosy. I want to see how Danny talks when he knows someone is listening.

"Who's winning?" I ask sarcastically, pointing to the only pawn that's been moved out of its starting position.

"Hey, I'm still thinking," Danny says, tapping the side of his head.

Chris lets out a sigh. "We're talking about Mari. I want to ask her out."

Lucky her. Her flirting from last night must have worked. That, or Chris really liked her answer about transcendent humanity.

"So do it," I say.

"But what if she says no?"

"That's the risk we all take."

"Easy for you to say," Danny says. "You didn't have to do anything. Grant told us last night that he was going to ask you out today."

I smile. "Okay, fine, maybe not all of us. Anyways, if you want my advice, don't think about what happens if she says no. Maybe she'll say yes. Or maybe she'll be the one to ask you out. Besides, if you wait too long, Danny might get there first."

Chris looks at Danny with a wounded expression, like, *Would you really do that?*

"Don't go there, Yoona." Danny laughs. "I was telling Chris the same thing. He just needs to hype himself up first. Anyways, I have other plans." Meaning he's going to ask out Sabine.

"All right, I'll do it. Maybe after lunch," Chris says.

I shake my head. "Why wait? Go do it right now. It's better on an empty stomach. You won't feel as nervous."

"C'mon, big guy. Let's go do this." Danny knocks over his own king. "You got me. I resign. That first pawn move was too strong."

He motions to the sliding door, and Chris reluctantly heads out to the pool.

Danny winks at me. "Come on, let's go watch."

"I already know she's going to say yes. Also, some free advice: when you ask Sabine out, no winking."

"Boring." Danny smirks as he follows Chris outside.

After he goes, I think about what he said about Sabine last night. *Girls like her tend to like me.* Maybe it's true, but there's still something off about that comment, even predatory. And Sabine is too vulnerable. Between her disappointment with the show format, and her demure backstory about growing up in Indiana or whatever, I can tell she's in a little too deep right now. I feel bad for her. I shouldn't go repeating words that I overheard by accident, but the least I can do is give her a fair warning.

SABINE

JUST BEFORE LUNCH, AS WE'RE ALL MILLING ABOUT THE LIVING room, the speaker pops up out of the coffee table again. Mari, who is on the couch sipping tea, shrieks in surprise.

"Good morning. I hope that you are all settling into your new life at the Hotel California."

The rest of us swiftly join Mari on the couch to hear what the lava lamp has to say.

"In about an hour, we'll be sending over a van for cast confessionals. Each of you will be called out of the house to speak to a producer about your first impressions. Remember that these interviews will be a part of the final show. You will be called in the order of your arrival. Have a wonderful day."

The lava lamp drops back into the coffee table, leaving us to ponder this message. This is yet another new wrinkle for the show.

"It's our chance to tell the world how we *really* feel about each other," Danny says dryly.

"Seriously. Prepare to burn," Yoona agrees.

They're joking (at least, I hope they are), but there's a grain of truth in their comments that leaves me uneasy. From what I know from most reality shows, these interviews get chopped up and spliced in at the exact worst moments, to make other people—or yourself—look as bad as possible. They wouldn't do that here, would they?

When the producer arrives, I'm the first person to be called outside. There's a trailer parked in the driveway, with blacked-out windows and a single door.

Inside is a mini studio with a plush chair and a wallpaper background of the palm desert. A woman in jeans and a blue blazer ushers me into the chair. She smiles and extends a hand for me to shake. I notice that she's wearing an assortment of bracelets and chunky rings.

"Hi, I'm Carrie Waters. Field producer for this season of *Hotel California*. It's a pleasure to meet you in person, Sabine."

"Nice to meet you, too," I say, shaking her hand. I settle into the chair, sinking in more than I expected to.

"This interview is very casual; nothing to worry about. We'll talk for about ten minutes, but I'm only looking to get a few short clips."

I nod. I look around, but I don't see cameras anywhere. Has the confessional already started?

"So first of all, welcome. I've been working on this show since the first season, and believe it or not, this is the first time I've ever spoken to one of our cast members."

My ears prick up. "Since the very first season? With Jay, Norah, and . . . what was his name? Penn?"

"And Tuya, and Alex, and Erin!"

At least there's one person here who gets it, who knows that wonderful first season. There weren't any dates or challenges back then; there weren't any rules at all. Even the cast members would wonder aloud what they were supposed to be doing in the house. Then they'd come up with silly activities to do together—holding a bake-a-thon to bake cakes shaped like emojis, writing haiku diss tracks of each other, putting on black clothes and eyeliner for "Goth Prom." It felt different from other TV shows: it felt like anything could happen. It was totally engrossing.

"Of course, I do feel like I know you already," Carrie continues. "I watched all your audition tapes during the final selection. I loved that tour of the mall you and your friend gave. You gave your hometown so much life!"

I smile, remembering that video. My friend Em and I pointed out the old mall standbys—the mall cops with their alarmingly tight short shorts, the slowly dying Sears that we were pretty sure was haunted, the woman at the food court who'd give you an extra sample of bourbon chicken if you could recite a tongue twister in Cantonese. When I taught Em how to do it, the woman was so pleased to hear her mother tongue on the lips of a foreigner that she bought us a double combo with extra rice.

For the big finale, we went to Macy's, where we filmed each other sneakily putting on makeup samples until one of the sales associates spotted us. The footage captures her hurrying over to ask if we need help, and Em and me panicking and running away. The final frame shows the bewildered look on the associate's face; then the video cuts to me and Em in the parking lot, laughing our heads off. The pièce de résistance was a close-up of me, still with my makeup on, my hair billowing in the breeze like a Taylor Swift music video. The camera pans out to show me poking my head through the sunroof of Em's car, until the wind eventually proves too much for me, and I shrink back inside.

"Thanks. I'm glad you liked it."

Carrie Waters pulls up a folding chair and sits across from me, still smiling. As she settles into the chair, she leans down and flips a switch on a side panel of the van. Behind her, a green light goes on, which I take to mean that the cameras are rolling.

"So, what do you think of your housemates so far?"

"They're unnecessarily attractive," I blurt out. Carrie laughs. "Seriously, it's eerie. I know it shouldn't matter, but it makes me feel like I'm on the wrong show."

"Are you getting along with everyone?"

"I guess so. Everyone seems pretty chill. Yoona scares me a little." Maybe I shouldn't have said that. The green light is watching. "I think Danny is nice," I add.

We chat about last night's dinner, first impressions, Mari and Chris. Then Carrie shuts the camera off again.

"For what it's worth, I understand what you're saying about the changes to the show," she says. "I feel the same way sometimes. For those of us who've been with the show from the beginning, this season feels like something of a U-turn."

"Yeah, I'll say. I mean, I get it: the show was kind of weird and tame when they were all just hanging out with no rules. But I *liked* that."

Carrie winces. "I did, too, believe me. Frankly, there have been some changes in creative direction at the top levels of our staff."

"Meaning?"

She purses her lips. "You've probably watched this show on one of our regional network partners. Well, this season isn't going to be distributed that way. Nothing has been announced yet, but this season is going to be on one of the big streaming platforms. I can't say which one, but I'll let you take a guess. And when the corporate players call you up to the big leagues, they send in some of their own people, who have their own way of doing things."

So that's what's going on. Everything clicks into place: the dating, the prize money, the hot contestants. Someone is purposely cranking everything up a few notches, trying to take this show big. *Hotel California* will never be the same.

I imagine seeing my face splashed across the home page of one of the huge streaming websites, and a chill runs down my spine. People at school might see it. I'll be right there in their living rooms, standing next to Yoona, Chris, and everyone else.

"Then why did they pick me?" I lament. "I belong in the old show, where they just talked and did weird hijinks. Not the *Bachelor in Paradise* version. No offense."

"I know this isn't what you signed up for," Carrie says. "But if you don't mind me saying, why wouldn't you be picked? You're an interesting young person, and you have a unique background. You're bringing a lot to the cast."

"Me?" I suppress a snort. Maybe if this show brought us all to Moline for *Hotel Illinois*, and asked us trivia questions about agriculture, I'd have an edge. But not here.

"I mean it," Carrie continues. "I'm excited about everyone in the cast, but you're the one that gives this season heart. Think of it this way, Sabine. Everyone who watches this show tends to latch on to a character, right? Some boys will relate to Grant. Some girls will relate to Yoona. I think a lot of people are going to relate to you. I know I do. You remind me so much of me and my girlfriends when I was growing up."

I try to picture Carrie as a child. She has a white-sounding last name, and I don't see a ring on her finger, so I wonder if she was adopted. Is she a Midwest Asian, too?

"As for the superficial changes, don't worry about them too much. Most of the staff working on the show are the same as before. Beneath the surface, this is still the same *Hotel California* that you know and love."

I work up a smile, and she lets me go. Once I'm outside again, the truth of the situation starts to come together. This news about the streaming platform solidifies what I already suspected: that everything about this show has changed, and I'm the one misfit piece that's carried over from the old way of doing things.

I got picked because one or two producers had a soft spot for me. That's the only explanation for how I ended up on the same show as the rest of these people.

Except now, I'm the one who has to live with the consequences.

When I come back inside, Yoona leaves for her confessional, and I try not to think about her *prepare to burn* comment. Meanwhile, Chris and Mari are playing in the pool. This is how I learn that Chris has a six-pack straight out of a men's fitness magazine. Obviously.

Danny and Grant are on the couch with me, looking at memes on their phones.

"Oh, here's one," Grant says. "Look up images for 'Asian baby boy' and tell me what you see."

When I do the search, I get a bunch of pictures of cute babies with dark hair and dark eyes. Danny shows us his phone, with pictures of the same.

"All right, now search 'Asian baby girl,'" Grant says.

Danny laughs. Without even making the search, he says, "That's pretty good."

"I don't get it," I say.

Grant raises an eyebrow. "You've never heard of an ABG?"

"A what?"

"Danny, please educate our friend."

Danny sits up. "No way, dude. I don't need that in my search history."

"We all know it's already there. I bet if you type 'Asian b,' you'd get the rest from auto-complete."

Warily, I look it up myself. Instead of bright-eyed infants, I get pictures of women with long eyelashes, crop tops, and shoulder tattoos. A lot of the pictures seem to have been taken with a rave in the background. Farther down in the results, though, are regular baby Asian girls.

"You don't have ABGs in the Midwest?" Grant asks, with a look on his face like I've told him we don't have running water.

"It's kind of a West Coast thing," Danny offers. "I only heard about it from shuttle Asian traits."

Grant takes this explanation in stride and asks Danny where he's from.

"Houston," Danny says. "But I go to school in New Hampshire." I make a mental note—Danny is a *Texas* Asian.

"What's shuttle Asian traits?" I ask, feeling thoroughly confused.

"Subtle Asian Traits," Grant enunciates, making me feel like a child. "You've really never heard of it? It's a page with memes about Asians."

"Oh."

"I'll add you," Danny says. "It's a double-edged sword. Proceed with caution."

"What else do you not have? Do you have bubble tea? And Thai food?" Grant asks.

"It's not like Moline is frozen in the 1960s," I say, frowning.

"We have stuff other than just McDonald's and Wonder Bread. My parents order pad thai for dinner all the time."

Grant smirks. "You hear that, Danny? She eats pad thai all the time."

"What's that supposed to mean?" I glare at Grant. On top of all the other ways that I don't belong here, now I don't know enough about silly memes, either.

"I'm sorry I don't know about the same meme pages as the rest of you. I don't have a group of friends to help me keep up with whatever's trending for the cool California Asians. I already told you what my hometown is like, so I'd prefer not to get picked on for it, please."

I can feel a few beads of sweat building up on my brow.

"You have to forgive him, Sabine." Danny smiles at me sympathetically. "He's just excited. It's not every day you get to spread the news to a fresh convert."

"No offense, Sabine," Grant says.

"How was I supposed to not be offended by that?"

"Because you know I'm a nice guy?" Grant says guiltily. "And I like to joke around? Besides, the pad thai thing was a setup; you walked right into that one."

"Uh-huh."

"Just keep on digging, bro," Danny adds.

I decide to head back to the girls' room before I can snap at anyone again. I didn't mean to get so worked up, and I don't want to burn any bridges. Right now, I need to be alone. As I'm walking up the stairs, I hear footsteps behind me. I turn. It's Danny.

"You doing okay?" he asks.

"Yeah, I'm fine. Just feeling tired. Jet lag."

"Not storming off because we made fun of you, right?"

"I mean, *you* didn't make fun of me. Grant, on the other hand . . ."

Danny chuckles. His smile is dazzling. He runs a hand through his hair, and when he looks at me again, there's a twinkle in his eyes. "So, listen, about the first challenge."

My heart rate quickens. It's happening. Even though I know what's coming, I feel a rush of anticipation for what comes next.

"Sorry I made you wait the longest," Danny says. "I was nervous, so it took me a while to get my act together. And, uh, it may or may not be helping that you have no choice but to say yes."

I blink. He was nervous to ask *me* out? I'm the one that's being forced to go out with *him*?

"Anyways, I would love to go on an outing with you."

Though I can hardly believe it, his voice seems to be shaky, as if he's genuinely nervous.

"Sure," I say, unable to contain a smile. "That sounds great."

I still feel embarrassed about the Subtle Asian Traits thing—both not knowing about it, and getting upset—but at least I got asked out. That feels good, no matter the circumstances. Out of all the small indignities that I've endured so far, there's one bright spot.

By nighttime, as we're about to go to bed, my imagination is running wild. Forget the potential attractiveness disparity that may or may not exist between us. I picture Danny and me on a date, holding hands, squeezing my face up to his for a selfie. I roll his name around on my tongue like I'm trying it on for size. Can I really see us together? I picture staring into those eyes, taking a bath in them, drowning just a little. Why, yes. Yes I can.

"Hey, Sabine."

It's Yoona's voice, coming from the bottom bunk. I peer over the edge of my bed and see her, sitting up to talk to me.

"What's up?"

"Danny asked you out, right?"

"Yeah! This morning, after my confessional." Thinking about it again puts a big, goofy smile on my face.

"Right. And you said yes?"

"Yes. Of course."

Yoona purses her lips, like she's disappointed. I wasn't expecting this reaction; my smile drops.

"Okay, that's done, then. Well, you should still go. Danny is just kind of . . . well, you know what he's like. Last night, I—anyways, just be careful, is all."

Just like that, I'm on edge again.

One nice thing happens to me in the house, and in comes Yoona to take it away. *You should still go? You know what he's like?* That makes it sound like he's too good for me, and I should just admit it and stay home.

Plus, there's the note of impatience that tinges all her interactions with me. She's the epitome of the new show—pretty, polished, effortlessly popular—and it's like she knows I can't keep up.

"Thanks for looking out," I mutter, hating how weak my voice sounds.

"Of course. That's what I'm—"

"But actually, I can take care of myself."

The words come out of some deeply buried, instinctual part of myself. Once spoken, they feel solid and heavy as stone.

Yoona frowns, stares at me for a second with her radiant gaze. For once, she seems thrown off-balance. I have to fight to keep eye contact, to avoid the urge to look away.

Finally, she shrugs. "Suit yourself." She rolls back over to go to sleep.

My face is warm, and my pulse is up. That whole conversation went by so quickly, too quickly to feel real.

I lie there and replay it in my head: Yoona catching me by surprise during a moment of bliss, trying to knock me down a peg. I know she was expecting me to be meek, compliant, to play my part. The thing is, I didn't let her. I don't know what got into me, but I stood up to her.

And it felt good.

YOONA

I DON'T THINK MY WARNING WORKED.

I feel like I made it friendly enough, but Sabine didn't seem to take it that way. Her reaction was pretty much, *Mind your own business.*

It's nothing new for me. The same kind of thing used to happen at church, when girls like Winnie and Maggie Cho and Sarah Yoo would call me a bully and say that I couldn't hang out with them. I always felt like *they* were the ones who started it, but I was the one who got in trouble, for letting it go too far. It hurt at first, but I told myself that they just didn't like me because I was prettier than they were.

With Danny, I feel like the red flags are pretty obvious. Overheard comments aside, there's the long hair, the earring, the superstrong cologne that he wears. Plus, his name is *Danny*—normal guys go for Daniel or Dan; only a certain demographic holds onto the "-ny." I shouldn't need to point that out. But who knows? Maybe Sabine's into that. To each her own.

On the morning of the outings, Mari and Sabine stand in front of the mirror, getting ready. They're both taking it really seriously: slowly, painstakingly pulling their eyeliner pencils across their eyes, frowning in the mirror, wiping their faces and starting over.

"Are either of you nervous? Do you have any advice?" Sabine asks.

"Just play it cool," I suggest. "Let Danny do all the work. Act like this is just another date for you."

Sabine winces, in a way that makes me wonder if she's ever been on a date before at all. Maybe that's why she's so uptight right now.

"Of course I'm nervous," Mari says. "We're at the beginning of the story, and anything could still happen. You feel it, too, right? This mixture of fear and hope, like you're on the verge of being unbelievably happy, but you also might be sick?"

"Big-time," Sabine says, nodding.

"Personally, I love this feeling," Mari continues. "It's one of the most vulnerable positions you can be in, where you just have to embrace the possibilities. You don't get to feel this way all that often. So every time you do, it's like you're tapping into this rare part of yourself that usually stays hidden."

Sabine pauses her makeup to chew this advice over. God bless Mari and her poetic takes on life, but in this case, I think that Sabine is already too much in danger of overthinking things.

"I know something that might help you, Sabine," I say. "I suggest you give it a try. It's called 'not giving a f—'"

"Are you guys coming or not?" Grant calls from downstairs.

I yank the door open to yell back. "Hey, be more patient! It's a process; you can't rush it."

For emphasis, I slam the door shut. I sneak a glance at Sabine, hoping that I made her laugh. But she's back at it with the eyeliner; perhaps ignoring me, perhaps just laser-focused. I have a sneaking suspicion that she's upset about last night, but I'm not sure what I did.

About fifteen minutes later, the three of us go downstairs.

The boys are dressed up. Since the first day, it's been all sweatpants and T-shirts, but now Danny and Chris are wearing polos, and Grant is wearing a short-sleeve button-down.

Outside, there are three cars waiting for us. We pair off and head to our respective destinations.

For our date, Grant and I have a painting lesson at an art studio with an enormous cactus garden.

"You said you hate exercise, so I chose something as sedentary as possible," Grant says. He gets points for being a good listener. Our canvases are even set up under umbrellas that block out the sun, like the studio knew I was coming.

Our teacher is a woman named Noor, who's wearing a lot of beaded jewelry and matching silk scarves over her hair and around her neck.

"I moved to the desert during an unbearably painful period in my life, when I felt like the city was an iron vise, closing in on me," she explains. "Out here, I found unexpectedly that I could breathe. It was as if after living my life in black and white for many years, I could finally see colors again, colors that I had not seen since I was a child. I planned to be here for a short while, a year at most. Thirty years later, here I am still."

I shudder. Thirty years in the desert would wreak havoc on my skin. I'll gladly take life in black and white, thanks.

Noor shows us how to layer the acrylic paints to create a rosy twilight sky. I don't do much drawing or painting anymore—since I started high school, my mom has kept my focus squarely on science and math—but I used to take art lessons when I was a kid. As I mix together various shades of green to fill in my prickly pear, I feel the faint but familiar traces of my old skills coming back to me. Maybe that's what Noor meant by seeing the colors again.

"Someone's done this before," Grant says, peeking at my canvas.

I look over at his; his sky is dark from mixing in too much purple, and his cactus is covered in white tick marks that look like spilled rice grains. I think they're supposed to be spines.

"Why is it on fire at the top?" I ask, pointing to the bursts of red on each of the cactus's arms.

"Those are supposed to be flowers!"

"Dude, those are *not* flowers." I laugh, probably a little too hard, because Grant gives me a sour look and asks for another canvas.

"You never answered my question the other night," he says, while he waits for Noor to get the canvas. "Why did you come on this show?"

"No special reason. Someone asked me to do it, and I said yes. It was a chance to get out of the house."

"You traveled all the way across the country just to get out of the house? You could have just gone to summer camp or something."

I roll my eyes. "So what you mean is, *why* am I here, what's my *motivation*, who am I at my *true* self."

"Yeah. Something like that."

"I don't know, man. Maybe I'm not that deep. Maybe I really just came here on a whim."

Grant smiles and shakes his head. Rather than getting discouraged, he looks more determined to dig into my psychology, like I'm a particularly challenging puzzle.

Before Grant starts painting again, he studies my technique. I use horizontal brushstrokes to color my sky, and he mimics my arm motion. I mix together yellow, white, and green on my palette, and he does the same.

"Watch your back, Yoona. I'm coming at you like Pablo."

"You're a fast learner," I say charitably, as a peace offering.

Grant grins. "I'm a sore loser, too."

He beckons Noor over and starts buttering her up—"Your cactus garden is really lovely," "You were so smart to get out of LA," "I saw your paintings inside and they were amazing and can I buy one?" Then he starts plying her for tips; what colors and brushstrokes to use to make the flowers look right, how to angle the spines so that they actually look like spines. He catches me watching with a raised eyebrow, and winks at me. The nerve.

"So what's so bad about being at home?" he asks.

"You really want to know about this, don't you? All right, it's like this. When I'm at the house, my mom is always on me. I'm the person who doesn't call my dad enough, who doesn't study enough, who's always making a mess. Then I get to church, and it's like this competition between the parents about whose life is going the best, who has the best kid. So I have to act like I'm really perfect and happy or whatever. Meanwhile, the kids are all competing, too. Everyone is polite, but secretly they all want to be that one excellent kid that all the parents fawn over.

"It's not that bad. I just needed a break from it. I wanted to have a couple of weeks where I didn't have to be that person."

Grant nods. "Why not just go hang out with your friends? Can't you all just, like, get on the subway and see each other?"

"You mean from school? My high school covers the entire city. People come in from Queens, the Bronx, places that are hours away. Plus, you have to apply to your middle school and high school, so there's lots of shuffling around, lots of new faces. Aside from church people, there's no one who I've, like, known for my entire life or something."

"So you don't have anyone that you're really close with."

"Sure I do. My mom. We're together all the time. That's the problem."

"And you just sit around at home all day?"

"I mean, we don't just sit around. There's stuff to do at home. Are you familiar with this thing called the internet?"

Grant laughs. "Very interesting."

I've been talking a lot. Most of what I'm saying is new to me, too. When I describe it out loud, my life sounds kind of sad. I guess it's no wonder that I wanted a break from it. Why else would I run off like that?

Meanwhile, Grant seems to have gotten what he was looking for. Now he's back to painting, and he's turned his canvas away from me so I can't see his progress.

"Hey, you never gave your answer, either," I say. "What are you here to do? What are you about?"

"What am I about?" Grant rubs his chin for a moment, deep in thought. Then he grins. "Right now, I'm about to do a better painting than you."

He turns his canvas toward me. His succulents are more finely shaped than before, shaded so that they look more three-dimensional. The sky behind them is delicately layered with color, and speckled with orange-tinted clouds. The techniques are simple, recognizable, but put together the effect is surprisingly strong. When Noor sees it, she's delighted.

"I find that I do my best painting when I'm concerned not only with capturing what my eyes see, but with putting a part of myself onto the canvas. Some would argue that art is a practice, a slow journey toward sharper and more refined technique. But art is also about expression, and the most worthwhile art is made when you pour in a bit of your own joy, your own suffering, so that when others look at it, they think, *There's a story there*. I might not know what that story is, but I can *feel* it . . ."

It sounds like she's building up to compliment Grant's painting, but she never quite gets there. Still, she doesn't need to. This painting is an obvious improvement over his first.

Grant winks at me. "Now let's see yours."

I show them mine; after I finished the prickly pear, I spent a lot of time trying to paint one of the short, squat ones, but I overdid it on the spines and it ended up looking like a moldy watermelon.

Noor puts a hand over her mouth. "Oh dear. Perhaps you've let your focus slip."

Grant smiles a wide, gleaming smile. "Mine's better."

"No fair. You distracted me with that question. You don't even care why I came here!" I *tsk, tsk* him and shake my head.

He laughs. "Not true! Of course I care. I heard every word you said. That's why I want to give you my painting, as a token of our friendship."

"Now you're just gloating."

Still, at the end of the lesson, when Grant signs his canvas *G.A.* and offers it to me, I accept. Noor gives us each a hug and thanks us for sharing our creativity with her.

"Our time is up, and we aren't likely to see each other again in this life," she says. "Whatever trials and triumphs we face from here on out, we must face them without the sunlight of each other's company. I bid you farewell, and I ask of you only this: be brave, my dears, be brave!"

After going off on that long-winded answer to Grant's question, I feel an unexpected kinship with Noor. Both of us came to this corner of the world as an escape. I'm definitely not planning to stay here for thirty years—there's not enough moisturizer in the world to keep me here for that long—but I know what she means about coming up for air, searching for some long-lost feeling.

I came here looking for something. But what?

SABINE

THERE'S SOMETHING ABOUT SEEING A BOY GET DRESSED UP FOR
you that just feels good.

I know it probably doesn't mean anything, that the boys probably just did this as another one of their pacts, but it's still nice to
see Danny wearing a polo, with his hair combed back, for his date
with *me*.

"You look nice," he says, when I come to the bottom of the
stairs. My brain's pleasure centers erupt in fireworks.

Once we get outside, into the bright glare of the sun, Danny
puts on a pair of aviator sunglasses. All of a sudden, he looks
cold, distant, intimidating.

In the back seat of the car, I take the left window, he takes the
right, and the middle seat is a vast chasm between us. As we turn
out of the neighborhood, Danny is taking the scenery in through
the window, resting his chin on his elbow. He looks bored already.

Danny turns to me. His sunglasses are like two black holes,
bending the light around his face.

"After I asked you out, they gave me a list of options to choose from. I picked something that I thought you'd like."

"A list? Why'd they only give it to you?"

"They said they gave it to whoever asked for the date. It's only fair, right? Plus, this way you get to be surprised. But if you're making a comment on the patriarchy, point taken."

"So what did you choose?"

Danny smiles. He tilts his head like he's winking at me, but I can't tell for certain since I can't see his eyes. "It's flat in the Midwest, right? I thought you might like to see some mountains."

Eventually, the car turns into a narrow road through a deep, rocky canyon. It lets us off at the base of a huge mountain, dotted with bushes and the odd tree. Snaking up the mountain is a series of rickety steel towers, connected by cables. I spot a cable car, dangling precariously from a cable as it winds its way up the mountain.

"I hope you're not afraid of heights," Danny says.

"I don't have much experience with heights. Like you said, it's flat in the Midwest."

"Well, just remember that no one's ever died on this thing. At least, not yet."

It's barely ten a.m., but there's already a long line of people queuing up. Luckily, the producers have already booked our tickets, so we get to cut the line, *and* we get an entire cable car to ourselves.

Well, except for the cameraman who's inside waiting for us.

When I see him, I stiffen. Danny and I aren't going on this

date alone. And yes, the situation is no different from how it is at the house, where the hidden cameras are watching. But this full-size TV camera is much harder to ignore, especially with a real live person behind it.

As the car floats up above the jagged face of the mountain, I'm impressed by how smooth the ride is. That is, until we pass the first tower. Our car jolts forward and then swings back, like a yo-yo. I lose my balance, and as I tap-dance backward, I can't stop myself—I let out a squeal.

Danny catches me by the waist to steady me. With his other hand, he's already gripping a pole for support. After I recover from the shock, I feel his hand pressing into my back.

"You knew that was going to happen!" I say, feigning outrage.

Danny laughs. "Sorry, couldn't resist."

I sneak a glance at the cameraman. I can't see his face behind the stabilizer vest that he's wearing to steady the camera, but his body language is cold and impassive. This is a first date on hard mode. Being alone with a cute boy is one thing; being filmed while I'm doing it is another.

I remind myself to breathe. Gotta stay cool, like Yoona said. Even if she was just teasing me, her advice makes sense.

As we rise farther and farther up the mountain, I take in the desert landscape, unfurling across the valley to meet the mountains on the other side. Cars inch their way up a distant highway. Small towns gleam in the sun.

"Does it beat the Midwest?" Danny asks.

"I don't know. This is an amazing view. But we've got some pretty great cornfields in Illinois. Plus, did you know that Moline is only a half-hour drive from the world's largest truck stop?"

"Oh, no way. We should have gone there instead. Forget about natural beauty or whatever. We could be looking at trucks!"

When we pass the next tower, I'm ready for it. I shoot Danny a dirty look as I brace myself against a handrail. Danny smirks.

At the top of the mountain, it's unexpectedly windy and chilly. After a few minutes on the outdoor viewing deck, my hands are turning numb. We retreat back inside the mountaintop lodge, and Danny gets us two hot chocolates from the café. He also buys me an oversize long-sleeve tee that says *Palm Springs Aerial Tramway* on it. That puts a smile on my face.

"Would you mind taking your sunglasses off?" I ask.

"Too intimidating?"

"I just want to be able to look into your eyes."

Danny folds his sunglasses and clips them into the neck of his shirt. "Very smooth answer," he says, with a cheeky grin. "So, can we work on our chemistry?"

I blink. "Our what?"

"Our team chemistry. For the first challenge. What did you think I said?" He looks at me innocently. Can it be? Are we *flirting*?

"It depends," I say. "How good are you at following orders and giving compliments?"

"You have a nice smile," he says. "I'm usually better at *taking* compliments, but how's that?"

I can feel that I'm blushing. Luckily, my cheeks are already flushed from the cold.

"What are your strengths and weaknesses?" I ask.

"Strengths? I can eat really fast. I know all the US presidents, in order. And"—he wiggles his eyebrows—"I can juggle."

"Who was the fourteenth president?"

"Psh. Franklin Pierce. Next question."

I don't actually know the answer, but that sounds believable enough.

"As for weaknesses, I'm not sure. I mean, I'm pretty great. Not much room for improvement."

"Aaand you've lost me. Next!" I drag my finger across the air, pretending to swipe left on Danny. He laughs.

Miraculously, my confidence is surging. Words are coming to me easily, and the energy between me and Danny is good. Even the presence of the cameraman feels like a blessing in disguise: this date is going well, and there's going to be video proof!

"I have a serious question, though," Danny says.

"Shoot."

"The other day when we were talking about Subtle Asian Traits. You got mad, right?"

"No!" I respond, too quickly. "Well, maybe a little. I mean, Grant *was* making fun of me."

"Seems like you took it personally, though."

A part of me hesitates over revisiting that moment. I had an outburst, and Grant easily could have embarrassed me for getting too worked up. I get the sense, though, that Danny wouldn't do that. He's nice to me; I feel like he'll be on my side.

"I told everyone on the first day how I feel about Moline. It's like, I already admitted that I'm different, and now you're calling me out for it? I wish I hadn't gotten upset, but I think I was justified."

Danny nods. "I get that. I should have spoken up. Don't be too hard on Grant, though. He's definitely gone through the same thing. We all just have different ways of dealing with it."

I hadn't considered that, and it makes me feel less sour on Grant. Danny's pretty perceptive. I think back to Yoona's warnings about him. She didn't know what she was talking about.

"Do you actually feel like you get shut out of things in your hometown?" he asks.

"Not overtly. Why, you don't believe me?"

"No, I get it. I'm a brown kid who grew up in Texas after 9/11. No hate on Texas; we're still the best state. We have the biggest trucks. And the hottest hot sauce. I'm just saying, you have to keep trying, right? Otherwise, you're shutting yourself out."

I see what he's saying, but I don't quite agree. The rules are different when you're as attractive as he is. I tell Danny my story.

When I was in middle school, my parents told me to run for class president. *It's a great way to show that you're a leader*, they said. *And besides, it's an honor to be at the head of your class. In our school, we were all fighting to be the student chairperson.* I tried to explain to them that in America, student government is for try-hards and the elections are basically just a popularity contest, but they still made me do it.

"I got really into it," I tell Danny. "I had to get twenty signatures to get on the ballot. I wrote a speech, and I put up flyers. My campaign slogan was 'Start the Year Off with a Zhang.'"

"That's cute!" Danny says, chuckling.

Too bad no one thought so at the time.

We all had to give our speeches at a special assembly. I was scheduled to go last, obviously. But Taylor Caputo and Greg Novak both went over time, and five minutes before the end, Principal Andersen got up onstage to dismiss everyone. I had to run up onstage and remind her that I hadn't gone yet, and then I had to rush through my speech and cut out my final line ("to keep the school on track, Zhang's got your back"). Obviously, I did not win the race.

Afterward, I tried to complain to the principal. More accurately, I tried to make her feel bad for screwing me over. I said she had to make it right, because she was the one who'd forgotten about me.

"She got mad. She said, 'Be realistic, honey. Look at the votes. You wouldn't have won anyways.' I can't prove it, but I just felt like what she really meant was, *Do you really think an Asian person could win president?*"

"Duuude," Danny says, shaking his head.

"So I'd say I gave it a fair chance. More than one. But you can only swallow that type of thing so many times before you get the message. *You're a guest here. This town isn't your town.*"

"That's so messed up." He doesn't sound doubtful anymore. As a matter of fact, he sounds impressed. Like I'm a veteran of some edgy war, showing off a cool scar.

"Hey, at least you didn't go down without a fight. Respect."

He goes for a fist bump, and I take it. Even though this is about as platonic as physical contact can get, it still feels significant. What he said about me is true. I don't go down without a fight. Even if most people don't notice.

We ride the cable car back down the mountain. The car picks us up to take us to our next stop, the town of Palm Springs, for lunch.

"So, uh, fair warning, I'm not sure if you're going to like the place I picked for lunch," he tells me. He's still leaving the middle seat between us, but at least this time he's turned to face me.

"What's wrong with it?" I ask.

"The food should be fine. But I picked it before we had that intense conversation just now. I thought we should go to a Thai restaurant. So you could get your favorite."

"Pad thai?" I roll my eyes. "You're the worst."

"I thought it would be funny!"

"Not funny," I say. But I smile. We're still flirting, I think.

Rude jokes aside, the Thai restaurant has a promising vibe—walls covered in vintage movie posters, Thai rock 'n' roll playing on the speakers, shelves lined with cans of coconut milk. Danny orders for us, and I make a big deal about ordering something other than pad thai: something called khao soi, which I've never heard of. While we wait, Danny tells me about his school, with its idyllic New England campus, its teachers preaching tradition and pride, its students oozing wealth and privilege.

"It's ninety percent a pipeline for various Sheldon Worthington the Thirds to take over the family hedge fund from Sheldon Worthington the Seconds, and ten percent minorities."

When the food arrives, I learn that khao soi is a dish of egg noodles, both boiled and fried, in a thick, fragrant sauce.

"Wow, this is so good," I say, after a couple of bites. "I've never had this before."

Danny just smirks.

"Wait, is this what Thai food is like everywhere? Does this mean that the Thai food in Moline is, like, the Panda Express version of Thai food?"

"I wouldn't go that far. Pretty sure pad thai is a real dish. Besides, why are you hating on Panda X? General Tso's is as real as it gets."

I shake my head. "Maybe Grant was right."

Danny waves his hand. "It's just food. It doesn't mean anything if you don't know about it. Matter of fact, the same goes for Subtle Asian Traits. You're not missing out just because you don't know what an ABG is. That group is mostly for East Asians from California. But we're from the heartland. So us Middle America Asians have to stick together, right?"

I feel warm happiness spreading all through my chest. Is it just the spicy food, or is there something growing between us? When I first arrived at the house, I thought it was weird that Danny kept trying to talk to me. But maybe it isn't weird at all. Maybe I was always interesting, capable of standing out, and I just needed to go to a place where people could see it.

Maybe it is possible that I like a guy, and for once, that guy likes me back.

The next day, a van picks us up early in the morning to take us to the first challenge. All of us are cranky from waking up to our alarms, so we're mostly quiet on the ride over. We nap or watch out the window as the sun creeps over the mountains, bathing the desert in an orange glow.

The van pulls into an empty parking lot. In the middle of the lot is a big white tent, with a few more cars and vans parked around it.

We come to a stop, and Carrie Waters slides open the van door.

"Rise and shine!" she sings out. We groan at the bright light shining rudely in our faces.

"Come on, where's the youthful energy? The sun won't kill you!"

We clamber out of the car and follow Carrie in single file. When she opens the tent flap, we're met with a blast of cool air. Inside, there's music playing. In the center of the tent is a stage set up with what looks like a round screen. Around it are a series of tables, covered in white sheets.

As we approach the stage, the screen flashes to life—it's a

digital carnival wheel. Each slice of the wheel is illustrated with a different symbol. I spot, among other things, a pair of chopsticks, a Ping-Pong paddle, and what looks like the outline of a storm cloud.

"Welcome to the *Hotel California* Olympics!" a voice cries out over a hidden speaker system. "For today's competition, you'll all be on the same team. Win together, and you'll share in the ten-thousand-dollar prize! The rules are simple. There are six challenges. Each person will spin the wheel and attempt to complete the corresponding challenge. To win the Olympics, you need to successfully complete three out of six challenges. Good luck."

As the voice explains the challenge, a few assistants dressed in polo shirts and baseball caps file into the tent. They crouch around the edges of the tables, looking like ball runners in tennis.

It's all so surreal. Games, prize money, big-budget dates—I feel like I've been swept up in a wave that originated far, far away, and was never supposed to reach my quiet, obscure part of the ocean.

Yoona is the first to spin the wheel. Since it's digital, this just involves flipping a lever sticking out of the side. A ticker whirls around the edge of the circle, then slows and comes to a stop with a cheesy *ding-ding-ding*, like we're at a casino. The symbol on Yoona's slice is a square root sign.

"Does that mean . . . ?" Yoona starts to say. Before she can finish, a couple of the ball runners dash over to one of the tables and rip off the white sheet. On the table are a tablet and a small television.

"Yoona has been selected for the math test!" the announcer cries.

"Unbelievable," Yoona says.

Everyone else starts to head toward the table, but I linger by the wheel. Chopsticks? A Ping-Pong paddle? A bowl of noodles?

Unless I'm very much mistaken, the *Hotel California* Olympics is a collection of Asian stereotypes. We're all going to be going through this strange pantomime of ethnic activities. It feels like an elaborate prank.

The TV and the tablet both flash on. I listen in horrified fascination as the announcer explains that Yoona will have sixty seconds to complete ten algebra problems. It's multiple choice; the question will appear on the TV, and the choices will appear on the tablet for Yoona to select.

"You have to work quickly, but also carefully. You're only allowed one mistake!" the announcer says cheerfully. One of the assistants hands Yoona the tablet, and a timer lights up on the screen.

"Bring it on!" Yoona cries.

The first problem appears: *Find y, if 12x - 2y = 18.*

No one else seems weirded out by the math challenge. They're all going along with it, watching in nervous silence as Yoona works her way through the math problems. Each time she answers correctly, her choice flashes up on the screen, with a green check mark below it. She breezes through the first five problems. Then the sixth question appears on the screen: *What is 22 times 17?*

"Are you frickin' serious?" Yoona groans. For a few seconds, she's frozen. Time ticks by.

"Just guess!" Grant yells.

"Quiet!" Yoona glares at him. She closes her eyes and whispers to herself, and when her eyes snap open again, she taps on her choice. *374* pops up on the screen, with a green check mark underneath it. I'm not sure if she did it in her head, or if she guessed, but either way, I'm impressed.

The rest of the questions are easier. Yoona gets the first nine, and the group lets out a cheer. She's done it.

"My parents would kill me if I failed a math test on TV," Yoona says.

We go back to the center of the tent. Next up is Grant: he spins the wheel, and it lands on the Ping-Pong paddle. The ball runners whisk in and uncover a Ping-Pong table, with a paddle on one side, and a robot ball shooter on the other.

"Grant has been selected for Ping-Pong! He will have to return twenty-five out of thirty balls fired off by the robot. And each return shot must hit the table!"

"Does anyone else think it's weird that all of the activities are based on an Asian stereotype?" I ask.

"Probably. Looks like chopsticks are coming up next," Mari says, pointing to the wheel. "It's kind of funny, right?"

"Not really. Math? Chopsticks? This sounds like a *Family Feud* survey of 'top things you associate with Asians.' I mean, it's funny in the way that doing a fake accent will make a white person laugh. They're still laughing *at* you, because you're different."

"Buzzkill alert," Yoona says. The group snickers.

As she walks away, I flash back to yesterday. We were in the bathroom together, I was getting ready for my date, and she made fun of me for caring so much. The comment was so fast, so blunt, and I didn't have time to react. This time I want to stop her, come back with some retort. But everyone else is with her, and no one else seems as bothered as I am. Once again, the moment passes, and I let it go without defending myself.

Maybe I am overreacting. There is something fun about leaning into stereotypes—and we're all doing it ourselves, so maybe that makes it okay. It just hurts me to see this show, *my show*, being so crude. This has to be another symptom of the acquisition. It's like the streaming people bought the Asian show and thought, *Just in case this isn't Asian enough, let's attach some blaring red signs, so everyone knows what we're going for here.*

At the Ping-Pong table, Grant picks up the paddle with a look of grim determination on his face. Chris pretends to massage his shoulders, while Danny rubs and blows on his hands.

"You got this, champ," Danny says. "You were born for this."

When the balls start coming, Grant doesn't look much like he was born for Ping-Pong. He sends the first ball whizzing far out past the table, and whiffs completely on the second one. His third shot looks better, but it still hits the net. The robot oscillates side to side, mercilessly firing off balls.

Grant manages to regain his composure and start hitting balls onto the table. Despite the poor start, I can tell he has good hand-eye coordination. He seems to figure out a technique, and once he does, his shots are all consistent. Most important, he looks completely focused. When the last ball comes, and he hits it cleanly over the net for his twenty-seventh return in a row, he's still bent over, anticipating the next ball, unaware that he's succeeded.

"That's my boy!" Chris cries, wrapping Grant in a voluptuous, muscular embrace. The rest of the group joins in, and even I give in and gently place myself at the edge of the group hug. We jump up and down a couple of times. I may not like this challenge, but at least we're winning.

Next up is me. I spin the wheel, and it lands on a picture of a take-out box.

"Sabine will be doing a blind taste test," the announcer explains. "She will be given five dishes to eat, and she must correctly match each one to the cuisine from which it originates."

I quickly whip my head toward Grant, to warn him off of making any more pad thai jokes. I wish I'd gotten a different challenge. I think I would have done okay on the math test, but if there's one challenge where I know my knowledge is lacking, it's this one.

One of the assistants blindfolds me and sits me down in a chair. As I wait for the food to arrive, it occurs to me that this challenge is oddly appropriate. This past week has given me a crash course in

Asian food, and now I'll be using that knowledge with everything on the line.

I feel a little funny as I, a high schooler, tilt my head back so that an assistant can spoon food into my mouth. I chew the first dish and taste spinach, together with a mix of spices.

"Indian?"

A *ding-ding* tells me that I'm right.

The next dish is soupy and hot. But as the flavors explode on my tongue, I smile. Normally, this would be a close call, but I happen to know exactly what I'm eating. Like that movie *Slumdog Millionaire*, destiny is showing me the way.

"Khao soi," I say. "Thai. Final answer."

The next one is mapo tofu, which is easy. After that is a dessert, icy and sweet, that I have trouble placing. It stirs a vague memory of a travel show that I once watched, but I still feel shaky about it.

"Is it from the Philippines?"

Ding-ding.

It all comes down to the last dish. I tilt my head back, and the assistant spoons a disk of food into my mouth. As I chew through the rice and the seaweed, a smile spreads across my face. All that money on the line, and they finish with a softball. Everyone in America knows what sushi is.

"Japanese!" I say triumphantly. I'm so excited that I don't notice the angry whine of the buzzer. It's only when I take off my blindfold and see the crestfallen faces of my housemates that I realize that something is wrong.

"Dude, you don't know what Kim Pop is?" Yoona asks, her arms crossed, in a huff.

"Kim Pop?"

Yoona points to an index card printed with the words *kimbap—Korean*, in front of a plate of round, multicolored pieces of sushi. Except it's not sushi. Which means that I've failed.

"It's okay. We still have three more tries," Chris says, patting me on the shoulder.

Even though I still object to the whole idea of these games, I feel like I've let the team down. Everyone else looks deflated; the exuberance that we felt during our group hug is gone.

Mari spins the wheel, and it lands on the slice with a pair of chopsticks. The ball runners unveil a table set with an array of boxes and plates.

"And now it's Mari's turn to show us some dexterity! She'll have to complete three out of five demonstrations of her chopstick prowess."

"I don't know about this, guys," Mari says. "My chopsticks skills are a little suspect. I don't hold them properly."

She shows us the way she holds chopsticks. It *is* weird: she crosses them, making an X, and gets her squeezing action by pulling up on one chopstick rather than pushing one down.

"I've always done it this way, and no one ever corrected me," she explains. "It works for me, but it's probably objectively worse than the normal way."

The five chopsticks challenges are: catching slices of bread out of the air, transferring an egg from the table to the floor, removing a Jenga block from a rickety Jenga tower, removing three ice cubes from a thin glass, and finally, a Pictionary-like challenge where Mari has to pick up a marker, draw a picture, and have the rest of us guess what it is. All in under two minutes.

When the timer starts, one of the assistants softly lobs three slices of bread at Mari. Mari's unusual chopsticks technique does not serve her well here; she sends the first slice flying, and manages to touch but not grab the second one. For the third and final attempt, she gives up on catching and tries to spear the bread. No luck.

Next is the egg. Mari struggles to get a grip on it, again because her crossed chopsticks create a difficult angle for securing something so big. Eventually, she's able to scoop up the egg and balance it on top of her chopsticks. She bends down, sinks to one knee, and tries to delicately lower the egg to the floor. It's all going well until her wrist wobbles with fatigue, her eyes are suddenly seized with panic, and the egg slides off the end of her chopsticks. It's a short enough fall that the egg doesn't just splat, but there's an obvious crack in the side.

"Partial credit?" Mari asks, grimacing. The assistant shakes her head.

Now there's no more room for error. Mari manages to slide the Jenga block out of the tower, and although the tower wobbles a little, it doesn't fall. The timer shows forty-five seconds left. For the ice cubes, Mari doesn't bother with finesse. Instead of picking up the ice cubes, she traps them against the sides of the glass and flings them up and onto the table. It works. Now it comes down to Mari's artistic skills.

Gingerly, she picks up a marker with her chopsticks and starts drawing on a sheet of paper. The lines come out crooked and imprecise, and once or twice the marker slips out of her grasp. When the timer goes up, she puts down the marker, with a look of hope, even confidence, on her face. Now it's up to us.

We each get one guess.

"A giraffe."

"A car."

"A hand."

"The letter *F*?"

I'm the last one to go. Mari's drawing is truly opaque. There are some shapes, to be sure, but there are also a lot of stray marks, and it's hard to tell what's part of the picture and what isn't. To be honest, "giraffe" was a pretty good guess. Mari looks at me pleadingly, as if to say, *Not you, too?*

"Is it a faucet?" I ask.

Mari lets out a cry of despair that lets us know we've failed.

"It's a hammer! See, this is the handle, this is the head, and this is the claw part you use to pull out nails," she says.

Grant shakes his head. "Dude, that's not a hammer."

Now we're two for four. Our air of inevitability is waning. Mari stands next to me and rests her chin on my shoulder.

"We're both failures," she says.

And apparently, we've started a trend. The next challenge is a geography challenge; the continent of Asia gets split up into twelve puzzle pieces, and Chris is supposed to arrange them together within sixty seconds. One look at the pieces and he freezes up. He makes an attempt, but in the end he's not close.

All our hopes are riding on Danny. For his challenge, he has to listen to clips of conversations and identify the language that's being spoken. There's one in Mandarin, a kind of *Hello, I am Wang Peng, I like to play basketball* conversation straight out of a textbook. But for the rest of the clips, I'm at a total loss.

Apparently, so is Danny. The only language he gets right is Urdu.

"So close!" the announcer calls out. "Unfortunately, that means that you've only succeeded on two out of six challenges. Thanks for playing! That's a wrap on the *Hotel California* Olympics!"

We've failed. The digital wheel goes dark, the assistants start to clean up and put the covers back over the tables. There's nothing left for the six of us to do but file out.

And yes, it's some consolation that there were a couple of near-impossible challenges hidden at the end of the Olympics. But I feel like everything turned on me, failing on kimbap, blowing our best shot at victory when it was within easy reach.

SABINE

THE MOOD AT DINNER IS DOUR, TENSE. THE LOSS HAS LEFT A BAD
taste in our mouths, and no one has much energy to chitchat
about anything else.

"It's like a double loss," Mari says. "We didn't get the prize
money, and we're bad Asians."

"Well, not *all* of us," Yoona says, pointing to herself and Grant.

"It's okay. We'll win next time. Or at least, some of us will,"
Grant says, smiling. "I doubt that we'll all be on the same team
for the next challenge."

Meaning there won't be anchors like me to drag him down.

Mari's right: the Olympics do feel like a double loss. I know that
if I came from somewhere more cosmopolitan, or even if I read the
right meme pages, I would have been able to pass the food challenge.

The problem is, I'm stuck in the wrong version of the show.
Five weeks of not knowing the right things, not having the right
personality. I was hoping to find a place where I fit in, and instead
it's the opposite. I stand out, and not in a good way.

And what's worse, with the streaming platform in the picture, millions of people are going to see it. Including the people back home.

Yoona, Mari, and I are in the girls' room, winding down for the day. Last night we all went to sleep early before the first challenge, so we didn't get the chance to gossip about our dates. Now we finally debrief.

"It was difficult at first," Mari tells us. "I kept asking questions, trying to find a way into his mind. I think I put pressure on Chris. He's not someone who likes to talk and talk. So finally, I let myself talk, and then suddenly the words were pouring out of each of us. We discovered one thing after another that we had in common. It was like catching up with an old friend."

Her voice picks up speed as she talks, and by the time she finishes, her eyes are misty.

"So it went well," I say. No surprises there.

Yoona tells us about her painting lesson with Grant. "He asked me that question again. 'Why are you here? No really, *why* are you *here*?' He also got really competitive about the painting part. That's his painting." She points to the canvas leaning against her bed.

My date with Danny feels like a long time ago now, but thinking about it still makes me happy.

"He put a lot of thought into planning the date. And he's a good listener. I had a nice time."

"That's great," Yoona says. But there's a hint of an ironic smile on her face. "I thought maybe he was the kind of guy that's really into himself. But I guess I was wrong."

Right on cue, she swoops in to remind me of my place, to make sure that I'm not having any fun unless I play by her rules.

Each time she's done this so far, there's been something else to distract us—dates to get to, Olympics to play. But not this time. Her comment hangs in the air like a challenge. Time is standing still.

I'm not going to let this go.

"What's that supposed to mean?"

Yoona shrugs. "Nothing. I was just talking."

"But you said this earlier, too. I want to know why you keep taking these swipes at me."

"Don't take it personally, man. It's not at you." Yoona is smiling coolly, like she's unfazed, like she's amused that I'm overreacting.

"But it *is* at me." The accumulation of all her drive-by comments is coming back into my mind. The moments where she made me feel like I wasn't sharp enough, or good enough, and I didn't get to respond.

This time, I'm going to bite back.

"Anytime I do the smallest thing wrong, you always point it out. Now you're trying to tell me how to feel about my date. I get it, I'm an easy target for you."

I let the accusation hang in the air. Yoona's smile has faded, and now her brow is furrowed. I feel a flash of fear. I poked the bear.

"That's not—I didn't mean to—I . . . I never said you were an easy target."

It's surprising to see Yoona—smooth, confident, beautiful Yoona—stumbling over her words. I thought she'd come back with more firepower. Now my own confidence comes surging back.

"I think we're all tired," Mari says. Yoona and I both snap our heads toward her. Her expression is calm but firm. "Let's not fight. We're all on the same side here. If there's too much negative energy right now, then we should just go to bed."

I don't respond. I'm not going to be the one to back down. Inside, though, I'm relieved that there's a third person around to keep the situation under control. It feels like Mari is cutting things short while I'm still ahead.

"Good idea." Yoona nods. She turns back to me. Her brow is still furrowed, and there's no more ironic smile—now she seems to be examining me, as if she's trying to understand what she missed before, where this hidden resolve of mine is coming from. "Sorry if I hurt your feelings, Sabine."

"You didn't," I say. I'm not letting that one go, either, in case it was meant as a parting shot about my sensitivity. "I'm fine."

We turn off the lights and go to bed. I spend a long time lying awake, too wired to fall asleep. My eyes are open, and I gaze up at the dark ceiling. A smile spreads across my face.

I stood up to Yoona again, and it felt good. Now I understand why.

Before, when Grant made fun of me about Moline, I was afraid to show anger. He could have called me out for being too sensitive, and I would have been embarrassed. But now I'm realizing that I was being too timid. My feelings are valid. I'm allowed to stand up for myself, to ask for respect.

Because even though Yoona seems flawless, unassailable, inside she's not any smarter or tougher than I am. I've been through just as much as she has, I bet. Probably more: someone like her has never had to fight just to be seen, the way I have. I can keep up with her.

Yoona is not as invincible as I thought.

YOONA

PEOPLE THINK THAT I DON'T FEEL ANYTHING.

They approach me warily, they see the way I look, the way I talk, and they decide that I have a cold personality. That they can push me away, and I'll absorb the hostility like it's nothing.

I smile and play it off out of instinct, to avoid showing weakness. But still, it *hurts* to have people I hardly know suddenly turn on me, as if they've been against me the whole time, and they were just waiting for the right moment to show it.

In the morning, as the group filters down from upstairs into the living room, I'm afraid to speak. Sabine's presence feels monumental, planetary. I'm more conscious about how the small jokes and observations I like to make could be taken as bullying. I don't want to say the wrong thing again.

"Hey, Sabine, I want to ask you something," Grant says when he comes downstairs.

"Me?"

"I said your name, didn't I? Listen, I want to take you on the next outing. I know it's a little early, but I like being first." He flashes a cocky grin, as if to say, *Yeah, I just did that.*

Sabine glances around the room, at Danny, then at me. Even though I'm surprised, I try to keep my facial expression as neutral as possible; even that could be taken as judgment.

I wonder if the boys had their own debrief about the dates already. Did Grant tell Danny ahead of time that he was going to do this? I try to read Danny's reaction, but he appears truly nonchalant. Then again, he always looks like that when he's with the group.

Sabine, too, is slow to process the situation. Given what she said about Danny last night, I'm sure she was hoping to go on another outing with him. She's in a tough spot, though, because there seems to be an unspoken code against rejecting anyone's date request.

Sabine shoots me one final look, as if she wants my advice, or my permission.

"All right," she says, smiling shyly. "I'd love to."

Once the air warms up enough, Mari and Chris go out to the pool. Sabine follows them outside. From the living room, I watch through the glass as Sabine pulls Mari by the arm, whispers in her ear. Mari's mouth opens in surprise, and the two of them laugh about this morning's unexpected turn of events.

I understand why Sabine stood out, what star qualities got her picked for this show. She has a wholesome, earnest manner, and she wears her heart on her sleeve. She seems to feel things deeply, unselfconsciously, with no attempts to hide how she's feeling. It's charming.

On top of that, she has a nice smile.

"What are you looking at?"

Danny sets himself down on the couch next to me. I glance back at the dining table, where Grant is pointedly not looking at us. He's staring at a chessboard. One pawn has been moved. Realization dawns on me.

"So, Yoona, I wanted to talk to you about the next outing," Danny says.

"Ugh," I reply, before I can stop myself.

"Ugh," he repeats, with a mock sagging of the shoulders. "Try to hold back the enthusiasm."

Sabine and Grant are paired up, and Chris and Mari are a sure thing, so in a way, I knew this was coming. Still, now that it's happening, a wave of nausea pulses through my stomach. I wonder if he called me any gross names, or said something to Grant, like, *Let's trade dates—girls like Yoona tend to like me.*

"We could just stay home. You shouldn't feel obligated to ask me out," I say.

"I don't feel obligated. I want to get to know you better. Maybe it'll be fun." For once, he's not wearing that smirk that he always puts on when he's talking to a girl. In fact, he sounds normal, without any of his usual affectation. "Give it a chance. If it's really unbearable, I promise we can come back early."

I know I'm not getting out of this one. "I get to plan the date," I say. "I'm picking where we go, where we eat, all of that."

If I have to go on a date with Danny, I might as well get free omakase out of it.

"Deal," Danny says. "But wait. If you're making the plans, then you have to be the one to ask me out."

Bam, the smirk is back.

"You've got to be kidding me."

"I don't make the rules, Yoona."

Ideally, I'd call for a judge's challenge, or consult with my attorney before proceeding. But fine. Let's just get it over with. "Will you go out with me?"

"Hmm . . ."

"Say yes now or I'm changing my mind."

"All right, jeez. Yes. Just trying to have a little fun."

"Yeah, yeah. Save it for the date."

Most of the date options are in LA. I pick out a screening of an artsy Iranian film about a retired detective who has to return to his grandparents' village to solve a murder. This is the perfect option because it (a) is indoors, (b) minimizes time spent talking, and (c) should be intensely dreary, thus killing the mood for the remainder of the date. Good stuff.

So, as the day begins, at lunch in a sushi restaurant in North Hollywood, I tell myself that I just have to get through an hour or so of chitchat and we'll basically be done with the talking portion of the date.

"So remind me what the activity is again?" Danny asks.

"We're seeing a movie."

"What's it about?"

I look him dead in the eye. "Murder."

"Is there anyone famous in it?"

"Maybe."

"Maybe?"

"Maybe they're famous in Iran."

"Why would they be famous in Iran?"

"That's where this movie is from."

"So you're into movies?"

"Not really."

He raises an eyebrow, but I just pop a piece of tuna into my mouth and keep a straight face. My confusion tactics appear to be working. The one-word answers are also a nice touch. Danny probably thinks I'm a freak.

"I'm really big into movies, you know," he says.

I look at him, still chewing.

"Mostly Pixar. *Coco* gets me every time. They know exactly what they need to do to make me cry. I'm still waiting for *Finding Nemo 3*."

I snort. I thought he was going in a different direction, probably about to tell me that he likes *The Godfather*, or *The Wolf of Wall Street*—something macho but also sort of refined.

"I have a question," I say. "How did you arrive at your current personal aesthetic? The hair. The earring. The calf socks. Did you choose all of this consciously, or is it just what spoke to you?"

"You're basically asking why I'm such a fuckboy, right?" He grins broadly.

"Not just why. *How*."

"You're pretty blunt, aren't you?"

I shrug. "I asked first."

"It wasn't really on purpose. Well, maybe it was a little. I got picked on a lot in middle school. It was mostly the usual stuff that brown guys get, like, 'Are you good at math?' 'Are you a terrorist?' There were these two kids that rode the bus with me, and every time I got off the bus, they would say, 'Thank you, come again,' in that Apu accent. It was *not* cool. I wanted to fight them so bad. I'd lie awake in my bed at night, dreaming of beating them up."

His expression darkens, and his voice takes on an edge, like he's right back there on the bus. "After a year, we moved to a town with a better school district. And I just decided that things weren't going to be like that for me anymore. So I started trying to be cooler. It's going to sound silly, but I started playing basketball and listening to rap. I thought that was the formula for being cool. Over the summer, I'd go to the park and practice my jump shot all morning. Then I'd go home and try to learn all the words to rap songs. It wasn't even popular rap. It was, like, the old stuff that comes up when you search for 'best rap.' Tupac and Nas and stuff."

"And apparently it worked. Now you're as cool as it gets," I say.

Danny laughs and throws up his hands. "Hey, it's not all my fault. I go to private school. Living in an all-boys dorm gives you a PhD in being a knucklehead."

I'll give Danny credit: he's not as one-dimensional as I thought. At least he knows how he comes off, and how he got that way. Self-awareness: it's what separates humans from animals.

When we leave the restaurant, I'm almost regretting the activity I've picked. I wouldn't mind talking for a little longer. After hearing a bit about Danny's story, I feel the urge to share some of mine.

We arrive to find that the theater is mostly deserted. Danny and I have a whole row to ourselves; we're by far the youngest people in the audience. The movie is made in a very cinematic and artsy way, but it's also horrifically boring. Less than an hour in, I catch myself nodding off. Danny is watching with mild interest, but when he notices that I'm falling asleep, he mouths, *Should we leave?* I try to make myself sit through just a few minutes more, but eventually I give up. We sneak out of the theater—no offense to the director. To make up for it, I say a quick prayer for this movie to win an Oscar.

We go back outside to Hollywood Boulevard and start ambling down the sidewalk.

"I have a question for you, Yoona. Be honest."

"Ask away."

"Is there something going on between you and Sabine? I've been getting some weird vibes lately."

"Is it that obvious?" I'm surprised that he's picked up on this. Sabine and I have had some awkward moments, but only in private. I don't know what's giving it away, unless she told him about my warning from earlier.

"No, that's why I asked," Danny replies. "I thought I was picking up on something, but I wasn't sure. It's mostly coming from you, if I'm honest. You seemed down this morning. Not your usual self."

"What's my usual self?"

Danny grins. "The way you were acting at lunch. Calling me out, rolling your eyes, giving me shit."

I laugh. "Sorry, I guess."

"It's cool. You keep me in check. I can tell you'll never let me get away with anything. I dig that." He pauses, looking thoughtful. "I guess it doesn't work with everyone, though."

It's almost evening, and the late-afternoon sun bathes the row of theaters in a golden glow. The scenery must be putting me in a good mood, because as Danny and I take in the sights, look for names we recognize on the Walk of Fame, I find myself thinking maybe he's not so bad.

"She thinks I'm . . . I don't even know what she's thinking." I shrug. "I feel like she started getting aggressive out of nowhere. Maybe she thinks I nitpick her too much. That could be true."

"You didn't know she'd get upset. It's not your fault," Danny offers. "She's a cool person, you're a cool person, you just haven't found the right wavelength yet. But you should still try. At least talk to her. Don't let things simmer."

"I hadn't thought about that."

It's a simple suggestion, but in a way, it's radical. I wasn't thinking of reaching out. Usually, when people cut me out, I let them. But it doesn't have to be that way.

Who is this calm, reasonable person that showed up to my date? Maybe that disgusting comment I overheard wasn't the real Danny.

"All right, I'll do it," I say.

"Good."

He pushes his lips into a slight pout, stares into my eyes with what I'm pretty sure is his smolder. I know what he's doing. I know who and what he is—or at least, I thought I did. But the thing is, it's working. There's something chemical about this whole bad-boy thing that wisdom and prudence cannot defy. Maybe there is actually something here. A real person.

What is it with these reality-show boys and getting me to examine myself?

I thought that I came to this place to get away from my normal life, to have a few weeks of silly, low-stakes fun. As it turns out, it's not so easy to make a break with my regular self. But that could be a good thing.

I have so many memories of being angry. Every time Winnie and I got into a skirmish at church, I'd stew on it at home, fantasize about dumping tea on her bible, or sneaking up behind her and cutting off one of her pigtails. One time in middle school, when our pastor announced that Winnie was going to a national debate tournament, I prayed for her to fail ("Dear God, please don't let Winnie win a trophy so that the whole church has to hear about how great she is again . . ."). I looked up the results online, and when I saw that she'd gotten eliminated in her second round, I made sure to ask, "Hey, Winnie, how'd the tournament go?" in front of her mom and all the other parents.

Small victories like that were fun at first. But rivalry is a pointless game, and even winning it gets old quickly. With Sabine, the same patterns from back home are playing out here. Instead of repeating the past, though, I can choose a different ending.

Maybe that's what I was meant to find here—a second chance.

SABINE

"CONFESSION—I MADE A SELFISH PICK FOR OUR OUTING," Grant says.

"Uh-oh. This better be good. I hope you know that last week, I was treated to a curated itinerary of experiences that I could not have had in Moline," I say.

We're in downtown LA. Our first stop for the day is an indie bookstore. The shelves are high and tight, and they seem to have been intentionally arranged at odd angles to create a jagged maze. The air is stuffy and smells of disintegrating book pages. Grant breathes it in and sighs with satisfaction.

"Well, today, you get to experience a curated itinerary of experiences that *I* could not have had in Moline," he replies.

Grant and I go to look at the rare books section. Everything is safely ensconced in a glass case, and the prices are eye-popping. There's a first edition of *The Sun Also Rises* by Ernest Hemingway that costs more than a thousand dollars. On one corner of the cover is the original price—ten cents.

"Apparently, it's so expensive because there's a typo in it," Grant explains. "There's one instance where the word 'stopped' is spelled with three *P*s."

"Stop-p-ped," I say. "I never really got into Hemingway. Too much moping."

We go diving through the stacks of dollar books, hoping to find something more in our price range. Grant tilts his head so he can read the titles on the spines.

"What's your favorite book you've read in high school?" he asks.

"That's easy. *The Catcher in the Rye*."

Grant straightens up and looks at me, incredulous. "You called Hemingway mopey, and your favorite high school book is about an angsty teen who goes around calling everybody a phony?"

"Holden is very relatable," I say defensively.

"You should read this, then."

He holds up a copy of *The Bell Jar* by Sylvia Plath. "It's sort of similar, in my opinion. A lot more depressing, though."

After he hands the book to me, Grant goes on looking through the books intently. Every once in a while, he'll pluck out an impressive title like *The Fire Next Time* by James Baldwin, or *The Unbearable Lightness of Being* by Milan Kundera, and ask if I've read it. When I say no, he offers me his opinion ("It was really readable for something so intellectual"; "It was beautifully written but felt artificial") and then keeps on looking for more books.

"You came here to show off, didn't you?"

Grant smiles. "Maybe. Is it working?"

"I'm very impressed." I nod. "But then again, there's no proof that you've actually read these books. You could have just memorized the summaries from Wikipedia."

"I guess we'll never know."

Before we leave, Grant lines up to pay for his books. He has four in total, including *The Bell Jar* for me. Before handing it over, he borrows a pen from the cashier to write a note.

You're welcome. —Grant

"How touching," I tell him.

We leave the bookstore and wander up the block, toward Chinatown. We pass by an optician, an import-export store, and a test-prep school. In front of a piano academy, we stop.

"This takes me back," I say. "My parents used to make me take piano lessons."

"No kidding. Want to go inside?"

"Why not."

We open the door and walk down a narrow hallway. At the front desk, the receptionist gives us a puzzled frown. "No lessons right now. Come back in the evening," she says.

"We're with the documentary crew," Grant says, pointing to the cameraman who's been following us. My eyes widen at the brazen lie. "Didn't they tell you about us? We're featuring the school for a spotlight on Chinatown's small businesses."

The receptionist's eyes narrow. "How old are you?" she asks.

She obviously doesn't believe him. But before she can ask more questions, the phone rings, and she picks it up. The conversation quickly gets heated, and she turns away and covers the handset with her mouth. Grant tilts his head to indicate that we should go farther inside.

We go into one of the classrooms. Instead of desks, there are rows of keyboards. At the head of the classroom are a whiteboard and an upright piano. The piano reminds me of the one we have back at home—the one that's been untouched since I finally forced my parents to let me quit. It's been gathering dust ever since, a reminder of the bragging rights that I was unable to bring home for the family.

"Do you remember how to play?" Grant asks.

"I went to piano school for a couple of years. And I took private lessons for, like, ten seconds. Then I started throwing tantrums, and that was the end of my piano career."

I sit down at the upright and open the cover. Slowly, tentatively, I tap out "Row, Row, Row Your Boat."

"Do you play?" I ask. I stand up and beckon him to sit.

Silently, Grant sits down at the piano. He takes a deep breath.

"Don't tell me—" I start to say. When his fingers hit the keys, my jaw drops.

He's playing classical music, and his fingers are *flying*. I've been duped. He's a prodigy. He even looks the part—his body sways as he climbs up the higher keys, and he closes his eyes as if he's really feeling the music. When the piece is over, I applaud.

"My parents never let me quit," Grant explains. He does an

impression of a finger-wagging parent. "'If you can't stick with anything, then you'll never succeed at life.' I told them that my friends all got to quit, and they told me that I should relish getting ahead of them. Anyways, here we are today."

"Do you like playing?"

"I like being good at piano. But I don't like practicing, and I hate when I first start on a new piece and I can't play it." Grant shrugs.

The door opens, and the receptionist pokes her head in. "Was that you?" she asks, incredulous. Grant nods.

"Spectacular! I thought it was Mr. Wong, coming in early to practice." She comes up to the piano, eyes shining with admiration. "Do you give lessons?"

As we make our exit from the piano school, Grant has to brush away business cards and offers to guest lecture. "Come back anytime!" the receptionist calls out after us.

"So it wasn't just the bookstore," I say. "You planned the whole day around showing off."

Grant grins. "No idea what you're talking about. How could I have planned on sneaking into a piano school? You think I called ahead and arranged that whole situation?"

"I'm not complaining. It was eye-opening. I always thought my parents' expectations were too high. But it turns out that there actually was one kid out there who did everything they wanted me to do."

When a car comes to take us back to Palm Springs, I'm feeling pretty great. One nice date could be a fluke, but two in a row has me thinking—maybe I'm good at this.

I used to get jealous of the girls at my school who had boy-friends, or even friends who were boys. I thought that it took some special ability or aura that I just didn't have. But the problem wasn't me. In a friendlier setting, talking to boys is easy—even the unrealistically hot ones that the streaming platform found for this season. I can make jokes, tease, maybe even flirt. I didn't know this about myself before.

I like it.

Back at the house, I sit by the pool and dip my feet into the water. It's evening, and everyone else is inside; I'm by myself, but I don't feel lonely. I'm taking a moment to enjoy my situation, how well things are going for me. I close my eyes, lean back, and take in a deep breath of the desert air.

"Mind if I join you?"

I open my eyes, look up at the twilight sky. I recognize Yoona's voice, and I sit up slowly, taking my time before responding. "Sure."

She's already barefoot, and she slips her feet into the water beside me.

"What's up?" I ask.

"Nothing. I just wanted to come outside. Grant is going to try to sell everyone on playing some super-complicated board game, then he's going to spend ten minutes explaining the rules, and then everyone is going to remember how annoying he is to play with, because he doesn't go easy on us even though he's the only one that's played before. And in the end we're going to watch anime. I figured I'd wait it out with you until we get to that part." I point into the living room, where Grant is currently making the hard sell, talking with his hands.

"Oh. Got it."

In spite of our last, tense interaction, right now I feel calm. I was at the pool first, Yoona came out to visit me. In a way, that gives me the upper hand.

"So, how do you like California so far?" she asks.

"It's different. I really like the plants here. The palm trees make me feel like I'm on vacation. Like I'm welcome, but I don't belong here, if that makes sense. Same with the cactuses. Cacti."

Yoona nods and stares into the water. She pulls her feet out and hugs her knees to her chest. For once, she looks small, hesitant.

"What about you?" I ask. "How does it compare to New York?"

"It's not bad. I'm with you on the plants, but I don't like the dryness. I think I'll stick with New York. Have you been?"

I shake my head. "I want to go there someday. It might sound weird, but I really want to ride the subway. When I was a kid, I'd see movies set in New York, and I thought the subway was the coolest thing. I just couldn't believe that there was an underground tube that just took you wherever you wanted to go."

"You can visit me. We can definitely take the subway."

I smile at the invitation, but it's strange to me that she's being so nice. If anything, I thought that she might want to get back at me after I called her out. It's like she respects me now. She knows that I'm not someone to be messed with.

"How was your day out with Grant?" she asks.

"It was fun. He was showing off a lot." I tell her about the bookstore, and the piano school. "He bought me a copy of *The Bell Jar*."

"Not bad. But I got a painting." She holds a straight face for a second. Then her mouth cracks into a smile, and both of us laugh.

"The book has a message in it, though. 'You're welcome.' You hear that, Yoona? I'm *welcome*. How thoughtful is that?"

"We'll call it a tie."

"And how was your date with Danny?" I ask.

"Better than I expected. He's surprisingly sweet. I guess I was wrong about him." She winces sheepishly, as if in apology.

"I don't blame you, though," I offer. "The long hair is misleading. It's like he *wants* you to think he's a—well . . . a—"

"A douchebag," Yoona suggests. We both laugh. It feels like we're making an unspoken agreement now: We're at peace. There won't be any more sniping.

And just like that, my final reservation about this season of the show melts away.

When I first arrived at the house, I was scared. I thought I didn't belong. But bit by bit, I fought for my place here, and I discovered that all my hopes for myself—that I was capable of so much more than I'd been allowed to do in Moline—were true.

Now, even Yoona can't deny it any longer. She sees that I'm on her level. That I'm not just someone who can get by in a place like the Hotel California.

I'm someone who can stand out.

"I wanted to follow up with you about our last conversation," Carrie says. "I've been thinking about what you said, and I feel that I may have been too dismissive."

"What do you mean?" I ask, stifling a yawn. It's the morning, I've only been awake for about fifteen minutes, and I'm still groggy.

"Your comments about the changes in casting, how you felt uncomfortable. You specifically mentioned some potential issues with Yoona. I took a look at some of the footage from the first week, and I can see what you were talking about."

I squirm in my chair. I forgot that I'd gone blabbing about that. Time seems to move more slowly at the Hotel California; that last confessional was about a week ago, but it feels like a completely different era. Carrie doesn't know about my confrontation with Yoona, nor about the truce that Yoona and I reached yesterday evening.

"The snide remarks, the way she poured water on your outing with Danny," Carrie continues. "I've seen the way she picks on you. I know it must be hard. The executive staff wants me to let it go, but of course, I can't help but feel somewhat responsible."

"Oh. I see."

So Carrie has seen some footage of the show already. A small part of me feels vindicated—Yoona *was* giving me a hard time at the beginning. Carrie must not have seen the more recent stuff yet, so to her, I'm still on the hot seat. And she said that she feels responsible: Does that mean that I was right, that I got on the show because she had a soft spot for me?

"Admittedly, there's not a whole lot I can do, seeing as I'm over here on the sidelines. But if there's any way I can support you, then please let me know."

"Actually, we're doing fine," I say. "She went after me at first, but once I stood up to her, she backed off. She's been much nicer in the last day or two. Maybe we'll even be friends."

"Oh. That's very interesting," Carrie says. She's silent for a moment, seemingly at a loss for words. I can tell she was planning to do more comforting, encouragement, but I took the wind out of her sails. She didn't expect me to figure everything out myself.

"Well, in that case, forget what I said," Carrie says, smiling warmly. "That's the beauty of reality television. There's no script. Anything can happen: and whatever happens, happens."

I smile, feeling triumphant.

"Amen."

YOONA

CHRIS AND MARI ARE NOW OFFICIALLY A COUPLE.

In the morning, before the second challenge, Mari finally tells Sabine and me about their date. They were supposed to go to a photography exhibit in the arts district.

"Chris was all excited, because we talked about the photographer on our first date. The exhibit closes next week, so the timing was really lucky. It was really sweet of him to find this for us."

But when they arrived at the gallery, they learned that the tickets were all sold out; they had gone on sale a week in advance online.

"He was *so* devastated. He kept arguing with the guy at the ticket booth, like, 'Come on, you have to let us in, I'll pay extra.' Eventually, the ticket guy told us that we had to leave, or he'd call security. Chris kept beating himself up, talking about what a disappointment he was. I told him it was no big deal, and I was just happy that we got to spend the day together. But he wouldn't stop, and I just had this feeling that there was something else on his mind.

"So I just told him, 'Chris, whatever it is, just spit it out. I'll never judge you for it. But right now, you're shutting me out, and you need to let me in.'"

So that's what Chris did. "He said that he felt like he was on his last chance," Mari says, her eyes shining, like just the memory is putting her on the verge of tears. "He said, 'I'm not smart. I don't do well in school. I play sports, but I'm not going to get into college with that. My mom always jokes with me that it's too bad that I can't sell my looks. And that's kind of what I'm doing now. So if I can't get that right, then it just feels like I'll never find what I'm supposed to do.'

"This might sound strange, but I felt so, so happy at that moment. Because I knew exactly what I had to do, and it was what I wanted to do all along. I told him that he didn't have to pull off some big success to prove that he was good enough. I said, 'The people who love you, they love you because you have a beautiful soul.'"

"Not to mention those arms," Sabine mutters. I stifle a laugh.

"And then what?" I ask.

"And then we kissed. And it felt like he was finally letting his guard down, letting himself be vulnerable."

After she's done filling us in, Mari flounces off, presumably so she and Chris can go skipping through a lavender meadow before the van arrives. Sabine and I stay in the girls' room.

"Wow. Young love," I say. Sabine laughs.

"Guess this is the new status quo," she replies. Meaning, Mari will be spending less and less time with us.

I rub her shoulder. "At least we have each other!"

The room feels emptier without Mari. But on the bright side, there's a more intimate, conspiratorial vibe when it's just me and Sabine.

"Have you ever been in a relationship before?" I ask.

She presses her lips into a thin line, shakes her head. "Nope. Have you?"

"Not really. Just a couple of summer flings. Very secret. My parents don't want me to date until college."

"Are they really strict?"

I shrug. "My mom is fussy about the way I do small things, but she's not really strict. I can still do what I want, pretty much. My dad is really strict when he's around, but he's in Korea most of the time."

"He doesn't live with you?"

"Nope. Not since he got his fancy job. I see him maybe once a year now."

"Oh, wow." She slides closer. In a lower voice, she says, "You must miss him a lot."

"Meh. I'm used to it." I lower my voice, too. It's like we're at church, hiding in our own corner, whispering our secrets to each other. A new feeling for me.

"When he first told me about the job, I got really mad. I always knew his company might ask him to go back, but I never thought he'd actually do it. It was his idea to move the family out to the US in the first place. I was like, 'Dude, why would you bring us all the way out here and then just leave?'"

She nods in sympathy. "I'm sorry."

"Don't be sorry. Life is fine. He still calls pretty often. Least he could do, right?" I shake my head. "Anyways, don't let me go off about that. Thanks for listening."

"Of course! Anytime. I didn't know any of this about you."

I smile. Then, on a wave of giddiness, I start laughing.

"What?" she asks. She starts laughing, too. The giddiness must be contagious.

"Nothing. I guess it sounds sad, so it's weird that I'm laughing. It's just that I've never talked about this before with anyone."

After the words are out, I wonder if I've said the wrong thing. It feels like an embarrassing admission, or at least overdramatic. But Sabine doesn't seem to mind. She looks happy.

It's incredible how quickly reaching out, trying to be nice in the face of animosity, can make a difference. So simple, yet so transformative. It's like a superpower.

And now I have it.

In the afternoon, the van takes us to a neighboring town called Rancho Mirage. We pull up to a house in a residential neighborhood, one that looks suspiciously similar to the art studio where Grant and I met Noor. It even has a front yard planted with grotesque, extraterrestrial-looking succulents. I catch Grant's eye, and he winks at me—he sees the resemblance, too. If this is a painting competition, I want to be on his team.

But inside, the house is dark. The windows are blacked out,

and the only light comes from fluorescent neon panels in the walls. Then the music starts playing, a thudding techno-metal hybrid that I'd recognize anywhere. My adrenaline spikes through the roof. I realize what's going on, but my heart can't quite believe it.

There's no way they're going to make us play *Starfall*. Don't they know who I am?

"Hello, challengers!" a voice cries out over a hidden speaker system. "Welcome to week two—BOYS VERSUS GIRLS. A reality deathmatch like nothing you've experienced before!"

Starfall is the hottest video game on the planet right now. It's a shooting game, set on a distant star dotted with space facilities and volcanoes. People eat, sleep, and breathe this game, and when they're not playing it, they're watching other people play it on stream.

My parents and I moved from Seoul to New York when I was seven. My first friends in America were the three Jeong brothers that lived upstairs. They played video games all day, and they probably thought it would be funny to teach the new girl who didn't speak English how to play as well.

They didn't think it was funny when I started beating them.

Eventually, I got so much better than them that they refused to play against me. Instead, we'd spend hours on Siege mode: the four of us defending our holdout from wave after wave of aliens wielding plasma guns and laser swords. The first time we ever survived the entire siege on Legendary difficulty, the Jeong brothers picked me up and paraded me around the apartment on their shoulders, belting out the melody of the main theme music. It's one of my favorite memories.

When the boys moved away to the suburbs, my mom bought me the same console and games so I could play online and stay in touch with them. I think she thought they were nice boys from a nice family, and she wanted to keep them on the roster in case I ended up marrying one of them. Unfortunately for her, the Jeong brothers have never made it past Gold II, and I haven't played with them in years.

Anyways, the point is, I'm frickin' sick at shooter games. God help these poor boys.

The music stops, and the lights go on. The room is bigger than I thought. In front of us is a massive TV, with two couches in front of it—one blue, and one pink. Is that for boys and girls? So tacky.

"For today's challenge, you'll be playing *Starfall* in duel mode. 1v1. But there's a twist," the voice on the speaker explains. "Team members will alternate turns at the controls. The three of you will divide up a three-minute shift, a two-minute shift, and a one-minute shift. The match will last thirty minutes. THE TEAM WITH THE MOST KILLS WINS!"

The TV flashes on with a countdown—ten minutes until the match starts. Sabine, Mari, and I huddle up on the couch to talk strategy.

"Do either of you play video games?" Sabine asks. "I feel like the guys might be at an advantage here."

"I've played a little. Not *Starfall*, but I've played other shooter games," Mari says. "Yoona?"

"Yeah, I'm really good," I say, trying not to sound too full of myself. "I made Diamond last season. I don't play much 1v1, but unless one of these boys is secretly a pro, I'm pretty sure I can dominate."

"What about you, Sabine?" Mari asks.

"Um, you've both seen me play Super Smash Bros. I think that's pretty indicative of my video game skills."

For the rest of the countdown, I try to give Sabine a crash course on *Starfall* controls and tactics.

"Left stick is to move. Right stick is to aim. Right trigger to shoot, right bumper for grenades. 'A' to jump, 'B' to crouch, 'Y' to melee. Try to stay on the move as much as you can. I'm a Roxanne main, so we should have the speed advantage. Got it?"

"Um, no," she says.

"Just keep moving this stick around. And if you see anything coming at you, run away," Mari says.

"Right."

I sneak a glance over at the boys. They look like they're going through something similar to us. Danny and Chris are whispering urgently to Grant, who looks distinctly stressed out. Assuming he's a scrub, Sabine might have a fighting chance in the one-minute shift.

I do my finger-loosening exercises, bending my thumbs back, cracking my knuckles, clapping my hands together to get the blood flowing. Mari and Sabine both look amused, like they can't believe that any of this could make a difference. Clearly, they've never met a beast gamer like me before.

The countdown reads *Three . . . two . . . one . . .*

"BEGIN!" the voice roars over the speakers.

The room fills with noise and light. On-screen, we watch through our avatars' eyes as we plunge out of the sky toward a glowing, pulsing star and crash-land in an abandoned space facility. Then the guns pop up, and it's on.

No holding back.

When I find the boys' avatar, a hulking steel robot with cannons for hands, I dash around behind it, peppering it with laser gun blasts and rockets from a miniature wrist launcher. In moments, the robot lets out a shuddering metallic groan and falls dead on the ground.

"Yeah, get some," I mutter. While the robot respawns, I sneak a glance at the boys. Chris's jaw is hanging open. Danny and Grant start berating him.

"Dude, do you even play this game?"

"I thought you said you made Plat!"

"I did! Once! Like two years ago!"

I smirk. Amateurs.

I know that my face twitches and my tongue sticks out when I get really into the game, and it looks embarrassing. But I do what needs to be done. You can't play *Starfall* and expect to look cool. You have to go to that dark place in your mind, open up the vault, let the evil spill out just a little. At least, that's what I always say if people make fun of me.

When I get the last kill of my shift—I activate my invisibility power and sneak up behind Chris, then stab him through the chest with a purple sword, triggering a gory animation of sprockets, gears, and engine oil shooting up into the air—I let out a feral cry. Even the boys are impressed, grabbing each other's shoulders and yelling, "OOOOH!"

Mari and Danny are next, for the two-minute shift. Mari seems competent at the game, but Danny has a clear advantage, killing her several times with a vaporizing blast from his cannon arms. Before I know it, two minutes are up, and Mari is shoving the controller into Sabine's hands.

What happens next isn't pretty.

She tries frantically to remember the controls, but they elude her. Watching her run into walls, get stuck in corners, and fire her gun uselessly at the ceiling as Grant murders her—it hurts to watch.

"Don't mash the sticks so hard. Just focus on moving. Run away if you see him. Shoot only in emergencies," I say, keeping my voice as calm as possible.

"I'm trying!"

It's no use. The robot kills her three more times before the timer puts her out of her misery.

The next few rounds proceed in similar fashion. I build up a lead against Chris, and then Mari and Sabine fritter it away.

By the third shift, Sabine is at least getting the hang of moving and turning, but Grant still gleefully Falcon Punches her with his robot arms. After a particularly violent death, she shoots him a dirty look.

"You're doing great," Mari says, in a voice so soothing that it helps me calm down, too. "Yoona can carry. The two of us just have to hang on. We can win this. Just keep your eyes on the prize."

I cannot believe that there is money at stake for this absurd challenge.

As the match nears its end, the score is still close. On my last shift, Chris finally gives up on regular fighting—he changes his avatar to a speedy, birdlike alien, and spends three minutes running for dear life.

"Stop running away, you wuss," I scream. "I can still snipe you!"

But Chris's tactic works. I manage to kill him only a couple of times, leaving my teammates with a dangerously thin lead.

"Stop shooting me!" Mari cries, as she charges at Danny head-on. Danny's bird-man launches himself into the air and peppers Mari with gunfire. But before he finishes the kill, Mari gets in close and throws a grenade. There's a flash of white light, and then both sides of the screen gray out with the message, *You have died.*

"Nice save!" I thump her on the back.

With one minute remaining, Mari hands Sabine the controller, with our team clinging to a one-kill lead.

"You got this, Sabine! Win it for us!"

Mari and I stand up and start chanting her name. Chris and Danny do the same for Grant, which sends him into a frenzy.

"Come out and die, Sabine!" he shouts. In response, the other boys start barking like dogs. This is what *Starfall* does to people.

"Just stay away from him. Run away and don't let him catch you," I remind Sabine.

She speeds around the map, doing her best to stay out of harm's way. It's all going well—until she steps on a land mine. As her lifeless body careens off the walls, my heart sinks. I forgot to warn her about land mines.

"It's fine! We just need a tie, and I can win the sudden death!"

"THERE AIN'T GONNA BE A SUDDEN DEATH!" Grant roars.

Sabine respawns, with just under thirty seconds to go. *Stay alive. Stay alive. Just thirty seconds.* She skulks around the space station, keeping an eye out for more mines. Grant finds her just as she's leaving a room and tags her with gunfire. She barely manages to make it out without dying.

"Power up! Power up! Left bumper!" I say desperately.

By some miracle, her finger finds the left bumper, and she activates our power-up, buying fifteen seconds of precious invisibility.

"Invisibility won't save you," Grant says. He follows Sabine out of the room and starts to spray the hallway with gunfire. The shots ricochet off the walls. If any of them touch her, the invisibility will waver, and then it'll be all over for her.

"Ten more seconds!" Mari says.

Sabine races through the space station. Grant stops firing, and the whole room goes silent. The two of them stalk around the empty space station, hunter and hunted, desperate to win the prize. Five seconds. We're almost there. Sabine sprints down a hallway, turns a corner . . .

. . . and runs smack-dab into Grant. The invisibility shield flickers.

"Dude! Behind you! Finish her!" the boys yell.

"Sabine, shoot! Right trigger! Right trigger!"

Sabine looks like her brain is melting. It's a lot of pressure; that much is obvious. Her fingers swim over the buttons, but she can't find the right one. My hopes shrivel.

But then, right before my eyes, a miracle happens.

Sabine's right hand is frozen stiff. So she brings her left hand smashing down on the keypad and mashes buttons at random. The camera pulls out into third-person on both sides of the screen, and our avatar, Roxanne, draws her glowing purple sword.

"NO FRICKIN' WAY!" I scream.

For the second time of the match, the assassination animation triggers. Our avatar plunges a purple sword into the bird-man's back. There's a puff of feathers, a feeble squawk, and then Grant's screen turns gray. *You have died.*

The clock at the top of the screen ticks three, two, one.

"You did it! You melee'd him! GG!"

I tackle Sabine onto the couch, and Mari piles on top of us. We get up and jump up and down in a delirious group hug.

"You did it! You did it! I'm so frickin' proud of you!" I scream.

"You're the one that put the team on your back. I just had a lucky finish." Her eyes are shining, like she might actually cry. At this point, *I* might cry.

"And also Mari made some important contributions!" Mari says, covering her mouth to do mock ventriloquism.

We laugh, we shout, we share in the euphoria of victory. On the van ride back home, we taunt the boys, sing "We Are the Champions," and talk about what we're going to do with our money. And yes, I was the clear MVP of the winning team, but the highlight of the night belongs to Sabine.

There's something about her. Call it determination, or resilience, or just straight-up luck—no matter the situation, even when she's in over her head, she finds a way to land on her feet. I underestimated her. She's so much more than that girl from the first day, complaining that the show wasn't living up to her expectations.

Our eyes meet, and she smiles at me shyly. I smile back, and it feels like there's something new between us, something warm that wasn't there before.

We're becoming friends.

SABINE

THANK GOODNESS FOR THAT VIDEO GAME.

At the end of the second week, there's a break in shooting for July Fourth. Because of the *Starfall* challenge, I get to go back home riding a high. I'll have a nice, relaxing week in Moline, and when it's time to go back to shoot the second half of the season, I'll actually be excited for it.

My parents pick me up at O'Hare and ask how the show is going. In between bites of the watermelon and take-out dim sum they've brought for me in the car, I tell them about the other house members, making sure to mention their high academic aspirations.

"You should learn from them. This is a chance to see how students from other schools are preparing for college," Mom says.

"Are you sleeping enough?" Dad asks. "I bet you stay up late, now that there aren't any adults around."

"We all go to bed early in the house. They schedule a lot of the challenges in the morning, so we don't have a choice," I say.

Thankfully, I'm pretty sure my parents will never watch the

show. To them, all TV other than the History Channel, the Chinese news, and *Jeopardy!* is just lā jī and luàn qī bā zāo. Especially a trashy reality TV show.

For the rest of the car ride, they ask me about college apps and remind me that after the shoot is finished, I'll be taking the ACT. I groan. I've already taken the SAT twice, and even though my score is decent, my parents have been insisting all summer that I try the ACT to see if I can do better on it. I blame their circle of Chinese parent friends for giving them this wretched idea.

Still, it feels good to be home. When we've made it into Moline city limits, and the river comes into view, everything looks familiar, but different. Not because it changed, but because *I* changed. Now that I've seen LA, the buildings, the streets, and even the people here all seem a little bit smaller. I've gotten out of this place, if only temporarily, and one day I'll be out of it again, living a new life that the Quad Cities can't contain.

After I get back to the house, the first thing I do is hit up Em.

Sabine:

Mall tomorrow?

Em:

You know it. Eastern Plaza or Northridge?

Sabine:

Let's go to Cedar Park

Em:

Oooh so you're bougie now? It's only been two weeks!

Sabine:

There are years where nothing happens, and there are weeks where years happen.

Also, I wanna try that new ice cream place.

I've been waiting over a year for the Painted Pony Scoop Shop to finally open a branch in Quad Cities. Em says yes by way of a paint palette and a horse emoji. She'll pick me up tomorrow after lunch.

Em:

Can't wait to hear more about Danny 😉

I smile. I've been giving her brief updates on how the show is going over text, but I'll be able to give so much more detail in person. I can't wait. It'll be good to have someone from my normal life to dish with.

On top of that, I'm kind of excited to be back out on the town. Now that I've been out west, experienced LA and khao soi and real bubble tea, I feel an aura around me, and I wonder if everyone else will see it, too. *You ain't ready for me, Moline. I'm about to take the town by storm.*

The West Coast jet lag keeps me up late. When I wake up, it's nearly ten a.m. I blink in the unexpectedly bright morning light and try to shake off my grogginess. So when I pick up my phone, it takes me a moment to recognize that something is very, very wrong.

My phone has gone haywire overnight. On my home screen, my messaging apps, texts, social media, and even my email are all overgrown with notifications. I click through them in a haze, trying to clear all the numbers and red banners. Through this, I manage to piece together what has happened.

First of all, episodes of *Hotel California* have leaked. I find an article about it on an entertainment blog, which explains that rough cuts of the first two episodes were accidentally posted to the streaming website. The blog explains that an engineer at the company was trying to upload the episodes to a staging version of the site as a test, but accidentally uploaded them to the real thing. The episodes were available for only a few hours before being taken down, but that was plenty of time for them to be pirated, downloaded, chopped up, and repackaged into GIFs and memes.

Second of all, I've got *mad* followers. Like, literally on the order of twenty times more than I had before. And that number is growing. There are strangers blowing up my DMs—some of the messages are supportive, while others are disgusting and possibly grounds for legal action.

Last one—the comments. I visit my go-to *Hotel California* fan-site to see what people are saying. It's a site that I've visited many times before, enough that it feels like a safe space, my space. Except now, I'm the one under discussion. Some of the comments are nice—Sabine seems sweet, Sabine and Danny are cute together, yadda yadda. But then, there are the trolls. I scroll through them with morbid curiosity. The typical comments suddenly feel a lot meaner when they're directed at me.

> This girl literally can't keep her fucking mouth shut
> How can a plain ass bitch like that be so mean
> I want to punch her in the face

I know I should stop, but I can't tear myself away.

Finally, close to the bottom of the page, I find a link to a website that pirates TV shows. I open the link, and there it is: *Hotel California S3E1.*

I press Play.

The footage is grainy, and the audio is slightly out of sync with the video, but it still looks and feels like the real thing. I watch, transfixed, as the show opens up with shots of the house in Palm Springs. A voice-over promises me that this will be the best season yet of *Hotel California.*

I'm the first to arrive at the house. I look around the empty living room with an expression of terror; I sit on the couch and fidget. Then I close my eyes, like I want to take a nap. God, I knew in theory that everything I was doing was being filmed, but it's still jarring to actually see myself on-screen, in my full awkwardness.

Chris, Mari, and Grant show up at the house one by one. When I see them introducing themselves—Chris shy, Mari unabashedly forward, Grant with his ineffable smoothness—I smile. It's all very endearing, especially now that I know them.

Then Yoona arrives.

She drops her head on Mari's shoulder, just like I remembered. Then the camera cuts to me, with my eyes bulging in surprise. She complains about traffic, and when I ask, "It took two hours?" my voice sounds accusatory. Yoona answers without lifting up her head, like she can't be bothered. As the conversation flows, I notice that every time she speaks, the camera then immediately cuts to me, looking tense and unhappy.

I mean, I *was* tense. But this editing is making it look like I immediately didn't like Yoona. When she finally looks my way, and we make eye contact, the camera focuses on me. I look away, but the camera lingers on me, like it's relishing my capitulation. Is that really how it happened?

I skip ahead, searching for more scenes of the two of us. In every one I find, I look moody, upset. When Yoona tells me to watch out for Danny, she sounds matter-of-fact, but I flare up immediately. I remember feeling good about that moment, like I was finally standing up to Yoona. But on the screen, it just looks like I'm lashing out for no reason. Yoona's reaction is puzzled, like, *I'm just a messenger, why are you taking this out on me?*

Finally, there's the scene after the Olympics, when I finally confronted Yoona.

"I thought maybe he was the kind of guy that's really into himself."

"What's that supposed to mean?"

Edgy rock music starts to play. The drumbeat is fast, like someone is trying to hurry the two of us into a collision; rough, distorted synths make the scene feel suddenly ominous.

"I want to know why you keep taking these swipes at me."

"Don't take it personally, man. It's not at you."

"But it *is* at me."

The music pauses, like the devil on my shoulder is taking a deep breath in.

"Anytime I do the smallest thing wrong, you always point it out. Now you're trying to tell me how to feel about my date. I get it, I'm an easy target for you."

The guitars kick in, a fiery sonic explosion.

In my memory, this was the moment where Yoona started to falter, where she realized that she was treating me unfairly. But the show tells a different story.

In the show, I get upset out of nowhere. At each step, I'm the one who escalates the situation, and Yoona is taken aback by my shrillness.

"I never said you were an easy target," she says, sounding perfectly calm.

She doesn't falter at all; when she pulls back, it's not because she feels guilty. It's because she's embarrassed for me.

And when Mari jumps in, it's not to be a neutral peacemaker. She knows that I've gone too far, and she's trying to protect me from myself. She's stopping me before I bury myself any deeper. That's where the episode ends.

I think back to my last conversation with Carrie: how concerned she was, and how surprised when I told her things had gotten better. If these two episodes are all that leaked, then they must have been in the works around that time—that's what Carrie saw. That's why she was worried about me.

I think I know what happened afterward. Yoona came out to talk to me by the pool, we made peace, we started to get along better. We were becoming friends.

But if I got the first part of the season so wrong, then maybe I was wrong about those moments, too. Maybe I was alone by the pool because I was radioactive, and no one wanted to be around me. Maybe Yoona felt sorry for me, and she was trying to treat me gently so that I wouldn't explode again.

It all depends on whose version of events is real—mine, or the one in these leaked episodes. Surely, it's the show, with its slick editing and music cues, that's the exaggerated one. With all the changes that the new production team made to the show this season, it should be no surprise that the editing has been reconfigured toward heavier drama, too.

I search through my memories, trying to find proof that I'm right. But it's surprisingly difficult. I *did* start to resent Yoona fairly early. I *did* make a lot of sour faces at the things she said. And I *did* go after Yoona out of nowhere—even if in my head, we had reached a breaking point.

What if everything in these two leaked episodes is true?

"This is *so* messed up," I moan.

"So awesome, you mean," Em says.

We're in her car, on the way to Cedar Park. Despair has settled into my stomach, and even the familiar comfort of riding shotgun in her hatchback isn't enough to put me back at ease.

"Dude, what are you talking about? They're making me out to be this atomic bitch-wagon. The commenters hate me. It literally could not be worse."

"Sounds to me like you're the star of the show. You know this is why people like reality TV, right? For the drama?"

"It's different when you're a part of it. You should see what these people are saying about me. It's truly heinous."

"Who cares what some online trolls think? Sabine, you're looking at this all wrong. People love you. Even if they hate you, it's because they love you."

"I don't know if that's true."

Less than twenty-four hours earlier, I was excited to be out on the town, casting my shiny new glow out to an adoring public. Now, as we pull into the parking lot, the crowds of people make me nervous. I wonder if anyone among them has seen the episodes, might recognize me. Maybe one of those commenters is here.

"I should have worn a disguise," I say.

"I don't think anyone is going to recognize you. The show was only online for, like, two hours. What are the chances someone from around here actually would have seen it? Let's just go in there and eat our ice cream."

As we walk through the mall, I keep my head down, sticking close to Em and avoiding any eye contact.

At the Painted Pony, I get one of their creative flavors, coffee-chip mint, and the combination is epic. In the rankings of humanity's greatest achievements, it's right up there with movable type and the polio vaccine. Even so, I can't relax. Every few seconds, I glance over my shoulder, checking if anyone is staring or whispering about me.

"Sabine, your eye is twitching."

"I know, I know. I'm sorry. What did I expect, right? If I'm acting like this now, what am I going to do when the episodes air for real?"

Em flashes a devilish grin. "Speaking of which, can we watch?"

I'm a little reluctant to relive the horror of this morning, but I figure that having Em there with me will help me put a positive spin on things. I pull out my phone, find the pirated links, and press Play.

"You weren't kidding about the boys," she says as they come to the house one by one. "Which one did you go on a date with? Danny?"

"And Grant."

"Daaaaamn. Both? Don't get greedy, Sabine," she says, laughing.

"I'm glad that my misfortune is so funny to you."

With Em watching with me, I don't feel quite as bad about my depiction in the show. The rough moments don't seem as serious when Em is here to laugh about them. And there are some bright spots, like my date with Danny.

"Oh, this is cute. I like this. The vibe is sweet," she says. When we get to the part where the tram car shakes, and Danny catches me before I fall, she smiles a big smile.

"Wow, he even bought you a shirt. I don't know what you're so worked up about, Sabine. Seems like you're doing just fine over there."

I have to admit, the date came out looking pretty cute. There, at least, the editors have been kind.

"Seriously, look at you. My little girl is all grown up!" She wipes a fake tear from her eye. "You've come so far."

"If only everyone saw me through your eyes."

Em isn't very impartial, after all. She and I met during one of the cruelest times in a young person's life: the beginning of middle school. I had just moved to Moline, and within a week I was already at my breaking point. On my first day of school, by some outdated, Byzantine PE requirement, I had to run a mile-time trial. I finished dead last, with a time so slow that I worried I'd get expelled for it, and afterward I dry-heaved into a trash can while Mr. Babcock pounded me on the back and roared with laughter.

Then in orchestra, the conductor, Ms. Haas, took attendance and kept calling out, "Kwee! Kew? Kewey?" It took me a full ten seconds before I realized that she was trying to pronounce my legal name, Qiu, and raised my hand. She muttered something about people not paying attention during roll call. Behind me, I heard a boy laugh. He was only one person, but it felt like the whole room was laughing along with him.

The girl next to me patted me on the shoulder and offered me a stick of orange-flavored chewing gum.

"Don't chew it unless she's looking away, or she'll throw you out," she whispered. Then she explained that Ms. Haas wasn't good with names; she'd done the same thing to her name, Ablema, which is how she started going by Em.

"How are you supposed to say it?" Em asked.

I told her. "It means 'autumn,'" I said. "But I go by Sabine."

"That's a pretty name. Both of them."

We knew, without saying so, that we were on the outside. That's not to say we didn't try to fit in; in fact, when we made it to high school, we agreed to give our honest best shot at turning things around. We dressed up for spirit week, went to a yearbook committee meeting, and tried out for cheerleading. And sure, one look at the uniforms and pom-poms and we both agreed, with a single glance, to leave the tryout and never speak of it again. But we tried.

As we get up to walk around the mall, we finally move on to other subjects. Em tells me about her summer courses at Augustana College.

"They're not as bad as I'd thought they'd be. It's kind of fun to be on campus every day. And I got out of that college essay workshop!"

"You were complaining *nonstop* about that—"

"Yeah, because I was stuck grinding out hundreds of words on why college is going to broaden my intellectual horizons or whatever, and meanwhile you were in California becoming a reality star."

"What are you taking instead?"

"I got that Intro to Africana Studies course I was telling you about! I don't think my parents would have let me out of the essay workshop otherwise. I told them that I need to connect with my heritage, and we're not going back to Ghana anytime soon, and they don't *understand* what it's like for us diaspora kids . . ."

"Shameless." I grin. "I gotta use that on my parents."

So now, instead of writing essays, Em is reading *Lucy* by Jamaica Kincaid.

"It's hard to understand because the prose is so dense," she tells me. "But it's worth getting through, unlike the stuff they make us read in school. Like *Lord of the Flies*. Can you believe that every kid in America has to read about a group of feral boys—"

Up ahead, I spot Brock Fernandez, walking toward us. Instantly, my body goes into fight-or-flight mode. Before Em can finish dumping on *Lord of the Flies*, I grab her by the arm and pull her into the nearest store, a Hollister.

"Um, excuse me? Since when do you still shop here?" she asks.

I shake my head and motion outside. After a few moments, Brock passes by. Only, it's not Brock, just someone who kind of looks like him. The boy is wearing an MHS varsity jacket, like Brock always does. I don't recognize him, though, so maybe he already graduated.

"Sorry," I say. "I thought I saw—never mind. I'm not feeling very well."

Em spots the varsity jacket, too. She nods. She may not know who I thought I saw, but nevertheless, she understands.

"There, there," she says, patting me on the back. "Why don't we go somewhere with fewer people? Where we won't run into anyone we might know."

"Maybe we should go home. I think I want to lie down or something."

It's all hitting me. When Carrie told me that the show was moving networks, it still didn't feel real. But it does now. Leak or no, the show is going to air for real eventually. And when it does, people at school *will* watch it. They'll see me among my own kind, and they'll think that the person on the screen is who I really am.

I came home on a wave of momentum, feeling like I'd found some inner greatness—or at least competence—at that house in Palm Springs. But looking back, it's hard to remember why I felt so confident. The big moments that got caught on camera tell the opposite story. What if those good feelings were only in my head?

What if, after all, I'm just as hopeless on TV as I am in real life?

YOONA

I THOUGHT ABOUT SPENDING THE WEEK OFF IN LA, BUT MY MOM insisted that I go back. The flight is long, and with the time change, I don't get back to our apartment until 8:00 p.m.

When I arrive, my mom is waiting up with dinner. She's made naengmyeon and bought a big take-out container of spicy blue crab, my favorite.

"Aw, Mom. You made a welcome-home feast for me."

"It's for me, too," she replies. "I always want yangnyeom gejang when it's hot outside. But I can't justify buying it when I'm by myself."

"In that case, you're welcome."

We start to eat. Even though I've had the show treating me to every meal for the last two weeks, it's still nice to taste home cooking.

"So, Mom, did you miss me?" I ask.

"Miss? No, I liked having some time alone. I can listen to my music, read my books, and spend more time at the church. When

I'm with you, we always have to leave right when service ends. Otherwise, you complain."

"That's your answer? Come on, Mom, try again. I'm your only daughter. You're devastated."

My mom shrugs. "What? Sure, I miss you. When I'm alone, there's no one to talk to. But it's only a couple of weeks. When you go to college, it'll be all the time. So I better get used to it, right?"

I always pictured myself going far away for college, putting a plane ride between myself and home so that I don't have to come back every week. After two weeks away from home, I'm more certain about that than ever.

It's painful to imagine leaving my mom here alone, though. My room is the only one in the house with any real decoration—I've got my wall of Polaroids, posters of my favorite girl groups, fairy lights strung up around the ceiling. Even the living room is all me, with the beanbag chair I asked for in middle school and my painting of sunflowers from freshman art hanging on the wall.

That's not to say that my mom is going to spend all her time staring at my empty bed, stroking my portrait and pining for me. She'll have more time for her hobbies, and she still has the church. But I'm the only person in this hemisphere that she's truly close to, and I'll be gone.

"You'll go back and spend more time with Dad, right?"

"Some. But he has to work. And I have to stay here, in case you need me. What if you get arrested? I have to be here so I can bail you out. That reminds me. Do you remember Kim Dae-won?

The one who goes to Ohio State? His roommate got arrested. He was selling the marijuana! They put him in handcuffs in front of everybody! He was international, too. Probably going to get deported. Poor Dae-won has no roommate now."

Suddenly, it's as if my mom remembers her duty to inform me of all of the potential life dangers that only she, with her valuable connections to the New York Korean grapevine, can adequately inform me of. I'm to carefully guard myself against scammers, kidnappers, and pianos falling out of the sky.

Normally, I'd tire of these stories quickly. But knowing that I'm just a visitor right now, that I'll be heading back to the house in a week, makes them go down a little easier. As she launches through scandalous tale after scandalous tale, I nod and half listen, throwing in an occasional "Wow," "No way," or "Are you serious?" to keep her going. Once or twice, the story is so obviously fake that I let out a real laugh. Then my mom laughs, too, slaps a hand to her forehead, and admits, "You're right, that one's probably not true—these stories get exaggerated. Well, unless . . ."

I missed these moments while I was away. Take away the constant contact, the frayed nerves, and the two of us can get along well. I'd spent my whole life with her up until recently, and it wasn't all bad.

After dinner, my mom checks the clock. Almost ten p.m., which means it's late Saturday morning in Korea. She calls my dad. I overhear snatches of the conversation—my dad just woke up; he was out late last night with his bosses, he thinks he might be able to get a promotion by the middle of next year.

Meanwhile, I start to do the dishes. My mom beckons me over to talk to him, but I hold up a soapy dish and plead for a special exemption, too busy being a great daughter.

Sometimes my mom forces me, but tonight she lets it go. She tells my dad that I'm doing the dishes, and that I'll call in the morning. "We talked about you. She's worried about you, living by yourself over there, working so hard. She misses you."

That's not exactly what I said, and my mom knows it. But it's the kind of thing my dad likes to hear, and my mom is much better at delivering the right message than I am.

After he moved away, we used to talk on the phone each night, me, my mom, and my dad. For a while it was fun, waiting for the clock to hit seven p.m., knowing that his alarm was going off at that very moment, then calling ten minutes later, knowing that he was awake and sitting by the phone. Then, as my dad got busier and busier, he'd hang up early, or skip the call altogether. It felt deflating, like we'd built up the whole evening around a big show, only for the main actor to not even take the stage.

When we did talk, the mood was more tense, less fun. My mom said I sounded sullen. Sometimes I'd make comments like, "Nice of you to join us," and my mom would tell me off.

One time, he didn't pick up, and I got mad. I knew he was on the other end of the line, letting the phone ring through. I called him again, and when he did pick up, I started yelling at him.

I didn't expect that he would yell back.

He said that I wasn't supposed to yell at my appa like that, I said that my appa wasn't supposed to abandon me, and by the time my mom took the phone away, I was crying. She said some things to soothe him and then hung up. I told my mom, "I hate him." I thought she would slap me, but she didn't. I think she understood.

Now, when we talk, I try to control myself, keep it formal and polite so no one gets too upset. I feel like my dad is the same way. So sometimes it's fine if we don't talk. At least, not on a nice night like tonight.

In the morning, our *Hotel California* cast group chat is blowing up. I scroll up a wall of messages and read from the beginning. Apparently, the first two episodes of the show leaked. And not to some sketchy pirate website, not even to the second-tier streaming website that you get for free with your internet subscription. It was on the big one. Yeah, *that* one.

Chris sends screenshots of texts from his agent. Apparently, *Hotel California* got bought out over the summer. The deal was done in secret, and the official announcement was supposed to happen in October. But then early edits of the first two episodes were uploaded to the website by mistake. A vague memory of the contract my mom signed comes back: "something something rights retained by Production Company, something something transferred at any time without consent of Talent." Never thought they'd actually do it.

Whatever plans I had for the morning are canceled. I find a link in the chat where the episodes are still up, and I press Play.

After the theme song plays, the season opens up with Sabine opening the front door of the house. There's no music, and since she's the only one there, there's no talking, either. The camera follows her as she takes off her shoes, places them gingerly on a shoe rack, and slowly, timidly wheels her suitcase into the living room. The episode is quiet, with the hovering sensation that something big is about to happen.

Our arrival order obviously wasn't planned—who knows, without my detour to a random hotel in LA, maybe I would have gotten there first—but there's something fitting about Sabine being first. She has a bright, innocent look that only comes through more powerfully on the screen, and her every thought shows up on her face. She's nervous but excited. When she sits on the couch and closes her eyes, I can practically hear the voice in her head, rehearsing her self-introduction, the one or two jokes that she has prepped. It makes me smile. Sabine has main character energy for sure.

Then I show up. I charge straight into the middle of the crowd and put my head on Mari's shoulder. It's a little extra, but also, it's funny.

And then all of a sudden, it's not.

There's something off about the way the show is depicting events at the house. Before the first scene even ends, it's clear: the edit is done to make it look like Sabine and I don't like each other.

The music, the jump cuts, the selective use of facial expressions, all of it makes it seem like she's judging me, and I'm judging her.

And then it gets worse.

"So what's our game plan for these dates?" Grant asks. The three boys are in their room, on the first night.

"I know who Chris wants to ask," Danny says, wiggling his eyebrows. Chris smiles sheepishly.

"That leaves Yoona and Sabine," Grant says. "I'm probably gonna ask Yoona."

"That East Coast connection." Danny nods. "That's all you, my dude. She has the New York vibe. The too-good-for-you vibe. She kind of scares me, to be honest."

Grant raises an eyebrow. "I'm basically from New York. You're saying I scare you, too?"

"Nah, no way. I like that British accent too much. Plus, it's different. Because you're my booooooy!" Danny reaches out to dap up Grant, and Grant pulls him in for a bro-hug. The universal language of teenage boys.

I realize that this is a part of the conversation that I overheard on the first night. The edit leaves out the worst of Danny's comments; there are no shots of me overhearing things, either.

So when I start to give Sabine warnings about Danny, it feels like it's coming out of nowhere. Actually, not nowhere: with all of the dirty looks that are flying around, it's coming off as another way that I'm trying to mess with Sabine, get into her head, stop her from having fun.

What a cheap way to manufacture drama.

I wonder how Sabine is feeling about this. Once I finish watching, I'll send her a quick text so we can laugh it off.

Most of the second episode features our first challenge, the Olympics. Watching it again, I finally realize how unhappy Sabine was during this challenge. Grant makes fun of her in an earlier scene, for not knowing about Subtle Asian Traits. Now, a mere twenty TV minutes later, we're going through a bunch of silly challenges that are thinly veiled adaptations of the top ten or so posts in that group.

When she complained about the changes to the show, I thought she was just being difficult. But really, she was insecure about fitting in after all the changes. I'm starting to get it now. She was afraid.

And I made it worse.

When she points out how stereotypical the Olympics challenges are, I make a joke about her being a buzzkill. I remember saying that. The thing is, I *did* mean it in a mean way. Like, yes, we get it, you liked the old show better, now stop whining. That's the kind of thing I say—always quick to hop in with a snarky comment. That's my sense of humor.

And yes, the editing is playing everything up, but the wounded look on Sabine's face is real. It's something that editing can't fake.

It bothers me. I try to draft a lighthearted text to Sabine, rolling my eyes at the editing, but I can't send it. This isn't something that we can just laugh off. We may be at peace now, but it's like the show is reminding us: There's something between you two, and you can't bury it away. It's real. And it's still there.

At church, my mom points out a conspicuously empty spot in one of the pews at the front of the room.

"Mrs. Um hasn't been here in three weeks! No one has heard from her. I texted her, 'Sorry about Jessica, you must be so upset.' Mrs. Hwang sent them a cake, didn't even get a thank-you."

"Not a single person has heard from her?"

"None."

My mom smiles, like this is great news. She always said that Mrs. Um was too arrogant, too selfish. One time, she invited a bunch of us over to her house in Astoria for dinner. She didn't make enough food, so she ordered more from a local restaurant, then asked the guests to split the check with her. My mom talked shit about that for weeks.

It's not like I love Mrs. Um, but I don't think she's some evil woman. Everyone wanted their kids to be the best, so she did, too. It's not her fault that her daughter was the only one who got into Harvard.

Then again, the moms probably say the same thing when the kids fight, and that never made a difference, either.

After the sermon ends, I follow my mom as she makes the rounds. Predictably, there's only one thing she wants to talk about.

"So we *still* haven't heard from her?" my mom says, pumping her voice full of exaggerated surprise. "I would have thought she'd be back by now."

"She might have said something to Mrs. Park. Mrs. Park

wouldn't say, but I bet they talked. You know they were close even before joining the church."

"Mrs. Um is being dramatic. After all the big talk from last year, she thinks it's some shame to show her face now." My mom shakes her head sagely. "Sure, we'll make a couple of jokes, but we won't shame her! She's still a part of the community."

My stomach churns. My mom has probably been doing this since the day I left: bringing up Mrs. Um, making high-minded statements about how we all need to stick together, all while getting her digs in. This is what she lives for. Surely, she must know that the other moms aren't really on her side, that they'd just as quickly turn on her the way they're turning on Mrs. Um. But either she doesn't care, or she's doing it *because* she knows that battle is the only truth in this place.

My mom starts talking about my dad's job, how he's on track to get a promotion soon. I scan the room for other kids, but most people my age are gone for the summer. I see some boys I don't recognize, running up and down the aisles, probably desperate to go home, and some middle school girls, looking at their phones together. A few feet away is another girl, standing by herself, watching those two. I don't recognize her, and she's too far away for me to see clearly, but I get the impression that she's glowering at the other girls.

I look at her, then back at my mom, still puffing out her chest about my dad and his fancy job. The thought hits me: *This is what I am, where I come from, how it's always been.* My mom and I, we're the same. We see everything as a fight, and we don't like to lose.

In our minds, we're simply defending ourselves, playing the same game as everyone else. But from the outside, we look like the mean ones. It's no accident that I'm seen that way here, and it's no accident that I'm seen that way on a TV show set in California.

And once people get that idea about you, it becomes the truth. A little nudge is all it takes; after that, everything you do confirms their opinion of you. I know that now, as surely as I knew it when Winnie Jung cried to my mom about how bad I was, how I couldn't keep getting away with it, how I had to be punished.

But that isn't the worst part.

The worst part is that small, persistent voice in the back of my head, whispering: *Maybe they're right.*

"Let's get going. It's still early. If we hurry, you can still call your appa before he goes to bed."

The postsermon buzz is winding down, and my mom is practically glowing with triumph.

"This late? He probably won't be up. He has work tomorrow, doesn't he?"

"We'll go just in case. You didn't call him at all from your show. Don't keep looking for excuses, Bae Yoona, you have to talk to him sometime."

"Okay, fine, let's go."

She frowns. "Why do you look so sad? Is church that bad?"

"I'm just tired."

On the subway ride home, my mom fills me in on the latest

gossip about Mrs. Um. Depending on who you believe, the poor woman cut off all her hair, applied to a military academy on Jessica's behalf, and swore to move the family back to Korea. My mom reels off more of her own stories about times Mrs. Um got too confident, bragged too much, set herself up for an inevitable downfall.

"Don't you think we should leave her alone? It's bad luck to talk about people like this. She's probably suffering enough as it is," I say.

"We have to talk about it," she replies, her face suddenly going serious. "It's important. We have to make sure it doesn't happen to us."

When we get home, my mom calls my dad. From what she says—"You sound sick," "You're not sleeping enough," "You need to drink less and eat more vegetables"—I can tell he won't stay on the line. Still, after a few minutes she hands me the phone. I try to shake my head, but my mom frowns and shoves the phone up to my face.

"Talk to your appa," she says.

I press it to my ear. On the other end, silence.

"Hey, Dad," I say timidly.

My mom, watching, glares at me for speaking English. I'm supposed to answer in Korean, but I sometimes forget.

"How was your flight?" my dad asks me.

"Fine. Long. I watched a movie."

"How long will you stay at home?"

"About a week."

Silence. The only sound is the low rise and fall of my dad's breath on the other end of the line. He sounds tired, like he's eager to get to bed.

Finally, he asks me to put him on speaker. "Remember to take your college applications seriously," he says. It's the cue for my mom to take over—the calls always end with a lecture or lesson of some kind. My dad goes on speaker, names a topic, and my mom fills in the rest.

"When school starts, you have to be ready," she adds. "Don't slack off. Your grades this year are just as important as junior year, at least in the first half."

"I know."

"Good," my dad says curtly. "Good night."

After I hang up, my mom scowls at me. "Why do you have such an attitude? You can't tell him about how you're doing? You can't even call him your appa?"

"He's tired; he doesn't want to hear it."

"You can't tell him about your show?"

"He won't get it anyways. He still thinks it's some kind of documentary."

"Tell him about church, then."

"What is there to say? I'm not going to tell him bad things about Mrs. Um. What does he care?"

"You should tell him that you miss him, that you're thinking about him. His life over there is very hard. You'll make him feel better."

"No one forced him to go there. I'm the one who asked him not to. If he wants me to say I miss him, that's his problem."

"Aigo, he's over there working for *you*. Why don't you appreciate that? Because of him, you have money to go to whatever college you want. People in the church respect us because they know what he's doing over there."

I hate this line of reasoning. "He doesn't get credit because the two-faced church people 'respect' his job. He came here because he wanted a promotion, and he went back because he wanted another one. But he won't even admit that it's all been about him—"

"Stop it. I don't know who told you that, or where you get this from—"

"I probably get it from you!"

My mom glares at me, and I glare back. Aaand we're back at it again, our old ways. At least we made it through one good day first.

It's all coming back to me now. When I'm here, I get sucked into the pattern of this life, this closed, dark outlook on other people, this cycle of expectation and disappointment. I want to change it, but that takes focus, energy, and I don't seem to have it right now. I need to get away again.

Only now, I'm beginning to question if the place I'm going is any different. Yes, running away got me some breathing room. But there are some things about myself that I can't seem to outrun.

SABINE

I LIKE TO SAY THAT MY TROUBLED RELATIONSHIP WITH MOLINE comes down to my being Asian, but deep down, I know it's not that simple.

In the year above me, there was this guy Coby Huang, who played baseball and hung out with the athlete-cheerleader supergroup. He even dated Claire Beaulieu, who was tall and cute and blond. To explain this, I used to think of him as a "whitewashed" Asian, a Twinkie, a banana. It wasn't really fair—I didn't know him at all, and it's not like he went around denouncing his culture—but I didn't know how else to understand how his being Asian could just not matter, like it always seemed to for me.

Maybe it was the baseball. But I suspected that it went beyond that, that Coby had a certain "it" factor that canceled out his ethnicity. I know that other people on the show have "it," too: put Danny or Yoona at Moline High School, and they'd be right there with Coby. I always hoped that I might have it, in the right setting. For a while there, I thought I did.

I try watching the leak again, hoping that it wasn't all that bad. But it's no use. I hate how strong my reactions are, how I let every little thing that Yoona does get to me. I have no control, no guile. Every last thing I'm thinking shows up on my face. Yoona, on the other hand, always keeps her cool. I could swear there were moments at the house when I had her flustered, but they don't show up in the leak. Nothing gets to her. It was all wishful thinking.

"Sabine, forget about the show. Come to the movies with me," Em pleads over the phone. "You can't hide in your room watching *Parks and Rec* forever."

"I beg to differ. It's going great so far. I feel safe with these people. April and Andy will never hurt me."

Em finally goes to her last resort—she'll take me to Culver's, her treat. "We can go to the one in Davenport. No one will know us there. You can wear a disguise."

"I can't. From now on, I'm not leaving any traces. I was thinking, if I skip the first couple months of school, maybe people will forget about me. No one will connect the dots and realize it's me on the show."

I can practically hear Em rolling her eyes. "Fine, starve. I'll go by myself."

When I finally drag myself downstairs, it's almost evening, and my parents are prepping dinner.

"Now she remembers us!" Mom says sarcastically. "It's so touching that our daughter misses us so much when she's away."

"Being a parent is so fulfilling," Dad adds.

"I'm sorry, I'm sorry. I'm just stressed about going back to the show."

"What's wrong, honey?" Mom asks. She dries her hands, wet from washing vegetables, and sits down with me at the table.

Even though she's being supportive, I know I can't tell her what's really going on. If I tell her about the leak, the comments, then she'll try to make my choice for me.

"I'm thinking more about what it's going to be like to be on TV, having people watch me and judge me. It'll be harder to go out in public. What if this show follows me around forever?"

"Only losers pay attention to reality TV shows. No offense." She shrugs. "Besides, how do you know they'll judge you? Maybe they will like you. You can show them that you're a nice person, and you care about your studies. Be nice to everyone in the house. If you have snacks, offer to share. And if people leave dirty clothes around, fold it up and put it away for them without making them feel bad. But also, be neat. Don't let the other girls feel you are a messy person."

I smile. My mom's advice is always like this—simple, sweet, and totally not what I'm looking for.

"Thanks, Mom."

"If you really don't want to go on the show, you don't have to go back. We didn't pay them anything. They can't sue us. Can they?" Horror creeps across her face as she thinks back to the forms she signed, trying to remember what promises she might have made, what rights she signed away.

I quickly assure my mother that the show can't sue us, putting an end to the conversation. Over dinner, we talk about college apps and picking a major, topics that feel incredibly distant right now. If I want advice about how to handle the show, I'm going to need to look elsewhere.

When I go back upstairs, I see a pair of missed calls from an area code I don't recognize. DMs are one thing, but there's no way some internet troll found my phone number, right?

Despite a creeping sense of dread, I call back.

"Oh, good, you're there. I was beginning to worry I had the wrong number," a woman's voice says.

"Who is this?"

"It's Carrie."

"Oh, Carrie!" I'm surprised, but not necessarily in a bad way. It makes sense that someone from the show is reaching out. "Hi. Sorry I didn't recognize your voice. Um, what's up?"

"First of all, I wanted to apologize on behalf of the entire show team for the leak. It shouldn't have happened. New systems can always cause difficulties, but that's no excuse."

"Oh. Yeah, sure. No problem. I mean, it *is* kind of, like, not great. I guess."

"You're very kind," Carrie says. From her tone of voice, I'm getting the sense that she's not really apologizing for herself—rather, she's blaming this on the new company, and she'd be perfectly happy to hear me pile onto them, too.

"More important, I wanted to check in," she continues. "My guess is that you've watched the two leaked episodes. We're doing our best to scrub them from the internet, but you can imagine how difficult that is."

"Yup, I saw them. Sorry. I guess I wasn't supposed to."

"Oh, please. I would have watched them, too, if I hadn't already seen most of the footage. The question is, are you okay? I was worried that you'd find the edit to be upsetting."

I should have listened to her when she said she was worried about me. Maybe it was too late to change anything by then, but at least I wouldn't have had these delusions of grandeur. I wouldn't have felt proud of myself for acting the way I did.

"You mean because I looked like a total loser," I say. "Way oversensitive and mean."

"Of course not. Is that how you feel? Sabine, I don't see it that way at all. If that's your perception, then I really am worried. I'm talking about the way that Yoona treated you. I don't think it's an exaggeration to call it bullying. I have a nephew who's in middle school, so I know exactly how cruel this can be."

"Bullying?"

"Yes, bullying. Going out of her way to make you feel unwelcome, like you didn't belong."

So she was concerned about me, but not for the reason that I thought. I don't like the idea that I'm being bullied; it still makes me sound weak. But if Carrie has her own take on what's going on at the house, then I want to hear it.

"You really think so? You don't think that I was getting upset over nothing?"

"Of course not. This was all by design, you know. The streaming platforms are very particular about the way they construct the cast. These shows always look for someone like Yoona: a commanding presence, someone who's not afraid to ruffle feathers. In fact, if you knew exactly what went into the casting process . . . well, let's just say that I'm not all that surprised about how things are going."

I'm silent for a moment, absorbing this new piece of information. The new showrunners again. They wanted this to happen. I'm *supposed* to feel the way I'm feeling.

"I thought that she and I were getting along better, though," I say. "We had a good time playing the video game together. Isn't the show exaggerating things? What do you mean, 'exactly what went into the casting process'?"

"I haven't seen the footage of the video game challenge yet, so I don't know what happened there. As for your question, it's hard to explain. Perhaps we can talk more in person. If you truly believe that she's come around, then that's wonderful. But I still have my concerns. I want you to be careful, Sabine.

"I know this is a lot to process. It's not my intention to add to your troubles; I truly just wanted to see how you are doing. And I wanted you to know that you're not alone. I'm on your side, and I'm rooting for you."

"Thanks. I don't know if you'll have anything to show for it, though."

"Sabine, listen to me. You're an extraordinary young person. You're smart, you're funny, and most of all, you're resilient. I know what you've been through, and I know who you are now that you're on the other side of it. You may not believe it, but I think that this situation gives you a wonderful opportunity. You have gotten the viewers' attention. It may be negative attention at first, but sometimes, that's what happens to the heroine. She goes through some lows. But that's what makes her interesting.

"Everyone who's seen the show is wondering what you're going to do next. Sure, there are some mean internet trolls, but for every one of them, there are ten girls who see a little part of themselves in you and want to know how you're going to make your comeback. Everyone loves a good comeback. If anyone can turn this situation around, it's you."

I'm stunned. I stumble through a few words of thanks, but they don't feel adequate. Carrie says once again that we'll talk more at the house. Then she hangs up, leaving my head swirling with thoughts.

Perhaps I was being too hard on myself. Not everyone is going to watch the show and see me as the odd one out. Some people are going to understand who I am, what I'm thinking. They're going to want me to succeed.

Carrie said that I was resilient, that everything I've gone through made me into a strong person. I want that to be true. I want to be a person that doesn't give up.

I watch through the leak again, but this time, I do it with purpose. I study the way the cameras see me, and I try to be honest with myself about what I need to fix. To my relief, it's not all bad, either. Anytime Yoona isn't around, I come across fine; my date with Danny even feels cute. He picked up on the same thing that Carrie did: that I'm a fighter. I like that. I need more of that in my life.

Above all, I can't be so obvious with my emotions. The cameras love that stuff; they'll pick up on every last grimace and frown and glare. I have to be cool. I have to be more like Yoona.

But who is Yoona?

She's hard to understand. The handful of moments where she was being nice to me felt real. They made me happy; they made me believe that Yoona was a straightforward, sweet person. But the moments where she was picking on me were real, too. If she was mean for no reason before, then she could be mean for no reason again. I can't even be sure about the moment by the pool, or during the video game. Maybe she was just taunting me, and maybe she just wanted me to play better so we would win. I don't know how those moments really looked; all I have are my memories.

Like Carrie said, I have to be careful.

YOONA

WHEN I GET BACK TO THE HOUSE, THERE'S ONLY ONE OTHER PAIR
of shoes in the foyer. It belongs to one of the boys; I go into the
living room and see that it's Danny.

"I was hoping it was you," he says.

Oh. My. God. This man. How does he say this stuff with a
straight face? It's such a ridiculous greeting that I can't even call
him out for it, so instead I burst out laughing. Danny laughs, too.

"Help me with my suitcase," I reply.

Danny dutifully lugs my suitcase up the stairs for me, and I sit
on the couch and send a "Thank you!" chasing after him. Good
for me, putting him to work.

When he comes back downstairs, I decide to grill him.

"So, you're scared of me?"

Danny winces. "Sorry. I wish they hadn't put that in there. I
didn't mean it. Well, I guess I did. But it's not a bad thing. It's like
I told you before, you never let me get away with anything."

154

"So it's not *me* you're scared of. What you're really scared of is having to look into the mirror."

"No, I think I'm also scared of you."

I roll my eyes. "Want to watch a movie or something?"

He raises an eyebrow, no doubt remembering the last movie I made him watch with me. "Only if I get to pick it this time," he says.

We go to the basement and Danny puts on a Bollywood movie called *Maine Pyar Kiya*. A poor mechanic's daughter goes to stay at the house of a family friend, a wealthy businessman. The businessman has some reservations about taking her in, because he has a son who might fall for her, instead of marrying rich. It's okay, the son says, a boy and a girl can just be friends. Meanwhile, the son is a hottie who likes taking off his shirt. Obviously.

"Do you agree with that?" Danny asks. "Do you think a boy and a girl can just be friends?"

"Don't even go there," I say.

"What?" Danny says innocently. "You don't believe it?"

"Danny, I don't know much about Bollywood tropes, but I'll bet you literally anything that these two end up together."

The son gives the mechanic's daughter a hat that actually says *Friend* on it! She says thank you. "It's a rule of friendship," the son replies. "No sorry, no thank you."

Danny explains that this line is very famous. "No sorry, no thank you." The mechanic's daughter responds with a tilt of the head, a shy smile, and a sugary, one-word response: "Okay!"

Aside from the disapproving father, there's one more person trying to throw a wrench into their plans: Seema, the smoking hot daughter of the businessman's partner. In contrast to the sweet, innocent mechanic's daughter, Seema smokes cigarettes, wears red lipstick, and has a quick temper. She's into the son, too, but you know she's not a threat. You're meant to not like her. A movie like this would never let her get what she wants.

"Here's a question," I say. "Did you have that 'I was hoping it was you' line planned out ahead of time? And would you still have said it if Chris were the first one back?"

"I thought of it while I was chilling here. In my defense, I was the only one here for a while." Danny grins sheepishly. "I should have known not to use it on you."

"Actually, you should have known not to use it on anyone, under any circumstances, ever."

Danny laughs, and I laugh, too.

I'm starting to like our dynamic. It's nice to be around someone who doesn't get upset when I make fun of him. That alone puts me at ease; I don't have to be hyperaware of my words, or my tone of voice, around him.

I hear the pitter-patter of footsteps coming down the stairs. It's Sabine.

When she sees us, her face falls. "Oh, hi. Is it just you two?"

I wait for Sabine to join us on the couch, but instead she stands there, looking at us, while the movie keeps playing. I feel suddenly self-conscious about being alone with Danny. There was nothing weird about the situation before, but things feel different when you have an audience.

"I haven't seen anyone else yet," Danny says, finally.

"Yup. Just us. Want to join?" I ask.

"What are you watching?" Her eyes dart back and forth from me, to him, and back to me.

I never ended up texting her about the leak; I wanted to see Sabine in person, to take her temperature first, and also because I was worried about seeming cold over text. Now, though, I wonder if that was a mistake: it gave Sabine more time to think about things on her own, and who knows what she came up with.

"It's a Bollywood movie. We're about an hour in."

"Which means that we've only got another two and a half hours to go," Danny says, finishing my sentence.

Sabine looks dubious. I pat the couch next to me, but she doesn't bite. She makes an excuse and dashes back upstairs. I'm pretty sure I did everything right, but I still get the feeling that I botched the situation somehow.

A part of me wants to go upstairs after Sabine. But Danny goes on watching the movie, and I decide to stay. I feel relaxed right now. There can't be that much harm in enjoying this for a little longer.

Danny and I keep watching for a while, but the movie is absurdly long. We're barely more than halfway through when the sound of conversation from above reaches critical mass, and we both decide to head upstairs.

"We should finish it at some point. There are some really classic scenes toward the end of the movie," Danny says.

"For sure. I want to see what happens. I'm calling it: Seema steals a motorcycle, and the rest of the movie is about her jetting through the Himalayas. Eventually, she gets a phone call inviting her to Prem and Suman's wedding. She sneers. The final shot is of her, snarling into the receiver, 'Eat my dust.'"

"Interesting theory. You're definitely right about the wedding, at least."

Everyone else is back now. Once we're in the group, the mood shifts.

"So do we talk about it, or do we not talk about it?" Grant asks. He means the leak. After a few moments of collective silence, he adds, "I think we should talk about it."

I look around the table. Sabine's expression is stony, and she's determinedly avoiding eye contact with me. Unexpectedly, Mari and Chris look uncomfortable as well. They exchange a wary glance, looking at each other for answers. I can't guess why; their portrayal in the show was angelic.

On their first outing, Chris and Mari go for a hike in a canyon full of palm trees. When they reach a vista with a view of the long line of palm trees, cutting through the desert floor, Chris says, "I think that going to a place with beautiful scenery is the best way to get to know someone."

"Yes!" Mari says. "It fills you with a sense of your own life's grandeur and significance. It makes each moment hum with possibility."

"That's a great way to put it."

"So what's your greatest fear?" Mari asks, as they make their way down a winding ravine.

"Not being accepted. I want to be an actor, and everyone in my life has been supportive about my dream. I know my parents had their own plan for me, since I'm the oldest son. But when I told them what I wanted, they believed in me right away. My fear is that I'll put the work in, that I'll make sacrifices and struggle for the best years of my life, and in the end, it still won't be enough."

"I'm sorry you have to live with that fear. But I'm so glad that your family supports you. No matter what happens in your life, there's always redemption in love."

The way the camera lingers lovingly on Chris's shy smile, Mari's dimples—to anyone watching, it's obvious that the editors love them. Every moment is mined for maximum cuteness and likability.

"My agent told me that she knew all along about the streaming deal," Chris begins. "She didn't tell me because she didn't want me to feel pressure. Being on a show like this will help me get more work. Maybe another TV show, definitely some ads at the very least. Someone at Lululemon already reached out."

Danny thumps him on the back. "That's sick! Congrats."

Mari rubs his arm, smiling. Chris doesn't look happy, though. I get the sense that he's repeating whatever his agent said about why the situation is great, without truly believing in it.

"It feels weird that it's coming from a role that isn't a *role*, though," Chris continues. "I'm used to learning fake lines for a made-up story. Acting is about learning to see yourself from the outside, the way the camera sees you. That way, you can give the camera what it wants. Except for this show, I'm still supposed to just be me."

Mari nods. "Now we know what the show is expecting from each of us. Chris and I are supposed to be the perfect couple. So if we fight, it's like we're letting the audience down. And even the good moments have to be played up, like they're meant to be seen. We don't have any privacy."

Around the table, almost everyone seems to be going through some version of what Mari is describing. The only one who doesn't seem to care is Danny. The show made him out to be an aloof, too-cool-for-school type, which we already know is exactly what he's going for.

We weren't supposed to watch the show while we're still in it. Before, the fact of the 24-7 surveillance felt abstract, to the point that we forgot about it. Now we know how our lives are being mined for content, how any moment can be turned into a story. And the story about me and Sabine—that we don't like each other, that we're fighting—is the most dangerous one of all. I didn't reach out while we were all at home, but I know that I need to now.

After we clear the table, I pull her aside.

"Hey, can we talk in the game room?" I ask.

Sabine studies me for a moment before responding. Her face is relaxed, blank, in a way that feels unfamiliar.

"Sure," she says.

Normally, she's easy to read, but right now I can't tell what she's thinking.

Down in the basement, the TV is still on: Danny and I forgot to turn it off. The couch still bears our impressions; they're closer together than I remember. We were sitting right next to each other.

"So what's up?" Sabine asks. She glances at the couch, smooths out the cushion, then sits down, right where I was sitting before.

"I want to talk about the leak. You watched it, right? You saw how they made us look."

"I watched it a little bit."

"Do you want to talk about it?"

Sabine shrugs. "What do you want to talk about?"

Out of all the ways I thought this conversation would go—nervous laughter, angry recriminations, crying—I didn't expect this nonchalant version of Sabine. It's good that she's so calm, but there's something off about her demeanor right now. She's so different from the girl who was here before the break.

"It's the way they made us look. Like I was picking on you, like you hated me. I think we should—I feel like we need to . . ." I hesitate over my words. I don't know what we "need" or what we "should" do, and I'm afraid of getting it wrong. I don't know how to fix this situation. Every time I get into a conflict like this, it always ends in either separation or hostility.

Sabine is silent for a while. The only clue to her thoughts is a slight tilt of her head, like she's thinking. In that silence, I get the sense that she's studying my tone, my demeanor, my phrasing—*I was picking on you; you hated me*—like a position on a chessboard, trying to play out all the possibilities before she picks her next move.

Finally, she smiles. It feels like a genuine smile, warm and friendly. "We don't need to talk about it," she says. "It is what it is. We weren't supposed to see it anyways. That's why it's a leak, right?"

I let out a nervous laugh. "Right."

"Let's not worry about how we looked, or didn't look," Sabine adds. "Let's just have fun. Leak or no, this is still supposed to be fun."

She stands up from the couch and pulls me in for a hug. I'm caught off guard, and I stand there, limp, for a moment too long. But it feels nice, and eventually I get control of myself and hug her back.

"Should we go back upstairs?" Sabine asks. "Everyone else is probably wondering why we came down here alone."

She's already walking up the stairs by the time I answer.

I follow after her, feeling happy, but confused. Maybe the leak wasn't that big of a deal after all. Maybe the good feelings from talking by the pool and winning *Starfall* were enough to get us past it.

But I'm not sure. I don't know what to make of Sabine's cool demeanor. The smile and the hug were nice, but they felt calculated in a way that I can't quite ignore. Like she was putting up a kind facade, while still keeping me at arm's length. Like she's already written off the idea of becoming genuinely close with me.

Back upstairs, I watch her from a distance. She drops down onto the couch with Grant and Danny, and within minutes the three of them are laughing, looking totally relaxed. It's a nice scene.

I try to shake off my unease. I'm just being paranoid; the leak hit a little too close to home. I shouldn't let it bother me. Like Sabine said, we weren't supposed to see it anyways. I should focus on having fun.

This is supposed to be fun.

SABINE

IT'S EVENING, AND I CAN'T SLEEP. I'M LYING IN BED, STARING UP
at the pale moonlight spread across the ceiling.

I've only been back at the house for a few hours, and already
I'm struggling to keep up with events, to process them quickly
enough to figure out how to act.

First was coming home to two pairs of shoes in the foyer: one
girl and one boy. Then walking through the deserted living room,
hearing the muffled sound of the television from downstairs, going
down and finding Danny and Yoona together on the couch.

For an instant, Yoona had a guilty look on her face. What did
that look mean?

I think I might know.

Yoona watched the same leak that I did. She saw how she was
treating me, how bad I felt, and yet all through the week off,
she didn't reach out. That means she wasn't surprised. She knew
exactly what she was doing all along.

She also saw that there was only one bright spot for me: my

date with Danny. And that was after she warned me not to go out with him, too. I have a suspicion that all of it—the warning, the leak, and the funny way she was acting when I found her watching a movie with Danny—is related. It all has to do with me.

Carrie's warning is still in my mind. Be careful. I can't trust Yoona. I won't.

"I know that I owe you more answers. I'll give them to you. But remember, once I tell you everything, there's no going back."

I'm in the trailer with Carrie. Over the phone, she hinted that there was more going on behind the scenes than I knew, that there were reasons that I had to be careful. Now it's time to find out what, exactly, she was talking about.

"I want to know," I say simply.

She takes a deep breath. "Keep in mind, I'm only telling you about this because you're familiar with this show. You understand what we did in the past. Our goal was always to reach young people."

I nod vigorously.

"I told you that we still have that goal in mind. But the new executives don't. They're tech people, you know, everything is 'AI' and 'big data.' For them, this show checked a couple of boxes: existing fan base, low cost of acquisition, the opportunity to reach more diverse viewers. But according to their fancy computer algorithms, it wasn't going to be successful enough for them unless they turned up the drama."

I figured as much already. The dates, the challenges, the hot cast: whatever changes the streaming people made, they weren't exactly subtle about it. I say this to Carrie, but she shakes her head.

"They didn't just change up the format of the show. They *studied* you. Everyone is online these days, right? You all have information on you out there, and it's not all that hard to find. So the company can take that data, feed it into their AI machine, and get it to spit out a cast that's literally *programmed* for drama. Each person fits into a type, and those types interact with each other in predictable ways. Take Chris and Mari, for instance. The soft boy and the sensitive girl? Last week, I overheard an executive producer *crowing* about how he knew that they'd get together."

I think about what the two of them said, about the pressure they were under to have a visibly perfect relationship. They were right about that, but they didn't realize how deep that pressure went. Their social media posts, their photos, their relationship status, all of it closely scrutinized to design a romance plot that would happen, seemingly organically, in front of the cameras. We were all chosen to play a part, using audition material that we've been slowly accumulating ever since we first went online.

"What did the AI say about me and Yoona?" I ask.

"It's not as simple as spitting out a description of you. For each person, the technology focuses on something different. It might notice that on social media, a person posts a lot of pictures, but very few of them are taken in a group. Or it might look at a person's friend network and find that they have a lot of second-degree connections but relatively few first-degree ones. That means that they're socially isolated. Relatively speaking. Combine a few salient observations like that, and a type emerges."

She's trying to speak in general terms, but she's clearly thinking about *my* specific profile. I'm not part of a group. I didn't post any prom pics. And "socially isolated"? Painful as it is to admit, that's me.

"So the algorithm chose me because I'm a loser, basically. And it chose Yoona, who's willing to point that out and go after me for it, all to create drama. Even if it means I get embarrassed all season long."

"I can't speak to the intention," Carrie replies. "But the editors do seem to have latched on to that narrative."

"Can't you do something about it? It may not mean anything to you, but I'd really like to be able to keep going to school without wearing a paper bag over my head. And you're letting this happen? Why are you doing this to me?"

My voice is speeding up. I'm starting to feel frantic.

"The editors are just doing their job," Carrie responds. "At the end of the day, they're only working with the real footage of what happened."

The statement splashes over me like a bucket of cold water. I sit there, numb. She's right. I can complain about the editors all I want. But they didn't force me to do anything on camera. I did all of it myself.

"This is why I was worried about you," Carrie continues. She sits down, leans in closer to me. "This goes deeper than a fight with a housemate, doesn't it? Tell me what's really bothering you."

Her voice softens, and she becomes the gentle Carrie Waters who called me on the phone, who said that she related to me. The one who's still on my side. Right now, she feels like my only life raft.

"I don't want to be on the bottom anymore," I say. The words come from some hidden place inside of me, but once they're out, I recognize them immediately. This is the real reason I came to this show. It always was. "I don't want to be at the back of the room, keeping quiet and staying out of the way. It's one thing if that's who I am in my hometown. But if that's who I am here, too, then maybe that's who I really am, period. I don't want that to be true."

"I understand completely," Carrie says. "I respect that. I work in Hollywood, Sabine; I know what it feels like to have people draw a box around you, as if you couldn't possibly have anything interesting going on beneath your surface. Not everyone has the willpower to fight back against that.

"I'm going to repeat what I said earlier: the editors are only working with the real footage of what happened. You should understand that, Sabine. In a way, it's the fundamental law of reality TV."

Hearing this phrase again makes me wince. Carrie's eyes, kind but firm, bore into me, as if she's trying to plant the words in my skull.

"What do you mean?" I ask.

"There's no script. Nothing is decided ahead of time. The only way to discover the outcome is to let it play out in that house," she says. "The editors have an idea of who you are, but that isn't enough to make it true. Nothing is certain until it shows up on the cameras. In a way, you have the final say. So if you don't want to be the loser . . . don't lose."

"But how do I do that?"

"That's up to you. You're the one in the house, making decisions, navigating situations. The ending depends on what you're capable of. It's a very difficult place to be in. I wish that I could change it for you, but I can't. Only you can."

The full weight of her words hits me, and suddenly it's hard to breathe. I'm trapped in the house, facing a deep deficit, and the only way to turn things around is to fight my way back, inch by inch. That's so hard. Impossible. All my life I felt like a lion caged in a zoo, separated from my own kind, misunderstood. But I didn't realize: If you're not in a zoo, you're in the jungle. And everywhere around you are claws.

"I can't do it. What chance do I have against Yoona? She's too good. At everything."

"Come on, Sabine, is it that bad? You should have more confidence. You know this show better than anyone else in the cast. The editors are trying to tell a story. They construct the story out of big moments, scenes that have an intelligible meaning to viewers. If there's a moment that's too juicy to ignore, they'll latch on to it, build an entire episode around it. You can work with that.

"Of course, you don't have to go this route. You could try to let the rest of the season play out quietly. Yoona is a classic alpha, but she's not a monster. As long as you accommodate her, she won't treat you too badly. You said that you two were getting along better, didn't you? You can be friends, in a manner of speaking."

Carrie is choosing her words diplomatically, but I can see how this situation would play out with the editors. They'd pick out my moments of submissiveness, cut them together with Yoona's self-satisfied smile, make it look like I've tucked my tail between my legs. I'm not going to put myself at Yoona's mercy again. She may have been nice for a little while, but she's still intent on keeping me down. Why else would she warn me away from Danny, only to cozy up to him the instant she realized that we actually had chemistry? She's only nice to me when she's on top.

"That kind of friendship isn't worth anything. I'm not here to make friends like that."

As I say these words, I feel a jolt of electricity course through my body. It's like I finally understand where I am, what I need to do. I came to the house hoping that life would be magically easy for me, that I'd discover a new self and float up to new heights. But life has never been like that for me. I've always had to fight. And right here, on the biggest stage of my life, I'm finally going to win.

YOONA

IT'S THE GOLDEN HOUR, ALMOST SUNSET, AND WE'RE HANGING out by the pool. Sabine and I are sitting on deck chairs, watching the others have a kind of water joust. Mari is sitting on Chris's shoulders, Grant on Danny's; Mari and Grant are trying to unseat each other using pool noodles.

"I'm afraid they're going to hurt themselves," I say.

I steal a glance at Sabine. She's wearing sunglasses, and I can't see her eyes. "Mostly the boys. Chris can carry Mari no problem, but I don't know about Danny and Grant."

"They'll be fine," Sabine replies.

Grant takes a big swing at Mari, but she ducks, then pokes him in the stomach. Grant doubles over, teeters wildly for a second, and then tumbles into the water. Mari raises her arms up in victory.

I shrug. "They're not that close to the edge, I guess."

Sabine nods. We watch in silence as Mari and Grant fight out another round, hammering each other with their noodles.

I want to have a normal conversation with her, some kind of proof that things are good between us. Something like our conversation at the pool, from before the leak.

"So how was your break?" I ask.

"It was okay."

"Did you do anything fun?"

"I mostly stayed at home. Went to the mall once or twice."

Sabine still isn't looking at me, and from behind her sunglasses her face is curiously blank. There's a faint smile on her face, but it's a distant smile, one that says, *I'll listen politely, but I wish you'd stop talking to me.*

I should go ahead and spit it out. "Is everything okay with us?"

Sabine pulls down her sunglasses, so that they're resting on her upper lip. She studies me for a moment, her eyes still blank.

And then, all of a sudden, she smiles the same wide, dazzling smile from our last conversation in the basement. It's so charming, and yet it's somehow off-putting.

"I'm totally fine," she says. "You asked me that already. Do I seem upset?"

"No, I guess not."

She pops her sunglasses back up to her eyes, and leans back in her chair as if the matter is settled. I still don't know what to make of all this. Twice, she's said that she's fine. She's right, there's nothing overtly wrong about her demeanor. But there's a layer of frostiness between us, and I don't quite believe that it's all in my head.

From the pool, I hear a splash. Mari is waving her pool noodle over her head in celebration, and Grant is underwater again. A moment later, he pops up, coughing because of the water he swallowed.

"Man down," he sputters. "I need a break. Been drinking too much chlorine."

Danny thumps him on the back. As Grant climbs out of the pool, Danny looks over at me. "Hey, I need a new rider!"

I don't really want to play this jousting game, but at least it'll take my mind off of Sabine. Besides, I want to hang out more with Danny, talk to someone I don't have to be careful around. I can make fun of him all I want, without fear of bad edits. Later, I can ask him for advice. He knows both me and Sabine, so maybe he'll have a better idea of what she's thinking right now. I bet he wouldn't get caught up in minute emotional drama—he'd just say something like, *Relax, you're both cool people, don't worry so much.*

I stand up—and at the same time, so does Sabine. The two of us stare at each other for a moment, and then I realize. She thinks he was asking her. By reflex, I raise my arms to the sky to pretend I was stretching, and let out a yawn.

Sabine smiles politely and then hops into the pool. A part of me hopes Danny will stop her and say, *I meant Yoona.* But of course, he doesn't. She dog-paddles over to Danny and tries to climb onto his shoulders. But then Danny loses his balance, and Sabine slips. There's a big splash, and she lets out a little yelp. When the water settles, she's full-on straddling Danny's back.

"Oops," she says. "Hi, Danny."

"This keeps happening," Danny says, smirking. He definitely did that on purpose. He definitely wasn't trying to ask me.

"Is this seat taken?" Grant sets himself down in Sabine's chair, a towel wrapped around his shoulders.

Grant tells me about his break: he went to Joshua Tree National Park with a friend from math camp who lives in Arizona (of course Grant went to math camp). He shows me pictures of purple sunrises over a rocky desert, fields of fuzzy cacti, the alien shapes of Joshua trees looming starkly under a starry sky. It's all very impressive. But I keep getting distracted.

My eyes keep drifting to Mari and Sabine, whacking each other with pool noodles. Each time Sabine falls, she pops out of the water, looking shocked that she's lost another round. It's a silly game, but she's so earnest about it, furrowing her brow in concentration, snapping her pool noodle wildly when she sees an opening. When she finally unseats Mari, she tosses her head back and lets out a full-throated victory scream. There's something magnetic about her. When her inhibitions drop, and she's putting her whole heart into something, you can't help but want to be around her.

Watching her makes me feel incredibly lonely. She won't act like that with me, not anymore. And I know that it's my fault, at least to some extent.

Mari's nose starts bleeding, bringing an end to the game. Mari and Chris go inside, while Danny and Sabine sit on the edge of the pool, dipping their toes into the water.

"Hey, Danny, can I ask you something?" Sabine asks in a syrupy voice that cuts through the evening air.

"Sure, what's up?"

"Can I take you on an outing this week?"

My eyes snap up onto them. Danny is grinning. "Sure. Sounds fun," he says. "But good luck topping the date I put together for us."

"I'll try."

And then I realize: of course I can't talk to Danny about Sabine. He isn't a neutral party; he's closer to her than he is to me. If I say the wrong thing, he'll tell her about it, and then she'll think that I was talking behind her back.

I wish I hadn't been so cool toward Danny. On our one date together, I was trying to push him away on purpose. I thought I was the one who was putting up with him, but maybe it was the other way around; he had to spend the day with me, the girl who was always making fun of him, instead of Sabine, the fun one. I wish I had never overheard that one comment that he made. In a way, all my troubles stem from that one moment.

I thank Grant for showing me his pictures, and then head back inside.

In the kitchen, Chris is brewing tea and microwaving a bowl of ramen noodles.

"Where's Mari?"

"She was feeling woozy, so she went upstairs to lie down."

"Aww, so you're taking care of her. That's so sweet."

Chris lets out a pained smile. "Yeah, I know. Hopefully, it's not just for show."

"Is that how it feels?"

"Not right now. When someone's not feeling well, it's easy. You take care of them. Even if it weren't Mari, I'd know what to do." He chuckles. "But other times, I have to ask myself, *Am I doing this because it feels right, or because I know it's what the cameras want?*"

"And right now, you also have to ask yourself, *Do they want me to talk about it out loud like this, or act natural?*"

Chris laughs. "I'm trying not to go there. Mari and I agreed that we have to try to forget about the cameras. She said that if one of us is upset about something, or even just uncertain, we shouldn't be afraid to say it. She put it in this really nice way. 'We have to live out real life as best we can.'"

The producers are trying to make him look *good*, and it still sounds hard. And then there's me.

"Hey, Chris, before you go up, can I ask you a question?"

"Go for it. Mari's probably sleeping. The tea needs to cool down a bit anyways."

"Am I a mean person?"

Chris scratches his head sheepishly. He opens his mouth, hesitates, and closes it again. Finally, he says, "I don't know if I can answer that. I can give you my impressions, but to get a real answer, you'd want to ask someone who really knows you, right?"

"Impressions are fine. You've known me for three weeks. You watched the leak. You saw how they made me look. Is it true?"

"I—those aren't really the same thing." He shakes his head. "It's not really a true-or-false question."

"So what is it?"

"There's a lot to it. Like, some people are pleasant to everyone. Uh, maybe you'd say they're nice, or, like, sweet? But you're not really like that."

I laugh. Can't argue with that.

"That's not the same as actually being nice, though," Chris continues. "Some people are like that, but it's fake. And then there are people who are unpleasant to everyone. Making fun of people, giving them a hard time about everything."

"So that's me."

"I'm not saying that. But maybe you're closer to that than you are to the first thing. If someone does something wrong, you'll point it out. It's not mean-spirited, but it might be unpleasant."

I nod. I know he's right, but hearing it still stings. It's not like I expected him to dismiss the leak completely, but I must have been hoping for something a bit more charitable.

"Yeah, okay. Thanks, Chris." I wave him upstairs so he can go take care of Mari. He starts to go, but at the foot of the stairs, he turns back.

"One more thing. I thought about it more. I don't think you're mean. At least, you don't try to hurt people on purpose. Sometimes you're nice, too. You were really nice to Sabine after you won the video game. So if you want, you can try to keep up that energy more often. I think you can do it." Chris shrugs. "You do you, though."

He leaves, and I'm alone in the living room. The others are still outside, hanging by the pool. I watch them, listen to the gentle hum of their voices muffled by the sliding door.

I've been here before. How many times have I sat waiting in my pew after church, watching from afar as the girls from the inner circle whispered in each other's ears? I'd always be struck by how comfortable they looked around each other, how much more at ease they seemed to be when I wasn't around.

I want this time to be different. But it's not so easy. I have habits that I didn't even realize I'd picked up, habits that add up to a person who's not easy to like. If I want to change that, it's going to take work. But I have to do it. Because I can't bear to have traveled this far, only to live out the same pattern that I did at home.

SABINE

THINGS ARE GOING WELL SO FAR. I KNOW THAT I GOT ON YOONA'S nerves in that scene by the pool. She even stormed out after I asked Danny on the outing; maybe she actually did start to like him after their date. Whatever the reason, that moment is definitely going to make it into the final cut. I picture the edited version, with me and Danny's cuteness interspersed with her scowls, the moment of her leaving heightened by an electric guitar.

I know what I have to do. The one promising part of the leak, the one place where I looked good, was my date with Danny. If I can pull that off again, then we just might have a story line. And if that happens, all else will be forgiven. I'll be Sabine, the girl who went on TV and dated a hot guy. It's like Mari said: there's always redemption in love.

"I need your advice," I say to Mari. "I'm going on a date with Danny, and I want to know how to make it go well. Like, how were you able to connect with Chris?"

"I see," Mari says. "I can try to help you. I'll tell you a bit about what it felt like to get to know him. But that's just our story, so I don't know if I'd call it 'advice.'"

"Try me," I say.

Mari takes a deep breath. "With Chris, everything was exciting from the beginning, because I like how he looks. But as we got to know each other, I realized that I understood him. I was able to get into his head and see the world the way he sees it. To him, the world looks like something mean, something that wants to hurt him. To face it, he has to always prove that he's strong."

See the world the way he sees it. Can I do that with Danny? As of right now, I couldn't say much about what the world looks like to him.

"And then what?"

"When I realized that about him, I told him that he never has to prove anything to me. My intention was to help him pull down the walls in his mind that keep other people out, but I also learned something about myself. I understood that it's incredibly important to me to make people feel safe, accepted. That's always been a part of me, but the actual words for it hadn't come to me before. The discovery was electric. It felt like seeing all the colors of the rainbow at once."

Okay, jeez. That sounds intense. I try to think of new understandings of myself that I can come to with Danny, but it's tough. The truth is, I can't picture Danny "pulling down the walls" with me. But if I do get there, I'd bet the editors would eat it up.

"Like I said, though, that's just our story," Mari adds. "If I did have to give advice, it would be to go in with as few expectations as possible. There's a lot of delight in getting to know someone bit by bit, discovering the texture of their personality without trying to pin them down."

"Right."

This last part, I'm not so sure about. Hitting the road without a map works for people like Mari, but for the rest of us, it helps to have a plan. Trying to understand Danny, then making him feel accepted, sounds good to me.

Later in the day, I get an email from the producers with a list of date options. I'm immediately drawn to one of the flashier picks—a polo lesson, covering the basics of riding and hitting, followed by the chance to watch a real match. I've certainly never played polo before, and doing it with Danny would be pretty unique. Of the sporty options (mountain biking, tennis lessons at Indian Wells), it seems like the least sweaty. But then, learning to play hockey on horseback won't give us many opportunities to connect emotionally.

Eventually, I settle on the other equestrian option—a sunset horseback ride through a palm canyon. As Mari once put it, the natural setting will fill us with a sense of our own grandeur and significance. Or something. Hey, if it worked for her and Chris, why not me and Danny?

On the day of the date, I spend a long time picking out what to wear. Yoona is in the room with me, flopped on her stomach, scrolling through her phone, and I can practically feel her eyes rolling as I go back and forth between outfits.

Before our romantic horse ride, the car takes us to the restaurant I've picked out for an early dinner. It's a Hawaiian place; inside, there's a miniature lake, with real swans swimming in the water. The host leads us to a table under a thatched roof.

"So, how are you feeling?" I ask Danny. Direct, if not subtle.

"Feeling? Feeling fine, I guess. Life is chill. I go to boarding school, so I'm used to the whole living-away-from-home thing. But this is better than boarding school. No zany traditions to navigate."

"Traditions?"

Danny tells me that on the first day of the winter semester, the male junior and senior varsity athletes have to run across the quad, naked except for shoes and school scarves. The first time he witnessed it, as a freshman, he considered quitting sports on the spot.

"So you've done it?"

"Once. It wasn't as bad as I thought it would be. Our quad isn't that big. It's more about being wild and doing it for the school."

I try to work out how this information can help me see the world through Danny's eyes. Running naked in the cold would definitely qualify as a way to prove to the world that you're strong. But Danny doesn't seem to have much angst about it—more like a thin layer of irony, beneath which lies actual pride. I can hear in his voice that he thinks that this particular tradition, at least, is kind of fun.

"How about you, Sabine?" Danny asks.

"I'm good. Well, I'm okay. The leak threw me off a lot. I still don't feel comfortable when I'm around Yoona. I never know where I stand with her."

Danny nods. "For sure," he says.

I know I have to choose my words carefully. It's not just Danny who's listening right now. I'm starting to wrap my head around Carrie's fundamental law—anything I say could be used to construct a narrative about who's right and who's wrong. I can't wear my heart on my sleeve; I have to be smart about which thoughts to reveal and which to hide.

"She's so hot and cold. Sometimes things are so bad between us that I have to ask myself what *I'm* doing wrong. And then sometimes, she's so friendly, and I wonder if it's all in my head. But I can't let her do that to me, either. That's, like, gaslighting."

Danny blinks. There's a glazed-over look in his eyes, and I wonder if he heard anything I said. Maybe I'm talking too much.

"Oh yeah," Danny finally says after a long silence. "No sweat, Sabine. It happens."

This doesn't exactly feel like an emotional connection.

After we finish eating, a car comes to whisk us off to our next destination. We enter the mountains and arrive at a ranch set on a low hill. When Danny spots the horses, his eyes light up.

"Do you know how to ride? Is this supposed to be, like, a taste of the Midwest?"

I chuckle. "Is that what you think we do in the Midwest? Ride horses and grow corn?"

Danny shrugs. "And milk your cows every morning."

I roll my eyes. "I just picked this because I thought it would be fun to ride horses. The other option was a polo lesson, which seemed like a bit much for this heat."

"Polo? You mean like horse hockey? That sounds dope."

Danny and I put on riding helmets and pair up with our noble steeds. I get a paint horse named Cha-Cha, with a soft brown coat speckled with white. Danny, meanwhile, gets a gray named Conrad the Great. The cameraman, poor guy, has to follow on foot, dodging grassy horse turds while still keeping the camera trained on us.

Our guide gives us a rudimentary lesson in horseback riding, which mostly amounts to "sit in the saddle and move as little as possible." Once we're off, my horse doesn't seem to be responding to me so much as following the guide. This gives me plenty of brain space to enjoy the rhythm of the clop-clop, and take in the scenery. We're taking a trail through a rocky gully, dotted with shrubs and palm trees. The sun is low in the sky, bathing the desert in a melancholy glow.

"This was a good choice," I declare. "Very peaceful. And I'm glad we get to be in nature."

"What was that?" Danny calls back from ahead of me.

That's the one unfortunate downside of this outing idea—we're riding in single file, which makes it difficult to have a conversation. For now, all I've got is a view of Danny's back and a horse's butt. No matter how much grandeur and significance this horse ride gives me, it'll all be for naught if I can't convert that into some deep conversation, or at least some sustained eye contact.

Luckily, we climb up out of the gully onto a flattened trail carved into the hillside. Now there's enough space for Danny and me to ride side by side. The only problem is that I don't know how to get to his side.

"Hyah. Whoa. Heigh-ho, girl," I whisper, trying to urge the paint horse into action. No response. I rack my brain, trying to remember horse stuff that I've seen in movies. I consider pulling on the reins, or slapping the horse's rump, but we're on a trail with a pretty steep drop, and I don't know if the horse is smart enough not to fall if her human starts distracting her. I'm starting to get anxious. Is the whole date going to be like this? If it is, then Danny and I are going to end it right where we started.

Finally, we come to a ridge with a view. The guide comes to a stop and brings our horses together on the ridge.

"Fifteen minutes until dark. Let me know if you want a picture," he says.

The sun is setting, turning the sky blue and purple. From up here, the desert looks vast and inhospitable. But as the darkness grows, lights twinkle on in the twilight, and the valley becomes a sea of stars. I'm still a little peeved by the circumstances, but now that we're here, I have to put that aside. I have to get to work.

"How does this make you feel?"

Danny looks at me quizzically. "Feel? Good, I guess. It's pretty. You don't see this every day."

I laugh, a little too hard. Danny pulls out his phone to take a picture of the scene. Then he reaches out for a selfie, angling his arm to include me, and my horse, in the scene. I throw up a duck face and a double peace sign, but inside I'm freaking out about the fifteen-minute time limit.

"What's your biggest fear?" I ask, hoping I don't sound desperate.

Danny chuckles. "Where is this coming from?"

"Just wondering. I want to get to know you better," I say weakly.

"My biggest fear is probably death. Or, like, serious injury," Danny says. "One of the sophomores on the track team blew out his ACL this year. That freaked me out. I'd be pretty bummed out if that happened to me."

The emotional part of this question seems to have gone over Danny's head, because his answer is *not* what I was looking for. I don't even know where the ACL is. "You won't," I say feebly.

"I mean, I hope not," Danny says. "I'm really serious about dynamic warm-ups, and I stretch a ton. But college track is going to be intense."

The mention of sports intimidates me. It reminds me of my own high school, where athletes are society's elite, and I am the girl who didn't have a prom date. It reminds me of how improbable a prospective romance with Danny is.

"What about you?" Danny asks.

"Me?"

"Your biggest fear. What is it?"

I have an answer prepared, but it's still a battle to get it out. "Not fulfilling my potential. I'm scared that I'm going to go through college, get a job, maybe even work hard, then wake up one day and realize that life has passed me by. And I'm not even sure how to avoid that."

In my rehearsals of this moment, Danny says something like *I totally get it*, or *I've felt that, too; we have so much in common.* Or he copies Mari's line and says, *There's always redemption in love.* Imaginary Danny certainly never says what real Danny does, which is, "Yeah, that would suck."

When the guide tells us it's time to go, I start to sweat. This date is a total bust. I haven't gotten a single cute moment out of Danny; no one is going to swoon over a conversation about torn ligaments.

We ride down the trail in single file under a rapidly darkening sky. Just when the darkness is strong enough to be scary, we come around a bend and onto a path that is illuminated by glowing globes of light. Someone—the ranch owners, or maybe even the producers of the show—has put up a row of lanterns, creating an avenue of ethereal beauty. I gasp, even though I'm despondent. In different circumstances, this would be highly romantic.

"Wow. It feels like we're on *The Bachelor*," Danny says. He turns to me and smiles. "Perfect setting for a confession."

A faint ember of hope flares up in my disbelieving heart. Maybe this is it. Maybe we'll salvage something out of this godforsaken horse ride after all.

"Do you have a confession?" I ask.

"Sure, I could have one. But I don't know how you'll take it."

"Try me."

"Well, the truth is . . . as much as I loved this horse ride, I kind of wish we'd taken that polo lesson."

It's a good thing it's dark, because in this moment, my face is twisting with unspeakable rage.

When we get back to the house, it's late. Danny says good night, and it's only when I'm alone does the full, crushing weight of this night hit me.

I wanted this date to be an exclamation point, but instead, it was a total question mark. Danny's been on a date with Yoona, too, and I saw how cozy the two of them were getting over that movie. What if he was still deciding between us, and this date sealed my fate? One thing's for sure—it had about as much emotional resonance as a curt nod, a slap on the back, a freaking handshake.

When the editors see this footage, they're going to see the real story, clear as day: that Danny doesn't like me, that the date was awkward and forced, and that the two of us don't have any couple potential. Why did I think that I could do this? Getting Danny to like me, as if there was some plan in place, as if I could come up with a script and he'd just follow along—it was a fantasy. What shows up on camera is all that counts.

And for me, the camera is showing that my storyline with Danny, my one bright spot, the one part of my time on this show that didn't look so bad, was just as devoid of hope as all my others.

YOONA

WHEN I COME INTO THE ROOM, SABINE IS SITTING ON THE FLOOR, staring blankly into space. Her eyes are unhappy, and when she sees me, her face drops even further. It's the first time I've seen her show her emotions, unguarded, since we got back to the house.

"Everything okay?" I ask.

"Yeah, I'm fine." She nods, and her expression tightens. She's trying to draw herself back in, show me the cool exterior that she's been putting up lately. I don't want her to do that. It makes me feel like I'm being pushed away.

"You look upset. I'm your roommate; you can tell me about it. Or at least let me try to cheer you up." I rummage around in my suitcase for the snacks that my mom packed for me. "I have shrimp chips, if you want. Or how about some sweets? I have those chocolate koala cookies."

I fish out the hexagonal green box and wave it in front of Sabine's face.

"I'm okay, thanks," she says.

"Come on, don't be like that. Have one!" I open up a plastic pack and pop a koala into my mouth. I make an exaggerated smile to show how delicious it is, then shove the pack toward Sabine. She finally relents and takes one. I know I'm forcing things a little, but seeing her eat my food still feels good.

"So, what's going on? Boy trouble?"

"No," she says, so quickly that it's like a reflex. "Well, maybe. I don't know."

She frowns, eyes slightly narrowed, as if she's afraid that she gave the wrong answer. She must think that I'm going to make fun of her. I did make fun of her before for getting so worked up about her date with Danny. The words rise easily into my mind: *Why do you care so much, do you even like him, aren't you going out with him to prove a point?* That's where my brain goes. It takes effort to change directions.

"That makes sense," I begin. I pause for a moment, calling up some nice things to say. "No matter what happens with him, you're an amazing person, Sabine. You're smart, and you're fun to be around, and you never give up. If things work out with Danny, then lucky for him. And if they don't, well, he's one boy. You're too good for him anyways."

Sabine's brow creases in confusion. She's still pulled back inside of herself, working out some private puzzle that I can't access. I have a feeling that I'm part of it, too, although I'm not sure exactly how. Whatever it is, I hope that she's tilting in my favor.

"Thanks," she says.

She looks uncertain. I think I said the right things, but they didn't come to me naturally. I was parroting the kind of comforting phrases that I've heard before, but never used. I was playing a part, trying to be someone who I'm not. At least, not yet.

"Oh, and thanks for the cookie," Sabine adds. "It was yummy. And the koalas are cute."

I smile. I think that was real. I feel a flicker of that warm feeling that I got, once or twice, before the leak.

So that's something.

In the morning, I get up early to do laundry. As the machines run, I can hear the sounds of scraping chairs and muffled voices coming from the living room; the rest of the house is waking up. When my clothes are finished drying, I start to fold them and put them into my laundry basket. That's how I notice a couple of casualties, mixed in with my clothes: a pink sock, a long-sleeve shirt that says *Palm Springs* on it. It's an XL, comically huge. One of the boys probably picked it up at a tourist shop.

I pull it on over my sweatshirt. The hem goes almost to my knees, and when I put my hands at my sides, the sleeves are practically touching the floor. I take a look at myself in the bathroom mirror and almost burst out laughing. Too good.

Upstairs, the others are having breakfast, or hanging out on the couch.

"Check me out, everyone!" I crow, flapping the sleeves around over my head.

When Sabine sees me, her eyes widen. "Where did you get that shirt?"

I point to my basket full of laundry. "Someone left it in the dryer. Probably one of the boys. How do I look?"

"That's mine."

"It's yours? Are you sure?"

"Yes."

I flash a devilish grin. "I don't know, Sabine. Finders keepers!"

"Give it back."

All of a sudden, the air has been sucked out of the room. Sabine's voice is quiet, hurt. Everyone is looking at me expectantly. As for me, I have no idea what's going on.

"All right, I'll give it back. Just give me a minute. I'm going to put my clothes away, and then I'll change."

"Why are you doing this?" Sabine asks, in the same voice. I can feel the tension rising between us, but it feels out of proportion to the situation. I took Sabine's shirt by accident, and she's acting like I slapped her.

"Doing what?" I ask. "Is it really that serious? I'll give it back in a minute. It's just a shirt!"

"You know that's my shirt. We were just talking about— yesterday, when you—"

She pokes the front of the shirt. It's a baggy fit, so her finger doesn't actually touch me, but the motion is hard and fast enough to still feel violent. I look down and give the shirt a closer read. Beneath *Palm Springs* is written, in a different color and font,

Aerial Tramway. After a moment, I remember: that's where Danny and Sabine went on their first date. I saw the graphic prints of snowcapped peaks, towers connected by cables, but somehow I didn't make the connection.

"Right. Sorry," I say, working out a smile. "I'll give it back right away."

"Did you take it on purpose?"

"What do you mean, on purpose?"

"You must know."

She won't let it go. I'm trying to retreat, but she keeps stepping forward. I'm starting to feel nervous myself. This shouldn't be going on for so long.

"I told you, I found it in the dryer. I thought it looked funny, so I put it on. I honestly didn't realize it was yours."

"Why did you have to make fun of me, then? 'Finders, keepers'?"

"Sabine, I have no idea what's going on. I just found the shirt and put it on."

"Yoona," Mari says, quiet but firm. "I suggest, with my love, that you make an apology."

My eyes snap onto her. I'm in shock. It's not only that there's a mysterious conflict unfolding between me and Sabine. It's that the room is judging, and I've been placed in the wrong. I took the shirt by accident, I didn't get to defend myself, but the verdict is decided anyways.

"But what am I apologizing for?" I ask.

"For making her upset." Her voice is gentle and encouraging—

this is Mari, after all—but I feel betrayed. Sabine is the one who kept pushing ahead; she's the aggressor. But no one is pointing that out. It's as if they'd never think of her that way in the first place.

I study the other faces in the room. Danny is wearing his usual mask of nonchalance, Grant looks excited by the potential drama, and Chris and Mari are glancing warily back and forth between us. It occurs to me that I don't know what the conversation was like before I arrived. Maybe Sabine was working the room; maybe she said something to Mari that primed her to take a side.

These people that I live with: I'd like to think that they know me, that they would think well of me, give me the benefit of the doubt. But if the mood is wrong, all it takes is a small nudge to make people see you as the villain.

"All right, fine," I say. "Sabine, I'm sorry. I'm going to change."

I hurry to the stairs, and no one stops me. When I get to the girls' room, I let out a deep breath. For a moment, I feel my face wavering. I squeeze my eyes shut.

"No," I say aloud, to the empty room. I'm not going to cry. After a few seconds of holding still, the feeling passes.

I pull the shirt off, fold it up, and leave it on top of Sabine's bed.

Later, I'm back in the trailer with Carrie the producer lady. The events of the morning still have a fuzzy, dreamlike quality to them; as I recount the memory to her, I half expect her to tell me that I'm wrong, that it didn't happen that way at all.

"And you feel that the rest of the room was against you, too?" Carrie asks.

"I'm not sure. It felt that way, but it could have been in my head."

"It could have been in your head," Carrie repeats. I'm not sure if she's confirming what I said, or simply mulling it over.

"There are two ways of looking at it," she continues. "Either you took the shirt by accident and Sabine overreacted, or you took it on purpose to be mean. To you, the facts are obvious: you found it left in the drying machine, you gave the shirt back, and you apologized. The first version is the truth. The trouble is, there's nothing about the facts that disproves the second version. The only difference is in your intentions. And no one else can truly know what those were."

"Yeah, exactly. Everyone is willing to believe that my intentions were bad. That's frickin' rough, Carrie."

"It fits with their expectations. For both of you. It's a shallow thing. I understand your frustration."

"Meanwhile, when I got back to the room, I was almost crying. But no one cares about how I feel."

"That still matters," Carrie says. "No one in the house saw it, but the cameras saw it. In the end, that could help your case."

That's a strange thing to say. No one in the house saw it, but the cameras saw it. The audience of the show will see it. As if that's what matters: covering my bases with them.

"Before you go, let me offer a word of caution. Sabine isn't as helpless as she'd like you to believe. She's very aware of how things look. So if you find that the situation always seems to be weighted against you, then you might want to consider that she's making it so on purpose."

I shake my head. I don't want to think about that. "Why would she do that?"

"I'm not sure. What do you think?"

I don't reply, but I know what the answer to her question is. Sabine is angry at me. She's been cold to me ever since we got back from break. It's like she watched the leak and that became the truth for her; the nice moments that weren't captured in those two episodes were forgotten. She's not even giving me another chance. That scares me.

Maybe I can't fix this after all.

SABINE

I LET MY GUARD DOWN AGAIN.

When Yoona and I were in the room after my date, just talking, I wanted to believe that she was really being nice to me. I opened myself up for a brief moment, and it felt good.

But it's like Carrie said: I can't trust her. I let slip the smallest scrap of self-doubt, and she pounced on it. She was wearing my shirt right in front of both of us, me and Danny, not to mention the rest of the house. Like she was saying to both of us: *Don't you remember your first date? It was so cute, what happened to you two?*

I feel lost. I let my emotions go after that, and who knows how the editors will make that look. The worst part is the way that Yoona does it. She acts like she cares about me, like she wants to be friends, and it's so believable. It's so easy for her to pull me in, toy with me, and then push me down again. The way she does it is infuriating: everything is fast, oblique, like it could have been an accident.

But I know better. If it happens again and again, it isn't an accident.

We're all sitting in the living room, waiting for the van to take us to the next challenge. It's the afternoon, and the mood is chilly. The memory of the morning still seems to be hanging over us— yet another confrontation between Yoona and Sabine. Mari's eyes are closed; she's resting her head on Chris's shoulder. Her fatigue might just be sleepiness, but I feel like part of it is directed at me. She had to jump to my defense again. She probably thinks I don't know how to take care of myself.

When we get into the van, Danny takes a window seat in the back, and Grant takes one in the middle. I freeze at the door, unsure of what to do. Then I dart into the seat next to Grant. I'm too scared to sit next to Danny.

Mari and Chris take the other two seats in the back, and Yoona slams the door shut behind them and goes around to sit shotgun. She must not want to be near me.

"Everything okay, Sabine?" Grant whispers.

"Fine," I say automatically.

"Fine," he repeats, mimicking my glum voice. "No offense, but I'm kind of getting a *Woe is me* vibe from you right now. You're staring off into space."

"Yeah, well, you saw what happened this morning."

"The shirt thing?" Grant says, loudly enough that I sneak a glance at Yoona. She's got her headphones in, though, so I think we're in the clear. "You took that pretty hard, huh? What's that all about?"

I sigh. "It's hard to explain. Anyways, I don't want you to have to take a side."

"I'm on your side, Sabine. Well, maybe I am. Depends on how they divide up the teams for this challenge." He winks.

I feel a little bit better. Whenever there's tension with Yoona, I think of my other housemates as a single unit, watching and sitting in judgment as one. But really, they're four individuals, and at least one of them is good old Grant, who's just trying to have fun.

The van pulls into the parking lot of an unexpected destination: a high school. Palm trees rise up between brown stucco buildings. At the end of the parking lot is a football field, the bleachers framed dramatically by the mountains behind it. A chill runs down my spine. For some reason, being at this empty high school, the site of someone else's drama and triumph and heartache, gives me the creeps.

"What do they want us to do in there?" I wonder aloud.

"Maybe it's another math test," Mari says sleepily. "Hope you've been studying."

There's no producer on-site to greet us. We look around, but there isn't a person in sight. With nothing else to do, we walk through the front doors of the school.

Inside, most of the lights are off. The hallways and classrooms are dark, the chairs are stacked up for the summer. A single trail of lights illuminates the path to an open classroom door. From inside the room comes the faint sound of music playing.

"This is like a horror movie," Chris says. "When you watch something like this, you're screaming at the characters not to go into the room."

"Guess we don't have a choice, though," Yoona says.

Grant takes a step forward and beckons us to follow. "Nothing to worry about. We'll go in there, get our money, and make it out of here in one piece."

In the classroom, the desks have been cleared away to the sides of the room. At the back of the room are a television on a wheeled cart, and a single desk with a red box sitting on top. In the middle of the room, six chairs are set out in a circle. On the whiteboard is written, *Hotel California: Challenge #3*.

We all take our seats. I glance at the walls and up at the ceiling, looking for cameras.

The school intercom crackles on, and a familiar voice begins to speak. It's the deep, smoky drawl of the lava lamp, echoing through the building like a robotic school principal.

"Welcome, contestants. Class is in session. Today, you will be playing *Hotel California* Mafia, a social deduction game. The rules are quite complicated, so listen carefully.

"There are no teams today: at least, no fixed ones. Instead, you will have to talk among yourselves, decide whom you can trust, and form alliances. Team up, and you increase your prize—but also your chances of betrayal.

"You may now open the red box."

We stand up and gather around the box. Grant lifts off the cover. Inside are six red envelopes. On each one is written one of our names in flowing calligraphy. We take our respective envelopes. I trace my finger over the golden *Sabine*.

"In each of your envelopes is a secret word," the intercom–lava lamp says. "Open them, without showing them to anyone else."

We take a few steps away from each other. I stand by the window and open my envelope. On the card inside, all six of our names are printed. By my name, my word is written in black ink; next to each of the other names is a blank space.

Sabine: **Vertebra**
Chris:
Mari:
Grant:
Yoona:
Danny:

"The object of the game is to find as many of the secret words as possible. Submit a card with less than three words, and you get nothing. Three words, and your prize will be one thousand dollars. For four words, two thousand; and for five words, four thousand. As you can see, the maximum prize this week has been doubled: if you all submit a full card, you will receive a total of twenty thousand dollars."

Phew. That's a lot of money. Us girls got over three thousand dollars each for the video game, and that was with only three of us splitting the prize. For six of us . . .

"That adds up to twenty-four thousand, if we get all of the words. Not twenty," Yoona says, frowning.

"There are only five secret words," the speaker explains, as if to answer her question. "One of you has drawn a blank card. This player is the mafia. The mafia's goal is to steal a secret word. If, at the end of the game, the mafia has found even *one* secret word, then the mafia gets a ten-thousand-dollar prize. Everyone else gets nothing."

"Yeah, but are you really going to do us like that?" Grant mutters. He glances around the room, no doubt searching each face for signs of deception.

"There is one more twist," the speaker continues. Of course there is. "Please visit the office room one by one, in the order marked on your playing cards."

At the back of the room, underneath a hanging American flag, is a door leading to an attached teacher's office. I'm first on the list. The order, I now realize, is the same as our order of arrival to the house.

"Wish me luck, guys," I say, before going into the office.

It's a cramped room, with only enough space for a narrow desk with a computer. I wonder if the teacher who uses this classroom will know about the creepy game we're playing here, come September.

When I sit down in the chair, the computer flashes on. After a moment, a clip begins to play. It's me, sitting in the interview chair for a confessional. Without the show's usual music and sound effects, the footage feels eerily quiet.

"I can't do it. What chance do I have against Yoona? She's too good. At everything."

Whatever I was expecting, it wasn't this. I recognize the words. I know what comes next. Carrie suggests that I can be friends with Yoona.

"That kind of friendship isn't worth anything. I'm not here to make friends like that."

I revisit that moment, trying to remember if the green light behind her head was on. I was checking for that for the first couple of interviews, but maybe I slipped up that one time.

I knew all along that none of this was private, that I was in the trailer with Carrie to produce nuggets of content. But I thought there was an understanding between us. She was helping me. This moment wasn't supposed to be saved up to use against me in this game. If Yoona sees this clip, it'll be all the reason she needs to become full-on hostile to me. And if the editors want to, they can put it in context to make me look scheming, pathetic.

In other words, there's a sword hanging over my head. I don't know how this clip fits into the game, but I don't like it.

One by one, the others go in and watch their clips. I study their faces, gauge their reactions as they come out. When it's Yoona's turn to emerge from the office, she's hard to read. She looks more alert than usual, but otherwise she has her usual poise. It figures. Nothing gets to her.

"By now, you have all seen a secret clip concerning yourselves. For now, those clips will stay a secret. If the mafia is able to steal a person's secret word, then that person's clip will be played. Otherwise, a clip will be chosen at random from among the people who fail to qualify for a prize. If all five players manage to successfully share their words, then the *mafia's* clip will be played.

"These are the rules to *Hotel California* Mafia. The game will last for one hour. Good luck."

With that, the intercom system clicks off. The TV flashes on and shows a timer: fifty-nine minutes and fifty-nine seconds, counting down.

"This is a messed-up game," Chris whispers. "It's like they're playing us off against each other."

"It's just a game," Danny says. "We're competing, same as the other challenges."

But, of course, this doesn't feel like it's just a game. Not when that clip is in play. If that gets out, the impact is going to last long after the game ends.

"This is the prisoner's dilemma!" Grant cries. He looks excited. "It's simple. We all team up, that's the optimal outcome. Whoever has the fake word, I'm sorry, but you have to give yourself up. Take one for the team."

Silence. We all look at each other, blinking foolishly in the face of this pressure. No one volunteers themselves as the mafia.

"If it's so simple, then why don't you show us your card," Yoona says mildly, with a small smile on her face.

Grant opens his mouth, then closes it again. Of course, he can't just flip his card over: then the mafia will have it, too.

As the seconds tick by, the realization grows. Whether for the prize money, or the secrecy of their clip, or simply for pride, the mafia isn't going to give up. As for the rest of us, I'm guessing we're not too keen on giving up our clips like that, either. Which means that, messed up or not, we're playing this game.

"Guys, we can figure this out," Grant says. "There has to be some kind of game theory or something we can apply here. I just need a piece of paper. We can do this."

He rummages around the room until he finds a piece of paper and a pen. Then he pulls his chair up to one of the desks and starts writing. The rest of us look at each other tentatively, not sure how to start playing the game.

I look from Mari, to Chris, to Danny. What secrets are they holding on to that they don't want to reveal? What dark ambitions, what cracks in the facade?

Finally, I look at Yoona. She's looking down at the floor, brow furrowed, shaking her head. For once, something is getting to her. She lifts her head up, perhaps sensing my gaze, and I quickly look away.

Whatever her clip is, it must be bad. And of course, it must be about me. In fact, it's obvious: her clip is the mirror image of mine, the moment where she admitted her intentions, admitted that she was picking on me, that she wanted to see me fall on my face. That little look of frustration says it all. For the first time this season, she knows she's in real danger.

But, of course, so am I.

YOONA

THESE FRICKIN' TV PEOPLE. I KNOW THAT THEY DID THIS ON
purpose.

Of course they made me the mafia: Who else would they pick?
The cold one, the one who's easy to suspect, to ostracize. And of
course, after keeping it out of the leak, they *would* give me the
one clip that could have changed how everything on the show has
gone since we got back from break.

A shot of me, standing by the door of the boys' room, leaning
in to have a closer listen. Cut to inside the room.

"I'll probably go for Sabine. She seems very innocent. Girls like
her tend to like me. But, I mean, they're all smokeshows. And with
the way the show is set up, they kind of have to go out with us."

We're almost thirty minutes into the Mafia game, and we've
done practically nothing so far. Mari and Chris, the two people
who have the most trust built up between them, have been sent
into the office room to try to figure things out as a pair. Grant is
scribbling away diagrams on his piece of paper. Occasionally, he

pops up with a new suggestion, showing off some probabilities and combinations we could follow to reduce our risk of getting exposed. But none of his suggestions can guarantee safety for everyone; besides, Danny points out, "*You* could be the mafia, bro, in which case we definitely can't do what you say."

"Well, we can't just sit around doing nothing," he says, throwing up his hands. "At least throw some accusations around or something. Make it hard for the mafia. It's hard to keep up a lie for a full hour! And if you're the mafia, put some effort into it. At least *try* to steal someone's word."

I don't want to, though. Yes, I'll win the game if I succeed, but I'll also have to air out someone else's secret. Another person who'll feel aggrieved, who'll think I screwed them over. In fact, the whole group will think that, since I'll be taking the only prize for myself. I'd rather not deal with that.

For that matter, I don't want to lose, either. I don't *want* my clip to be aired. It'll be such a middle finger to Sabine. She's sad about whatever happened with Danny, and I'll be embarrassing her, pushing her down further, *and* telling her that I was right all along. I don't want to do that to her.

Sabine probably thinks that my clip is about her. That's the ironic part about this game. I have to keep this clip from getting out. But if I have to fight to do it, it'll make her even more suspicious. So there's no winning for me. My best bet is to let the timer wind down and hope that chance spares me. If there's any justice in the universe, we'll pick at random and air Grant's clip. His is probably something harmless, like he cheated at a board game, or he secretly already knew how to paint before we met Noor.

Sabine, Danny, and I are sitting in the chairs in the middle of the room. Danny keeps smiling, like he thinks we're all making too big a deal out of the situation. Meanwhile, Sabine won't look at either of us.

"Grant, if you're going to keep telling us what to do, the least you could do is hang out with us," I call out to him. "Pull your desk up to the middle. Society is counting on you."

He stands up, staring at the paper and shaking his head, like a scientist who can't believe what the experiment is telling him. "There has to be some way for the non-mafias to establish trust with each other."

"What if we say what's in our secret clips?" Danny suggests. "Isn't that what's holding us back?"

Grant's eyebrows perk up. "That might work."

Sabine looks nervously among the rest of us. *Her* secret clip is probably about *me*. A part of me is curious. What might she have said or done that was so bad?

But that's not a healthy impulse. I don't really want to know: that's the whole point of it being a secret. As long as it doesn't get out, it doesn't matter. Some stones are best left unturned.

"I don't know how that builds trust, though," I point out. "Can't we all lie about our clips? Including the mafia? Besides, don't we want to win this game so that our clips *don't* get out?"

"We want to win this game to win!" Grant says grouchily. He

crosses his arms and slumps in his chair, looking so grumpy that I want to chuckle. Now would be a bad time for that, though.

"Twenty minutes remaining," the lava lamp says over the intercom. I'm starting to hate her. She's finally showing her true colors, meddling like she always wanted to.

The door of the office opens, and Mari and Chris come out. They look excited. Grant stands up from his chair, hopes renewed.

"Did you figure something out?" he asks.

"Figure out? No. We went in there to make out," Mari says, smirking. "We thought you'd have come up with something by now. It's just the prisoner's something something, right? Game theory?"

Grant looks about ready to collapse to the floor.

Chris, who must be feeling merciful, holds up his red envelope. "Actually, we did come up with something."

He and Mari pull their cards out of their envelopes and, without revealing them to us, show them to each other.

"Look, we're giving each other our words. You can see us doing it. So you know from that that we're both not the mafia." He pauses to let us absorb this information. "Mari and I are both cleared now. The rest of you can all join us. Show us your words one by one, and then we'll all share, and you'll be cleared, too. Only the mafia won't be able to join."

I feel a little bit of blood drain out of my face. That idea sounds smart. That idea sounds like it will work.

If they do all team up, then I can at least claim innocence. I didn't *want* the clip of Danny to air; the game just played out that way.

But that's not good enough. I know I owe it to Sabine to at least try to protect her. And I have to say something fast.

"I'm not saying don't do it," I begin. I try to keep my voice calm, to hide the fact that I'm winging it. "But I feel obligated to point something out. You guys were in there for a long time. If you had shown each other your words right away, you could have come out a lot faster. One of you could be the mafia. Not making accusations, but I'm just saying, it is possible that you teamed up and agreed to split the mafia prize. If it's ten thousand dollars between two people, that's more than you'd get by working with the good guys."

Chris's face falls, and I feel a pang of guilt. "You really think we'd do that? That's evil," he says.

"It's all fair in the game!" I add quickly. "You wouldn't be evil. If you did trick us like that, I'd be annoyed, but I wouldn't hold it against you. That's just how Mafia works."

Grant circles the two of them, like he's scrutinizing them for physical signs of their duplicity.

"I don't think you're lying," he says. "I'll join you, but I'm not going to show you my card first."

"But you have to," Mari protests. "You could be the mafia, too. The whole point is, the two of us are a safe bet. We've already earned your trust."

She shoots me a dirty look for disrupting the plan, and I flash what I hope is an apologetic smile.

Grant scratches his chin, every so often referring back to his paper full of diagrams. He keeps flipping his envelope over and over in his hands, starting to pull it out, almost handing it over, then slipping it back inside again. Just watching him is stressing me out. Finally, he rips his diagram to shreds and lets out a battle cry. The rest of us watch, incredulous, as he pulls his card out of his envelope and shows it to Mari and Chris.

"Yes!" Mari cries happily. "Guys, Grant is safe. We're a team of three! We're in the money."

Mari and Chris reveal their cards to Grant, and the three of them high-five and pump their fists. In a way, I'm happy for them. It's got to feel satisfying to have a breakthrough like this.

"This is perfect! Now the rest of you can join us, too," Grant says, grinning broadly. "You know we're all telling the truth."

"Ten minutes remaining," comes the voice from the intercom. "At the end of the game, you will drop your completed playing cards, inside of their envelopes, on the teacher's desk.

"As a reminder, once the playing cards are scored, one secret clip will be revealed to all of you. But there is a way out. If you wish to protect your secrets, then you may elect not to play the game at all, by crossing out your name on your playing card. If at least half of the players elect not to play, then the game will be ended, all prizes will be forfeited, and no secret will be revealed."

"No need to worry about that," Grant says happily. He writes in Mari's and Chris's words on his own card, and then passes around his pen so that they can do the same.

It's not looking good. Danny reveals his word to the group, leaving just Sabine and me. Once she joins, everyone else will be safe, and I'll be the odd one out. My clip will be played. I know that'll crush Sabine, that that'll be the end for us. Airing out Danny's smokeshow comment will exonerate me somewhat, by giving the justification for the warning that I tried to give Sabine. But I have a feeling that that won't make her forgive me. If anything, the fact that I was right all along will make her feel worse.

I have to act quickly.

"Are we sure about this? I want to take some time to think about it more. I want to understand the game theory a bit better," I say.

"Take all the time you want, mafia," Grant says gleefully. "If you can't show your word now, that means you don't have one. Come on, Sabine, do you really think that one of us is the mafia after we teamed up like this?"

Sabine shakes her head. Her face is a confusing mix of emotions, but most of all, she looks relieved. Her own secret is safe. She can share her word, fill in her playing card, help the group lock in the twenty-thousand-dollar prize. She'll get to celebrate beating me with everyone else.

"Congrats, guys. You got me," I say. "You won."

Grant pats me on the shoulder. "Don't take it personally, Yoona. This is just business."

"Do we have to do this, though?" I ask feebly. "I mean, can we still agree not to play? I know it's a lot to ask, but I'd really like to keep this secret from getting out. You won, fair and square, so you deserve to claim your prizes. But if you're okay with giving them up, I'll be grateful."

With no cards left to play, I'm reduced to begging for mercy. I probably look desperate, but I like to think that there's a certain dignity in laying it all out on the line for someone else. Inside, I feel like a heroine—even if no one else thinks so.

I search each face one by one, looking for sympathy. Grant and Sabine avert their eyes. Danny is looking at his phone. But Mari and Chris are wavering. My final hope.

"I don't know, guys," Chris says at last. "Yoona is asking us not to play. I don't know if we should go ahead with this."

Chris, you saint, I think to myself.

Grant shakes his head. "We have to. It's like Yoona said, we have to claim these prizes. It's for the collective good."

"This is all going to end up on TV. Put yourself in Yoona's shoes. If you had something you really didn't want out there, then you'd have the right to keep it private. The prize is nice, but it's just money. We all live in the same house. We're like . . . we're like a family. We should stick together. Otherwise, it's like we're putting ourselves up for sale."

"That's exactly the truth. I absolutely am for sale," Grant says, chuckling sheepishly. But I can tell Chris is getting to him.

"But if we're all sticking together, then Yoona should be willing to make a sacrifice for the rest of us," Sabine says. Her expression is steely, and a prickle of fear tugs at my throat. "You're asking all five of us to give up this game for you. What did you do that's so bad? I don't know, it just strikes me as kind of selfish."

Rage ignites my brain, and I fight to hold it in. I'm doing this for her. Calling me selfish is so callous. A retort comes to mind: *You just want to see what's in my secret clip so you can watch me squirm, so you can hold it over me.* It's so easy to find bad intentions in other people.

"I'm with you, Yoona. If you don't want to play, I'll cross out my name," Chris says.

I close my eyes, take a deep breath. It hurts, but I know this is the best way. I nod.

Mari gives me a hug and says she'll do it, too. It feels nice, but I can't fully enjoy it. Not with Sabine orbiting us like an angry planet.

It's over: half of us are choosing not to play. Grant, smiling ruefully, crosses his name out on his own card, too.

"If I have to go out like this, I at least want the dignity of hammering the final nail into my own coffin," he says.

When the time is up, two of the game assistants come into the room to collect our cards. When they see the crossed-out names, they usher us out. Our secrets are safe.

"I finally figured it out, too," Grant moans on the van ride home. "We could have all covered up our words except for the first letter. Enough to prove we had a word. Then we could have teamed up right away. The good guys would have won in, like, five minutes."

"But then we would have screwed the mafia over," Mari points out.

"Yeah, but who cares, they're the mafia!"

"Let's forget about it," Danny says, yawning. "We basically won the game anyways. We're winners on the inside."

The mood is relaxed enough, given the circumstances. I got the outcome that I wanted, but something about that game still isn't sitting right. For the second time in one day, I felt like I was going against the whole house. Only this time, an apology wasn't enough from me. Sabine had to call me selfish. It was so unfair; I was the one who got stuck being the mafia, I was fighting *for* her, and she still had to slip in the worst possible comment. Chris took my side, but who knows what the others were thinking.

Sabine isn't as helpless as she'd like you to believe.

Carrie warned me that Sabine is aware of how things look, that she knows how to weight situations against me on purpose. I didn't want to believe it then.

Now I'm not so sure.

SABINE

"THAT CLIP WAS SUPPOSED TO BE PRIVATE. OR AT LEAST between us. How am I supposed to trust you now? Is everything I say to you fair game for the editors?"

When I finish my rant, I'm out of breath. I know I should be more careful with my tone around Carrie—she is trying to help me—but after that Mafia game, it's hard to keep my composure. The moment at the end, when I called Yoona out for being selfish, still gives me chills. I could feel her anger bubbling up, and I felt like I'd finally pushed too hard, like it was finally open war. I wasn't ready.

"What's the big deal?" Carrie smiles. "Nothing bad happened. Remember what I said about the fundamental law of reality TV? The only thing that matters is what shows up on-screen. If a secret clip doesn't get out, it might as well not exist. It was just meant to get you to play the game. And it worked!"

"That light is supposed to let me know when the cameras are on, right?" I point to the green light behind Carrie. "You always flip it off so we can speak in private. But you didn't do that when we talked after break. That was on purpose, wasn't it?"

Carrie's smile falls. "You were upset. I felt guilty about what was happening to you, so I was focused on comforting you. I must have forgotten to turn off the camera. I don't have control over the footage, Sabine; everything from the cameras goes straight up into the cloud, or something."

She waves her hand over her head, to indicate "the cloud."

"I want to know if you're really on my side."

"Sabine, what's gotten into you? You're doing so well now. Better than I expected, if I'm being honest. I thought you'd be coming in here to celebrate."

I blink. "I'm doing well?"

"I certainly think so. On the Yoona front, it sounds to me like these last two situations put her in the wrong, not you. Wouldn't you say that the rest of the house took your side? Quite clearly, in fact, in the case of the Mafia game." She shrugs. "It shouldn't be very hard to use that to your advantage.

"And that's not to mention your date with Danny. I thought it was wonderful! A nice heart-to-heart at dinner, and then a romantic horseback ride? It doesn't get better than that."

I stare blankly back at her.

"You look confused," Carrie says, smiling. "It's much less clear to you, I'm sure, since you're the one who's in it. Think about the fundamental law."

For a moment, I don't get it. I thought the date with Danny

was a disaster. I could hardly get a word out of him at dinner, and once we got onto our horses, we didn't talk at all. Yes, the sunset was nice, but no one who saw the actual date would say that it was any kind of cute.

Then it hits me. Carrie *didn't* see the actual date. She only saw clips of the date, and that's all anyone else will see, either. From an outside perspective, Danny and I rode our horses through one stunning visual set piece after another. Most of the bad aspects of the date were in my head, or were throwaway snippets of conversation. Quiet moments don't make for good TV; cut them out, and only the flashy ones remain.

I wanted the date to look cute, so I tried to make it cute *for real*. That's why I felt like such a failure. But what happens for real doesn't matter: the only thing that matters, in the end, is what shows up on tape.

"Do you know why we shoot these confessionals, Sabine?" Carrie asks.

"To find out what the cast is thinking?"

"That's one way of looking at it. But another way is: for exposition. Sometimes it isn't enough just to film what's happening. We need a narrator, someone who'll spell it out for us. We can't tell you what to say, but most of the time, we get enough material to make do. Do you understand?"

I nod slowly, chewing this over. In other words, the confessionals are exactly like the rest of the show: the editors can only work with what they're given. That means that I'm in control. If I bend the truth, twist events in my favor, then they'll have to find the clips to match. Whatever I say will become true.

Carrie switches on the green light and mouths, *Camera on.* It's like she's offering a truce after I complained about the Mafia clip. But it isn't just a truce. After what she's just explained about confessionals, it's like she's telling me, *Now, let's hear your side of the story.* She knows what she's doing; she knows how much she's helping me. So maybe I really am doing as well as she says.

"My date with Danny was perfect," I say. "I'm really, really happy about how it went."

And on and on. When I finish recounting the Mafia game from my perspective, Carrie flips the green light off with a nod of approval.

"But there's still one problem. My date with Danny wasn't that good. What are we supposed to do when that fizzles out?"

"So you like him, do you?"

"I just—I thought it would help—the leak, you know, those were the only . . . the only good scenes."

Carrie nods. "I understand. Well, nothing that we can't take care of. I'll talk to him."

"What are you going to say?"

"Nothing too intrusive. I'll just make it clear that you like him. That's all it takes sometimes. He may have gotten mixed messages after you chose to go on the second outing with someone else. I'll help clear up any misunderstandings, nudge him in the right direction."

I open my mouth, then close it again. That doesn't sound so bad. Best to let Carrie take care of things.

Right now, I need to focus on my next move. I can build on the shirt incident, the Mafia game. Yoona is getting closer to the edge; I would love to crack that cool facade, get her to blink first, make the first outburst. One big, messy scene and our roles will be solidified; Yoona will be the clear antagonist. The editors might even go back over old episodes and emphasize her as a bully so that the buildup makes sense.

First, I need to provoke her. I saw in her eyes how much she hated that "selfish" comment. I could practically hear the retorts forming in her head; if Chris hadn't been around, who knows what she might have said.

If it isn't on camera, it didn't happen. I open up my phone, pull up my messages with Yoona. There's nothing in our history, not from when we first met, not from over the break, when the leak came out. I send her a message, something the cameras won't see.

Sabine:

What was in your secret clip

I want to know what you said that was more important than the entire group

I know it was about me

YOONA

MY PHONE VIBRATES. EVEN THOUGH I'M SAFELY LYING IN BED, IN
a quiet, empty girls' room, the sound makes my adrenaline spike.
I bet I know who's texting me. A storm has been brewing since
the end of the Mafia game, and sooner or later it's going to break.

But when I pick up the phone, the message isn't from Sabine.
It's from my mom.

> We need to talk. Call me.

When she sends texts like this, short sentences with a period at
the end, I know it's urgent. My mind instantly goes to Dad, back
in Korea. What if something happened to him? I call, and my
mom picks up at the first ring.

"I saw your show," she says.

My blood goes cold. "You *watched*—"

"Everyone at church was talking about it. You should have seen

Mrs. Lim, smiling like a dog when she brought it up. I knew I shouldn't have let you go back."

This wasn't supposed to happen. My parents would never have watched the show on their own; they don't even watch *Korean* TV. But I made a classic mistake—I underestimated the radius of the church moms' gaze. They were bound to get bored of dumping on Mrs. Um at some point. Now they've found a new victim.

"Mom, it's no big deal," I plead. "It's a TV show; they have to make it look dramatic."

"It *is* a big deal. People are going to watch this! What do you think they'll say when they see you fighting with that girl from Illinois? It's such an embarrassment—"

"Mom!" I shout, as my temperature shoots way up. "Don't say that. I'm fine here, I'm telling you. Who cares if there's a little gossip at church?"

"Bae Yoona! Don't be so naive. You think your reputation doesn't matter? Wait until everyone turns their back on you, every door slams in your face, then see if you still think so."

"Well, what do you want me to do about it?" I ask.

"Come home now."

"I can't just leave! What am I supposed to tell the producers?"

"You don't have to tell them anything. Just walk out the door."

I'm pretty sure she's bluffing, but I don't have the energy to compose myself, talk it out with her calmly. It's still exhausting to have to fight with her about this, on top of everything else.

"Mom, let it be. It'll be fine."

She tsks loudly. "You still don't listen. And you have no control over your temper. You only think you're okay because you can't admit when you're wrong."

My mom hangs up before I can respond, leaving a cold, jarring silence in her wake. For a moment, I'm in shock, and I stare numbly at my phone. Then the shock wears off, and the frustration comes in a big wave. I feel sad, too. No one is on my side; no one is coming to my defense. I'm alone.

I press my eyelids together to stop the tears from coming. I don't want anyone to see me cry.

The door opens. Sabine walks in. She stares at me, and even though I'd like to hide my face, I hold her gaze.

"Sorry," she says. Of course she does.

She asks what's wrong, and I do my best to keep it together. She's just here to grab a book. On her way out of the room, I whisper, "Talk to you later, Sabine."

After she's gone, I take deep breaths until I've recovered some semblance of composure. I crack open the window to get some fresh air, and the sounds of everyone else, hanging out by the pool, drift into the room. When I look down at my phone, I finally see Sabine's texts.

I read the messages in disbelief. She sent them before coming into the room. Did she seriously come at me like this over messages, then see me in person and act like nothing was wrong?

The noise in my brain thickens into a roar. She's been so shady since we got back: acting fake nice whenever we talk face-to-face, but never really working to make up. I've tried to reach out, but she stonewalls me every time. *She's* the reason why there's still so much tension in the house.

In the back of my mind, a small voice urges me to stay calm. I know I'm not thinking clearly. I know I'll probably regret this later.

But forget that. I've tried to hold myself back, and Sabine has done nothing but take advantage. She doesn't want to be friends. She's already decided who I am. Well, so be it.

Now let's see if she can handle it.

SABINE

AFTER RATTLING OFF MY TEXTS, I'M FEELING WIRED. MY housemates are out by the pool, but I'm too on edge to be around them. I go upstairs to the girls' room to be alone for a little bit—maybe I'll read *The Bell Jar*, or dash off some lines for my college essays.

When I push open the door, I freeze. Yoona's in there, sitting on her bed, bent over her phone. When she looks up at me, her eyes are puffy and red, and her mouth is twisted with grief. She's been crying.

"Sorry," I say instinctively.

Yoona shakes her head, but doesn't speak. She turns away like she doesn't want me to see her.

Intuition tells me she hasn't seen my texts yet—she wouldn't be crying because of what I wrote. Internally, I curse myself for coming upstairs. I assumed she was at the pool with everyone else, but I didn't check. It's the late afternoon. Yoona would never go to the pool while the sun is still out.

"Everything okay?" I ask tentatively.

"Fine," Yoona croaks out, her voice thick with mucus. "It's nothing."

"Do you want me to leave?"

"Do what you want."

I take *The Bell Jar* from beside my bed and leave the room. As I'm closing the door, Yoona says, "Talk to you later, Sabine." Her voice cracks in the middle of my name, turning the "bine" into a whisper. I like the way it sounds—intimate, as if it's a secret known only to her and me.

What was that about? I rack my brain for memories of family issues, parental pressures, or other demons Yoona is facing. But I come up empty. Whatever struggle she's facing, it's not for me to know.

It's disarming to have seen Yoona in that state—to remember that she's not only a human being, with fears and weaknesses, but also a human being that I might like, under different circumstances. The untouchable aura created by her stunning appearance has worn off because of familiarity. Now when I see her, I just see Yoona Bae, the girl I live with, the girl I hate and love and hate again. I almost regret what I'm doing. Almost.

Because we're still at war. Wolves and sheep can share no meeting of the minds. There's only one way out of this mess we're in, and it's to fight. I have to see things through.

I go out to the pool. Mari and Chris are having a rematch of the chicken fight with Grant and Danny. They beckon me into the pool, but I shake my head and point to my book. I sit on one of the chairs to read, with the sounds of laughter and splashing in the background. Esther Greenwood stares up at the fig tree full of futures, unable to choose. The figs start dropping. She starves to death. Grant said I would like this book, but he never warned me it would be such a bummer.

I hear the house door slide open. I'm mid-sentence, and I read up to the next paragraph break before I lift my eyes up from the page. By that time, Yoona is practically on top of me.

"You wanna talk?" she sneers, her voice dripping with venom. "All right, let's talk."

I'm caught off guard, especially because she seems to be ready to have it out in front of everyone. Doesn't she understand how this will look? I wonder, wildly, if this is some kind of trick. But if it is, I can't spot it. There's no time for caution: I have to meet force with force.

"You asked us not to play the game—fine. Like Chris said, it's about sticking together. But there are two sides to that. The rest of us gave up a lot to protect you. I think we deserve an explanation. Or at the very least, an apology."

"What exactly do you think was in my secret clip? I want to hear you say it out loud."

I take a deep breath. "Sometimes it seems like you're trying to be nice to me. And every time you do it, I get sucked in, because I want to believe that we can finally be friends. But then you do something mean, like you want to put me back in my place. And you always do it in a way that could have been an accident, so that you can reel me in and do it all again."

I pause to let the implication hang in the air. In Yoona's secret clip, she's revealing her true colors, laughing with Carrie about my helplessness, or talking shit about me to Danny. It's even more damning now that we'll never see it. It can be as bad as the imagination will allow. It's her word against mine.

"So that's what you really think," she says, glaring at me. "What was in your clip, then, if you're so innocent?"

She isn't even denying it. She has no idea what I'm doing; she's letting me tell the story however I want. And her emotions are out of control, her voice is dangerously close to a shriek. My hopes are rising. In any scene between the two of us, the calm one wins. Right now, that's me.

"I was angry. I was with Carrie, and I complained about you. I said that I didn't want to be friends with you, because I didn't trust you anymore. It was a bad moment. I'm not proud of it."

It's partly true, but after what I just said about Yoona, my anger sounds reasonable. I wasn't scheming against Yoona; I was protecting myself from getting burned again. Context is everything.

Yoona sputters for a response. Fear is creeping into her eyes. She's starting to realize that the situation is stacked against her.

She should cry, I think to myself. *Play the victim. When you're losing this badly, that's your only way out.*

"You guys good?"

It's Danny. He's climbing out of the pool, dripping like a

swimsuit model. The others are in the water, staring at him. I hope they're enjoying the show.

"We're fine," I say, smiling at him. "Just talking some things out."

"Okay, well, sorry to interrupt. I promise it'll be worth it." He turns to me. "Sabine, I want to take you out again. On a proper date. Something special."

A huge smile spreads across my face. Carrie must have talked to him already. His timing is impeccable.

"I'd really like that," I say.

"Sweet. Well, I'll let you get back to your . . . chat. Remember to play nice." He winks at me, then heads back into the pool.

Yoona's eyes are full of confusion. She seemed to have a thing for Danny before, and now he's definitively put himself on my side. That has to hurt. I feel a flash of pity as I remember her crying in our room. Whatever that was about, it probably threw off her judgment, caused her to miscalculate.

But there's no room for hesitation.

"I know you don't like me, and that's fine. But you can't push me around anymore. That's all I have to say."

She stares at me. To someone who didn't know her, she'd look calm and composed. But I see the strain in her mouth, the wetness building up in her eyes. She forces out a bitter, defeated smile. I'll give her one thing—she always keeps her pride.

She turns and walks back inside the house. The pressure inside of my chest is enormous; if I were alone right now, I might cry, too. It's over.

I should be happy. I got what I wanted. I told my side of the story, I made Yoona crack, and I even landed my next date. But something doesn't feel right.

I wasn't expecting to win so easily. I thought that Yoona would put up some resistance, show up with tricks up her sleeve. And when she didn't, I pressed forward harder. I twisted the knife. She reacted like she didn't see it coming at all.

A long time ago, I thought to myself: *Yoona is not as invincible as I thought.* But now I wonder if it goes beyond that. I even said it to her: "You always do it in a way that could have been an accident." It was a clever turn of phrase, but now I'm wondering if it was true.

Maybe, behind the great and terrible idea of her that existed in my mind, was a person who didn't know that she was fighting me at all.

YOONA

I'VE DONE FAR TOO MUCH CRYING FOR ONE DAY.

The last hour or so has been a total blur. It's almost like it happened to someone else. But I know that that scene by the pool was real. That it happened to me.

It's over now. I've embarrassed myself with Sabine, and the worst part is that Danny helped her. The whole house is probably against me. I'm just like Seema in *Maine Pyar Kiya*: relegated to villain status while the sweet, innocent girl gets the guy, and the adulation, and the happy ending.

I wallow in self-pity for a while, wondering if I shouldn't just follow my mom's advice and leave. Then at least one person in the family would be happy.

The window is still open from earlier. I can hear the conversation below, Sabine holding forth as everyone else questions her.

"It's fine, really. We may not get along, but I genuinely don't have any ill will toward her. I still don't believe that she has bad intentions. She's just very aware of how things look, and she knows how to weigh the situation in her favor. It's natural to do that a little bit, but I had to let her know that she couldn't do it on purpose."

Hold. Up.

I've heard that shit before. Those aren't exactly the words of a teenager. And I know exactly who said them first, because of how creepy and intense they sounded even then. It was Carrie Waters. What the hell?

Something doesn't feel right. Sabine saw me coming from a mile away. It's almost like she set a trap for me, waiting at the pool in front of everyone, with Danny close by and ready to rush to her aid. But of course, she couldn't have. There was no way she could have known ahead of time that Danny was going to ask her out.

But Carrie could have. I already thought she was sus for "warning" me about Sabine. And if she's going around giving both Sabine and me the same snake talk about why we each need to watch out for the other, then something is up.

This would explain why Sabine changed so suddenly after the leak. She was scared, and Carrie took the opportunity to sink in her hooks. She's a producer for a reality show: her job is to manufacture drama.

I still have my confessional this afternoon. If I can get myself together, I can try to figure out what's going on. But Carrie is dangerous. I have to be sneaky.

Before I go into the trailer, I open up the voice recorder on my phone and hit Record. Once I'm inside, Carrie asks how I'm feeling in the wake of the last challenge. I'm guessing she's looking for some shade on Sabine. So I play along.

"Sabine is the most two-faced person I've ever met. She pretends to be nice, but inside she's rooting for bad things to happen to me. You saw how she acted during the Mafia game. When my back was against the wall, she kept quiet. But once Chris took my side, she went after me."

Even though I'm pretending, it feels good to fire off some shots at Sabine. She'll forgive me later.

Carrie nods coolly. She's hard to read, but based on the way she doesn't press, I'm guessing that she's gotten what she wants.

"And how about your next outing? Who do you want to go with?"

Now there's a leading question. Grant is the only one left. Mari and Chris are one couple. Danny and Sabine are on their way to being another.

I have a spark of intuition. "Danny," I say.

For a split second, a shadow of irritation crosses Carrie's face. She pauses and then, just as quickly, adjusts.

"Since when are you interested in him?" she asks, raising an eyebrow.

I think I'm onto something. From the way Danny swept in during that pool scene, I suspect that he's part of Carrie's plan.

Sabine is supposed to end up with Danny—that much is clear. But judging by Sabine's reaction to their last date, that storyline is a bit shaky. Danny might not play along—he doesn't exactly seem reliable when it comes to matters of the heart. And there's a loose end: me.

I went on a date with him, too. Technically, I even stole the shirt that he bought for Sabine. Suppose I had an ulterior motive there, after all. Suppose I like him, and I'm not going to let Sabine take him so easily.

"I know it sounds unbelievable. I didn't want to like him, either, especially after hearing the way that he talks about women," I begin. "But that date in Hollywood showed me something different about him. He didn't turn out the way he did by chance, or by an innate affinity with dumbbells and hair gel. He is the way he is because the world hurt him. I want to help him heal.

"Technically, he's already going out with Sabine, but I think that if I tell him how I feel, he'll come around."

Carrie tries to talk me out of it. She all but calls Danny boy trash, unworthy of a strong, independent woman like me. She looks calm, but I can sense the urgency lying beneath the surface. She's problem-solving, right here in this interview.

If there's one thing I'm naturally gifted at doing, it's being a problem.

"You don't know what you're talking about, Carrie Waters. That's just how he seems on the outside, if you don't understand people. People are different these days, so someone your age wouldn't get it. In fact, I don't even think Sabine gets it. Only I do. And I think deep down, Danny knows that."

If I really am a difficult, angry person, then I have to use it to my advantage, right?

Gradually, Carrie's patience wears thin. She doesn't want to deal with me. Eventually, she looks for an easy way out.

"Can you keep a secret?" she asks. "Here, let me show you something. If this doesn't make you see sense, then I don't know what else I can do for you."

She opens her phone, finds what she's looking for, and then shows me.

"This is Corina Bowdoin," she says. "They went 'on break' for the summer, but she's waiting for him when he gets back. This is all a game to him, Yoona. You're better off staying away."

Jackpot.

So apparently, Danny has a girlfriend. Rough. For the record, I never actually liked him, so *I* have nothing to be embarrassed about. Anyways, that's over. I wish the man nothing but happiness.

I go back to bad-mouthing Sabine, saying I never should have wasted my time trying to help her, that I hope Danny spills soy sauce all over her precious shirt.

"Don't worry, she'll get what's coming to her," Carrie says. She sounds relieved to have me back in line. "Sabine is the real villain of the show. It's a classic TV narrative: the repressed, seemingly harmless individual who finally gets the chance to be bad. The executive team loves it. When the final cut is released, you'll see."

Carrie is helping Sabine, all right. She's helping her down the road to perdition. Sabine will finish me off, end the season with the bad boy on her arm, and go home thinking she overcame the evil queen bee. That *is* what happened, in a manner of speaking. It's just not the version that the final cut is going to tell.

At first, I'm surprised that Carrie is being so unguarded. But I get it. In this room, I myself can easily forget that I'm being recorded. Carrie is the master of this little world, the one pulling the strings. She doesn't need to watch her words. Why should she suspect that the chess pieces might actually turn against her?

When I was really young, I was closer to my dad than I was to my mom. If I wanted to eat junk food or get a new toy, I'd ask him, because he'd always say yes. My mom, meanwhile, was the parent who told me off for talking too loud, or chewing with my mouth open, or leaving my dirty clothes on the floor instead of putting them in the hamper. She was the one that I was afraid of.

After we got to America, though, things started to flip. I realized that my mom was the one who had to do all the work around the house: cooking our meals, washing our dishes, scrubbing our messes off the floor. My dad, meanwhile, got to sit around waiting for food to show up on the table, got to sit on the couch, drinking beer and watching baseball while my mom cleaned. Some days, he would stay out late with his coworkers, and I wouldn't see him until he woke up late the next morning, eyes red, rumpled clothes smelling of cigarette smoke.

When I pointed this out to my mom, she explained that he was the one who worked, so it was only fair that he got to relax around the house. But I wasn't convinced. I stopped being nice to my dad, and I tried to snub him in little ways to show him how I really felt. Eventually, it became a habit. My mom yelled at me about it, but I couldn't go back to how I'd been.

When my dad told me that he was leaving to go back to Korea, I was angry. But a part of me wondered: *Is it because of me? Because I didn't do enough to change, to be sweet, to make him stay?*

I don't think that way anymore, but I do still think that there was a lesson in that idea. Sometimes you have to make nice, even if it's hard. You have to hold on to the good memories, the promise of a better future, if only you can get through to it.

Sabine is in trouble, and I'm part of the reason why. I teased her. I knew she was uncomfortable, and I picked on her anyways. But I've also tried to bridge the gap between us, and in moments, I've succeeded. I can still help her. I owe it to her to try. Maybe I owe it to myself, too.

I pull my phone out of my pocket and open the recording I made. With this recording, I can turn things around. It may be too late for us to be friends, but I can still give Sabine the power to choose. With what little time we have left in the house, I'll do my best to give Sabine her happy ending.

SABINE

IN THE EVENING, DANNY STOPS BY THE GIRLS' ROOM.

"Your room feels bigger than ours. And the lighting in here is way better," he says, shaking his head enviously. "That ain't right."

Yoona has retreated elsewhere in the house, to gather herself or to sulk, so it's just me and Mari listening to him.

"Seems fair to me," Mari retorts. "The girls are more than pulling their weight on this show. You guys couldn't even win at *Starfall*."

Danny chuckles. "Anyways. Sabine, I wanted to talk to you."

"What's up?"

"For our date, it's going to be a really nice dinner. So I'm warning you that I think you should dress up. Do you have the, uh, equipment for that?"

Mari and I both chuckle over his word choice.

"Yeah, I think I'm equipped," I say. Thankfully, I packed a dress when I came back from break.

"Okay, good. Can't wait. Have a good night."

After he's gone, I pick up one of the pillows and press my face into it, then keel over onto the ground so I can die of satisfaction. I feel a little corny, but I can't help myself. Having a boy come by your room and tell you that you need to dress up for dinner is immensely pleasing. I luxuriate in the knowledge that I am precious and unique.

Now I can safely laugh at how silly I acted on my last date with Danny. I was trying to emulate the moments that Mari and Chris have had, but all that deep-emotional-connection stuff isn't really my speed anyways. Danny and I have fun together. That's what we do. And that's more than good enough.

I think back to the early days in the house, when I worried that Yoona and Mari were forming a coalition and shutting me out. If I could go back in time, I'd tell that Sabine not to worry so much. It all works out in the end. Now, a mere four weeks later, I feel like they may as well crown me the queen of California.

In the morning, a notification pops up on my phone—a new message from Yoona. I hesitate for a moment, wondering what she might have said. Then I decide to ignore it. I don't have to think about her right now.

Throughout the day, I observe that while everyone is polite to Yoona, they're treating her carefully, like she might explode at any moment. The bad vibes from our confrontation linger; the house is still in a somber mood.

At one point, Mari and I are in the kitchen, and Yoona is sitting on the couch alone, staring blankly into space. She cuts a tragic figure: beautiful, composed, but alone.

"I'm worried about her," Mari whispers. "She seems to have gone to a dark place, right before our eyes."

My eyes drop down to the floor. "Oh. I don't know. I mean, she has. But I think she'll be fine. She never stays down for long."

"You didn't seem to take it too badly yourself."

"Should I have?" I ask, a little too quickly.

Mari shakes her head. "No, it's good that you withstood that situation so well. But Yoona, not so much. People don't act the way she did unless they're in pain."

"Right."

"The tension between you two is getting stronger. I think now is the time for you to reach out."

Her eyes are warm and forgiving. Almost like she knows what I've done. I quickly look away.

"I've tried! It doesn't work. It's not my fault."

Mari takes my hand and squeezes it. "I believe you. No matter who's at fault, you don't owe her anything. But she needs healing. Maybe her lowest point will also be her turning point. Isn't that a nice thought?"

"I don't know. I think I should give her space," I say. I still can't meet Mari's eyes.

"Perhaps. But I think she needs to hear from you, too. I was afraid to get involved before, because I didn't want to do harm. But at this point, the harm is already done." She gently puts a finger under my chin and lifts my head up. "Think it over. When you're ready, we'll do it together."

A day ago, if I had seen Yoona looking so desolate, I would have gloated. But now I'm not in the mood. In the afternoon, I try to distract myself with reading, but I still can't brush away the guilt that Mari's comments make me feel. Finally, I decide to open Yoona's text.

I swipe open my messages and tap on *Yoona Bae*.

Yoona:

I know about u and Carrie

Something is weird

We need to figure it out together

This is not what I was expecting. At. All.

My heart is pounding at the accusation. How much does Yoona know? I try to remember if I somehow let something slip. But it's impossible to say. I remind myself that I need to be wary of Yoona. She's smart and tenacious. After yesterday, she should be itching for a counterattack.

Sabine:

What do you mean, me and Carrie?

I send out the text, and immediately I see the "typing" bubble. Yoona knows that she has my attention. I retreat upstairs to the girls' room to dig in against whatever's coming next.

Yoona:

The way you talk about me sounds like her

She talked about u the same way

She's been giving u advice, hasn't she?

She's been giving me advice too

I can feel my throat constricting with horror. I want to throw the phone down. This has to be a lie.

Yoona is still typing.

Yoona:

She wants us to keep fighting

It's all part of this big plan

To turn u into the bad guy of the season

She's been telling you what to do, hasn't she?

I know that Yoona is making this up, that this is her way of throwing me off my game. She knows I don't want to look bad, so she's trying to make me feel guilty. I won't get sucked in again.

Sabine:

I don't know what you're talking about

No one told me to do anything

I try to push her out of my head, but a kernel of truth is already burrowed deep. The part about Carrie is too right to just be a lucky guess. Yoona knows something that I don't.

I sit in my bed for a few minutes, eyes closed, taking deep breaths. Trying to calm down. I'm going to ignore Yoona, and I'm going to go back downstairs. But when I open my eyes, she's already sent her next message.

It's an audio file. My phone downloads it; it's four minutes and thirteen seconds long.

Yoona:

Listen to it in secret

Pretend it's music while u work out

I'm sorry about yesterday

About everything

I'm shook. How does she do this? How is it that at every turn, even after I've thoroughly destroyed her, Yoona finds a way to reach into my being and grip my very soul?

Downstairs, it's surreal how normal everything is. Grant is at the dining table, writing on his laptop. Mari and Chris are in the kitchen, baking chocolate chip cookies. Danny is lounging on the couch, looking at his phone. Yoona is there, too. She doesn't even look up at me when I come down. From looking at her, you'd have no idea that she's just been firing off shocking texts to her biggest rival in the house.

Which, when I think about it, makes sense.

Yoona knows what I was doing when I provoked her over text yesterday, instead of in person. Now she's beckoning me into another private conversation, hidden away from the showrunners' omnipotent gaze. And in spite of my better judgment, I want to follow.

"Hey, Pack Pact. Does anyone want to get a workout in?"

Danny and Grant both look at me, amused.

"What? I'm serious," I say. "I do nothing but eat and sit around all day. I'm trying to be healthy."

"Why not," Grant says. He closes his laptop and heads upstairs to put it away and change into workout gear. Danny, who's already in athletic shorts and one of those tech-fabric T-shirts, nods without getting up from the couch.

"How about you, Yoona?" I ask, testing her.

Yoona looks up from her phone and eyes me coolly. "No thanks. I don't do exercise."

As far as the cameras are concerned, we're not on good terms. We'll probably need to do some kind of apology-and-make-up scene to reestablish normal relations. But as for our real relationship, I'm not so sure. All I know is that I have to find out what's in that audio file.

We go downstairs to the game room, and the guys put a

workout video onto the big screen. The instructor is a cute blonde with an amazing body that looks like it was made for crop tops and yoga pants. I suppress the urge to roll my eyes. No wonder the boys are so into ab workouts.

But thirty seconds into the video, I'm dying. This isn't a workout; it's an exquisitely designed form of torture. I complain and try to slack off, but Danny and Grant have adopted ultra-macho workout personas, and they won't let me quit.

"You gotta love pain!"

"Mamba mentality!"

"The question is, how bad do you want it!"

Not that bad, I mutter under my breath. The ten minutes we spend folding and unfolding our bodies, hardening ourselves into various plank positions, are the longest ten minutes of my life. God, I hope they don't put this on TV. Maybe if I yell out a stream of curse words, they'll have no choice but to edit it out.

When it's over, I lie on the floor, panting in agony. Grant and Danny look tired, too, but they're at least sitting up and breathing at a regular speed.

"Good call, Sabine. We needed that," Grant says.

Danny nods in agreement. "The Pack Pact has been losing steam lately. I'm glad we're starting it back up."

"*You're* starting it back up. *I'm* retiring from exercise. The woman in that video isn't human."

"How dare you speak ill of our queen?" Grant cries in mock outrage.

Once my body recovers, I sit up and start to stretch.

"You guys go on without me," I say. "I need a few more minutes. If I try to climb the stairs right now, I'm going to pass away."

Once they're gone, I pop in my headphones and play Yoona's recording. Meanwhile, I bob my head and mouth fake lyrics, pretending I'm listening to music.

"I get it, I really do. But it's for your own good that I'm telling you to forget about it. No offense, Yoona, but I think you're letting a pretty face cloud your judgment. Believe me when I say that that boy is about as emotional as my left shoe."

It's Carrie, and she's talking about Danny. I recognize her voice, but she sounds like a completely different person: aggressive, domineering. The clip gives me chills.

"It was hard enough to get him to ask out Sabine. I had to spoon-feed him instructions. I'd like to put an earpiece in his ear."

The blood drains out of my face. Carrie said she would talk to Danny, but I thought she was going to nudge him, not give him orders.

And then, finally:

"Sabine is the real villain of the show. It's a classic TV narrative: the repressed, seemingly harmless individual who finally gets the chance to be bad. The executive team loves it. When the final cut is released, you'll see."

I want so badly for this all to be a lie. Yoona is clever, after all. She could have tricked Carrie into saying something she didn't mean. I could tell her that I don't believe her, that I don't want to hear any more.

But I know, in the clearest of terms, that everything Yoona has said is true. That my date with Danny is a hollow pantomime. That Yoona never actually had it out for me. That Carrie cast me as the villain, and I turned out to be perfectly suited to the role.

SABINE

TIME IS PLAYING TRICKS ON ME.

Before I know it, it's evening, time for my big date with Danny. I go change into my dress, then go to the bathroom to put on makeup and look at myself in the mirror. It's strange, considering how I feel, to see myself looking so good. I look like someone you could root for.

In an hour or so, I'll be in the middle of my date, doing the best I can to pretend that I've gotten everything I wanted. It'll be difficult to keep up the charade, but I can't let the cameras know what I've learned. Carrie is still watching.

Yoona and I have been texting. Somehow she isn't angry at me, despite everything that I did to her. She wants to fight back. But I'm scared. I don't trust myself anymore, not after what I've done.

I go back to the girls' room to wait. When Danny knocks on the door and comes in wearing his khakis and navy blazer, it feels like a bad dream. He takes my hand, gives it a squeeze.

"You look really beautiful," Danny says to me.

We go downstairs, where a black car is waiting for us. On the ride over, Danny tells me about track recruiting, which colleges he's considering signing with. He talks about what it means to be a Division I athlete, how intense the lifestyle will be, but what an honor it is to put on a uniform and represent a school. I nod along numbly, smiling and giving an occasional "Wow, that's interesting," or "I never thought about it like that before." It feels painfully obvious to me that I'm acting, but Danny doesn't seem to notice.

The car pulls up at a luxe resort. Danny makes me wait so he can hold the door open for me as I get out of the car. We go inside to a French restaurant with beautiful plates and enormous, plush seats. Our waiter is named Dominic. My table setting has two forks, two knives, and two spoons, all of differing lengths.

"You should go to the bathroom in the middle of the meal," Danny says. Seeing my frown, he explains, "To try out the hand soap and the hand lotion. And then when you get back, you can see whether or not they folded your napkin."

"I'll start chugging water now."

Dominic helps us order. He recommends a salad with goat cheese and anchovies, which he pronounces "on-show-vees." I would find this all very entertaining if I weren't empty on the inside.

"Do you know when I realized that I liked you?" Danny asks.

I'm mid-bite of a buttered roll, and I have to swallow an

uncomfortably large pill of bread and wash it down with water before I can answer.

"No. When?"

"It was during our horse ride, when we were coming down the avenue of lights. You were riding next to me, and I turned to look at you. But you didn't notice, because you were looking up. So I was watching you admire the lights, and that's when it hit me."

Danny is smiling like he knows this is exactly what I want to hear. Did Carrie feed him this line? Because that is *not* how I remember that horse ride.

"Was that before or after you told me you wished we were playing polo?"

Danny frowns. "I don't know. Before, maybe. I don't remember."

When the oysters come, Danny takes a picture of the half shells fanned out on a bed of ice. By the time we're done eating them, I'm able to work out a smile. That turns out to be all the encouragement Danny needs.

"Sabine, I like you. I wanted to ask you out on this date and make it special, so I could tell you that."

This is the part where I say *I like you* back. It's easy. I've done it dozens of times, imagining a moment just like this. They're just words.

But I don't say them.

"Why me?" I ask.

Danny hesitates, and I see a shadow of annoyance cross his

face. This night is supposed to be easy for him. A triumph. He isn't supposed to have to work for it.

"I like the way you make me feel," Danny says quickly, as if he's testing out the words. I look at him blankly. He quickly clears his throat.

"And you're the prettiest girl in the house."

It's almost insulting, the way he expects me to eat up corny lines like this. And yet just a few hours ago, I would have. That's one more way this situation hurts: it makes it painfully clear how much of a sucker I was, back when I wanted Danny to like me. I was starving for validation. It's pathetic.

The back-and-forth proceeds through dinner—Danny turning up the charm, me unable to match it. At one point, I ask him to tell me more about track, because I just find it *so* interesting. Danny gets going about distance runs, volume versus speed training, whether he wants to focus on the eight hundred meters or go full-on cross-country. That buys me some time to tune out and get myself together.

Eventually, Danny runs out of things to say about running, and I can tell that he's loading up to try to get me to say I like him again.

"Um, I have to go to the bathroom," I say.

Danny's face falls.

"Gotta try that hand soap!" I dash out of the restaurant before he can reply.

On the way down the hall, I pass by hotel rooms, and the sight of the key card receptacles makes me think of road trips with my family, stopping for the night in little towns off the highway.

In the bathroom, I lean over the sink and see my reflection in the mirror. Once again, it's strange to see my own face, looking so made-up and put together. Given the state my mind is in, running mascara or wind-rumpled hair seems more appropriate.

I text Yoona again.

Sabine:
Why aren't you angry at me?

Yoona:

I'm a big girl. I'll live.

And I'm tired of fighting

Don't worry about me

We'll work things out later

Right now u have to be careful

All of Carrie's focus is on u

And that's the most frightening part.

At this point, maybe it's too late to resist. My storyline is hurtling along on its track, and the most damning part is already written. Maybe I should go along with it. Forget about Yoona, forget about Carrie. Tonight is about me and Danny. *Just tell him you like him back. Yes, someone else is pulling the strings. But what difference does it make? When he looks into your eyes, when he puts his hand on your back, that will be real.*

I take a deep breath and head back into the restaurant.

"Look," Danny says excitedly when I'm back at the table. He points to my napkin, which has been folded into a neat triangle.

"You were right," I say. I'm relieved to find that my voice sounds light, even cheerful. I can do this.

"Let's go out to the lagoon," Danny says. "We can watch the sunset. Then if we want, we can come back for dessert."

Danny and I go through glass double doors onto a boardwalk by the water. The sun is dipping down behind the mountains, and the sky is pink and orange. In the fading light, Danny's pretty eyes seem to glow. *The producers couldn't have asked for a better shot to cap off the night,* I think bitterly.

We look out over the water, at the mountains and the setting sun reflected on its surface. At the other end of the lagoon are a pair of swans, one white and one black, drifting side by side.

"Hey, Sabine."

Danny and I are standing face-to-face. I see the cameraman in the corner of my vision, with his usual quiet stoicism. I brace myself. *Three little words, Sabine. That's all it takes.*

But Danny isn't talking. He's staring deep into my eyes, as if he's trying to hypnotize me. He starts to lean in. I realize what's happening.

When I was still at home, daydreaming about how my time on *Hotel California* would go, I pictured a moment like this. I dared to hope that I might get to kiss someone. But now that it's happening, I can't do it.

I inch away from Danny. He takes a step toward me, puts a hand on my shoulder, and I plant a hand on his chest to hold him off.

"What's wrong?" he asks.

"I'm sorry. I can't do this."

"But I thought—you said that—"

He blinks in confusion, letting his mouth hang half-open in surprise.

"I'm sorry," I say again.

A dazed smile spreads across his face, like this is all some big prank. Carrie must have talked to him, given him certain assurances, and now here I am doing the exact opposite of what he expected.

"I don't get it," he says, shaking his head in wonderment. He looks at the cameraman, like, *Do you believe this chick?*

"You sure?" he asks one last time. "It doesn't have to be, like, serious. We're here to, like, have fun, right? Ha ha."

I'm not sure what world he thinks we're living in, that fear of being "like, serious" is what's holding me back. But I feel for him a bit. My strange behavior must be giving him emotional whiplash.

I shake my head. "I just . . . can't."

Danny stares at me for a long time. I want to curl up into a ball until he looks away, but I'm still on camera.

Finally, Danny shrugs, sticks his hands into his pockets, and walks back through the double doors of the restaurant. I don't follow him; I don't want to face the end of the dinner, the awkward car ride home, just yet.

I turn and face the lagoon, gazing out at the horizon until the final, fiery trace of the sun disappears behind the mountains.

SABINE

"I'M READY, MARI. TO MAKE UP WITH YOONA. I NEED YOUR HELP. You said you'd help." My voice sounds low and desperate. I've just gotten back from my disastrous date. Yoona is already asleep, and Mari is getting ready for bed, but I know this can't wait.

Mari smiles warmly at me and places a hand on my shoulder. "Of course, Sabine. I'm happy to hear you say that. I'll take care of everything."

The prospect of talking to Yoona, of having it out face-to-face, is daunting. But I had to do something. I'm reaching a breaking point. Somehow, this feels like the right thing to do.

Fifteen minutes later, we're down in the living room, along with Chris and a bedraggled Yoona.

"Did we really have to do this now?" Yoona whines. "My brain is closed down for the night. Normal business hours are from ten to four."

"This is an emergency," Mari responds. "Besides, it's a full moon. No better time for a séance."

"You mean like calling up the spirits?" When I took up Mari's offer of healing, I didn't realize she meant the supernatural kind.

"You could say that. A spirit is merely a name you give to an energy that you cannot otherwise comprehend. Where does compassion come from? Where do the highest highs of the human heart come from? Call it what you like—that's what we're calling up tonight."

Coming from anyone else, the concept would be easy to dismiss. But Mari has a knack for backing up her floofy talk.

Chris instructs Yoona and me to face each other. Simple words, but even this is difficult. Holding Yoona's gaze, all I can think about is the way I tried to destroy her. Our last interaction was that blowup by the pool. She said over text that she wasn't angry at me, but I still don't know what she's thinking.

She keeps yawning and blinking away sleep. When our eyes do meet, I see her pupils darting around, itching to look somewhere else. Her mouth twitches with indecision, now curling into a smile, now pressing into a thin line.

It's hard for her, too.

"Reach out and touch your fingertips," Chris says.

Seriously? I look to Mari for confirmation, and she nods. Did these two plan this out ahead of time, or are they just vibing off of each other?

Yoona holds out her hands. I reach out with mine. When our fingertips touch, I feel a jolt of electricity run up my arm and into my shoulders. Yoona shivers like she's feeling the same thing.

"As long as you two touch, there will be a connection between you," Mari says. "Hold on to it, and trust the other person to hold on to it with you."

Chris observes as Yoona and I hold our arms in place. Once we're sufficiently connected, he gives the next instruction. "Ask the other person the one question you've been afraid to ask. Something that will challenge them, but also help you understand them."

Here we go. Spirits, take me now.

"Me first," Yoona says. "Sabine, how do you want people to see you?"

Like everything Yoona says, this question sounds casual on the surface. But if I read into it, try to guess what's going on behind that cool exterior, then there are myriad implications: *you care too much about what other people think, you try too hard to be someone you're not.* Even now, the flow of angry, defensive thoughts is hard to shut off.

Ever since we got back from break, I've been scheming out my actions, calculating my words to tell my own, skewed side of the story. All of that is out the window now. It's like I'm back to my first day in the house, searching for a way to explain who I am to a stranger whose heart I don't know.

"At school, people assume I'm quiet and boring. I want people to at least give me a chance to be something more than that. For one thing, I'm really adaptable. I may have no idea what I'm doing at first, but give me enough time, and I'll figure out my own path. And no matter the difficulty, I don't back down."

"I can see that," Yoona says.

Of course, Yoona is not a stranger, not anymore. She knows me, at least a little.

"Also, I'm funny," I say, my voice growing. "Or at least, I'm always willing to laugh. So funny things happen to me. It may not seem like I'm doing them on purpose, but I'm pretty sure I kind of am."

Yoona smiles. "I think you are, too."

There's a chance that, after living with me for three weeks, she really does see me the way I want to be seen. But, of course, she's also seen me at my worst. A part of her might be rolling her eyes, wondering how I could expect such generosity after all I've done.

"Anyways, that's not to say I think I'm really smart or good at everything," I add. "I can be pretty clumsy, too. It's just—"

Chris holds up a hand, stopping me short. "No need to qualify it. We're talking about how you'd like to be seen. I think you gave a good answer."

"Your turn to ask a question," Yoona says.

I want to ask what she's thinking, how she feels about me now that she's figured out what Carrie is up to. How much of the blame does she still place on me? I wish I could have some final confirmation of what's inside of her head, so I wouldn't have to guess anymore.

But we are not alone. This house has ears and eyes; everything we say reveals what we know, what we've done. I can't let slip to Carrie that Yoona has tipped me off.

"Why were you crying the other day?"

It's not the most pressing question in my mind, but it's safe. Or at least, I thought it was. After I ask it, Yoona stiffens.

"I don't—it's not really important," she says quickly.

Mari frowns. "Come on, dear, you have to try. Even if it's hard."

"Trust," Chris adds.

Yoona bites her lip. She thinks for a second, like she's trying to find a way out. But Mari and Chris keep nudging her, and eventually she gives in. "All right, fine. I was crying because of my mom. She called me because she had just seen the leak."

"Go on," Mari says.

Yoona looks at me fearfully. "She thinks I have no control over my temper. I'm always getting into it with the other girls at my church. People tend to assume that I'm mean. Maybe I am. Anyways, I was crying because my mom said I was an embarrassment."

My stomach drops. This all happened just before our big blowup. No wonder she was so flammable that day.

"Does she say that a lot?" I ask.

"No! Well, not the embarrassment part. She *is* always telling me to lower my voice, and be less surly with the ladies at church. But it doesn't matter; it's just because of her gossip network. I know I was crying, but like I said, it's no big deal," she pleads.

Now I see why she didn't want to answer the question. It wasn't to protect her own secrets. It was to protect me.

So all this time, when I was trying to provoke her, thinking I was so clever, I was really subjecting her to the same treatment she gets back home. No wonder the editors made me the villain of the show. Carrie had me believing that I was the plucky protagonist, navigating a jungle of judgmental Plastics, when in reality, *I* was the judgmental one, the one who fired the first shot with no provocation.

"You didn't know," Yoona says simply.

But that doesn't make me feel any less guilty. I want to admit what I did, say that I'm sorry. But it's hard to find the right formula, the words that will show how I feel without giving too much away.

"Good evening," a familiar voice says from behind me. Yoona cries out in surprise, and I almost jump out of my skin. It's the lava lamp. I turn to look at the glowing band of purple light.

"The producers would like to speak with Sabine. A van is waiting outside. Go now."

Yoona, Mari, and Chris are frozen still, staring at me with bewilderment. None of them knows how my date with Danny went. Carrie must want to talk about that.

"I'm sorry," I say to them all, one more time. Then I head for the door.

Under the night sky, the silhouette of the confessional trailer looms over the driveway like a desert monolith. When I open the door, Carrie's expression is flinty, with none of her usual warmth. This is the Carrie from Yoona's recordings.

She slams the door behind me, and I feel like she's locking me in.

"What the hell was that date about?" she begins. I flinch. "Did I not help you? Did I not give you advice? Are you not getting *exactly* what you wanted, down to the very last inch?"

"I don't know," I whisper.

"You said you liked Danny. Now you can't even kiss him? Are you some kind of prude?"

"He doesn't even like me. I couldn't pretend."

Carrie shakes her head in disgust. "Listen up, sweetheart. I've been giving you the kid gloves so far. Every time you have a problem, I come in and help you solve it. Everyone here is playing their part, and it's all to set *you* up. I'm giving you the happy ending. I'm serving it to you on a silver platter. And you're trying to throw it all away."

She's dropped all pretense now.

"I could tell he was just going through the motions," I say weakly. "You told him to go out with me, didn't you? This would have been my first kiss."

"That's a really sad story, Sabine. I'd hate for you to have to kiss someone that got a little nudge from me first. What did you expect? That Danny was going to tell you he liked you, then ask for a high five?

"I don't think you understand what's at stake. This is going to be the biggest season of *Hotel California* in the history of the show. You're going to make a lot of money, you're going to be famous, and you're going to look back and wonder why the hell you cared so much about this one little boy. But for that to happen, you need to fix this. Tell Danny you're sorry, that you were just scared of how much you liked him. You've been hurt before, or something. Whatever you want. Just don't tell me that crap about how you're the victim, about how you're not getting your perfect first kiss. I can't stand self-pity. It makes me sick."

"Why are you doing this?" I ask, my voice hoarse. "You said you were rooting for me. You said you cared about the old show, and you didn't like what the new editors were doing. Why are you telling me what to do?"

"Me? Listen to me when I say this, my dear. *You* wanted this. You wanted your date with Danny. You wanted to stop being a loser. Well, this is what being a winner feels like. Yes, there are people that have to get hurt, but you and I both know you'd rather be on this side than the other one, don't we?

"We're the same, Sabine. We say we're content being the sweet, kindhearted outsider, but the truth is, we both want more. Yes, the old show was fun. But do you think I came to Hollywood to work on G-rated fluff for fifteen viewers a night? No, and neither did you. You came here because you wanted to be seen. Well, if you want people to watch you, you have to give them something to watch. So be a big girl and do it."

I'm right on the precipice. For now, all Carrie knows for sure is that I had second thoughts about Danny—but if I wanted to, I could tell her everything that Yoona told me. That name, Corina Bowdoin, is on the tip of my tongue. I bet Carrie would be shocked if I threw *that* in her face.

One thing holds me back. I don't want to expose Yoona to Carrie's wrath, too. I've done enough to Yoona already.

"Tell me what I have to do, then," I say.

I listen, numbly, as Carrie lays out the plan for the season's final act. The editors will clean up my date with Danny, make it look like it was all cute and happy, even though it didn't end with a kiss. The two of us will get together in the season finale.

Carrie emphasizes that I only have one last chance to make things right, and I tell her that I understand. Then, just like that, she releases me back into the night. It occurs to me that she probably didn't want to reveal something by accident, either. Both of us are hiding what we know. For now, it seems, I'm safe. As far as Carrie is concerned, the botched kiss was the one hiccup; otherwise, I'm fully going along with the story she's written for me.

Not that there's much I can do to go against it.

I don't have a plan of my own, and I don't know how I can

reverse what's already done. The editors have the final control, and I've given them almost everything they need to tell the story Carrie's way.

Back in the house, Mari and Chris have gone to bed. A small table lamp is the only light in the living room, and it casts a dim glow over Yoona, who has fallen asleep on the couch. She must have been sitting up, waiting for me. I watch her sleep, her breaths rising and falling. She looks so small, with her knees curled up to her chest.

I take a blanket and lay it gently over Yoona's sleeping body. As I tiptoe up the stairs, I make a decision: whatever comes next, I won't involve her in it. I won't let her come to any more harm. Yoona has already given me more help than I deserve. The rest is up to me alone.

SABINE

IN THE MORNING, THE LAVA LAMP ANNOUNCES THE FOURTH AND final challenge. Once again, the prize is twenty thousand dollars. Only this time, there won't be any splitting.

"There will be no teams for this challenge. It will be a battle royale: every person for themself. We will have only one winner."

My housemates are abuzz with excitement. Twenty thousand dollars for one person? That's a full year of tuition at a state school! And, like, one-third of a year at a private school. Generous.

I don't feel excited, though. I sit in silence as everyone else guesses what the final challenge will be. Yoona shoots me a questioning look. I smile and shrug, like *No big deal*, and look away.

Before the van arrives, Danny pulls me aside to talk.

"Listen, I'm sorry about last night," Danny says. "I shouldn't have acted that way. I messed up."

Maybe Carrie has already reached out to him, told him that from now on I'll be more compliant.

"I didn't make things easy on you," I say carefully. "Everything is confusing right now. I think I just need time."

Danny nods. "I totally get that. Take as much time as you need. One thing I want you to know, though. I meant what I said. I really like you. I hope you'll give me another chance."

It's painful, having to pretend. Carrie's narrative is closing in on me like a vise. I have to find a way out, but I don't know how.

And I don't have much time.

On the van ride to the final challenge, I close my eyes and try to come up with a plan. Carrie has taught me the rudiments of manipulating the show—bank some kind of narrative thread, build up momentum, force the editors to tell the story the way *I* want it to be told. The trouble is, I have so little in the bank.

To change the ending of the show, I need to come up with something better than what Carrie already has in mind. I need to find a new ending to my own story—a full-on hijacking. Something irresistible, something so good that it blows the editors away, but that also tells the showrunners in no uncertain terms that I'm giving them a big, fat middle finger.

The van takes us to the edge of town. We pull off at the last exit before the highway opens up into a long stretch of barren desert. In the distance stands a line of wind turbines, turning stoically in the breeze.

The van pulls into a lot marked with an ornate wooden sign that reads *Welcome to Palm Springs' Largest Hedge Maze.* At the end of the lot are a lawn and the promised wall of hedges. The park is an unnatural isle of vibrant green, in contrast to the browns and yellows of the desert.

Some producers are already set up at the entrance, unpacking boxes of equipment. I see light-up vests, each of which is attached by a cord to a small plastic gun. Laser tag.

Standing by the entrance of the maze, holding a microphone attached to a black speaker box, is a woman in a white jumpsuit and towering heels.

"Challengers! Welcome to the fourth and final challenge of *Hotel California* season three!"

I blink. It's the voice of the lava lamp. For whatever reason, she's finally decided to show her face. Maybe she's here to gloat after what she did to us in the last challenge. Hearing the familiar voice come out of this unfamiliar human makes my head hurt.

"Today's challenge is capture the flag—with a twist! Inside the hedge maze are five stations, each of which may contain the digital flag. Your goal is to seek out the flag. The first challenger to find it and return it to the entrance wins. But if you get shot with a laser gun, your own gun will deactivate for thirty seconds, and the flag will be sent back at random to one of the flag stations. Also, while you're carrying the flag, your vest will emit a noise that everyone else in the maze will be able to hear. So you'll have to be crafty!"

This challenge sounds suspiciously like exercise. From the outside, the hedge maze looks huge. Runner Danny is going to have a distinct advantage. Then again, I saw what Yoona is capable of in *Starfall*. Maybe all that video game marksmanship will translate to real life. As for me, I'll probably make easy target practice for the eventual winner.

As we line up at the entrance of the maze, the boys are all doing intimidating athletic movements, like high knees and leg kicks. I'm just thankful I wore real shoes.

"Friends, I bid you all good luck. Whatever happens in that hedge maze, I hope you'll still remember me fondly when I beat you," Grant says.

Yoona shakes her head. "There are no friends in the hedge maze. Only targets."

Even though I don't care about winning, my stomach is queasy, and my hands are vibrating with tension as I grip my plastic gun. I say a silent prayer that this will all end quickly, and I brace myself for the yell of the announcer.

"Begin!"

We all charge into the hedge maze, splitting off down diverging paths. I run for a little while, but I soon tire out and slow to a trot. The maze is tighter and more claustrophobic than I expected. As I make my way deeper inside, I spot cameras perched on wooden poles, or peeking out of the neatly trimmed hedges.

I try to think if there's anything subversive I can do from inside the maze. It would feel wonderful to turn this challenge upside down somehow. I have my phone—I check, and I even have service. Maybe I can order a pizza into the hedge maze, or call in the fire department. It would only be a temporary holdup, but it would be hilarious. Still, it wouldn't make it past the editors.

As I wander through the hedges, I hear occasional scattered laser fire, always a few hedges away. Eventually, I turn a corner and stumble upon a metal box, glowing with fluorescent lights, with a screen on top. It reads *Flag Station*, and below that, *Status: Empty*. On the side of the box is an impression where I can put my gun. When I do, the box flashes and tells me, "Ammo replenished. The flag is not here right now."

I keep on walking past the flag station, but I stop when I hear footsteps. They're coming from ahead of me. In a panic, I take a turn and try to escape into another row of hedges. It's a dead end. The footsteps come closer. My heart rate is spiking, and my hands are sweaty as I grip my gun. The footsteps come around the corner. It's Yoona.

We stare at each other. She raises an eyebrow, asks wordlessly what's going on with me. She was up late last night, wondering what Carrie wanted to talk to me about, but I never did get to tell her. Too late now. I shake my head to say, *Not the time*.

Gradually, Yoona's face lights up with amusement. She puts a finger over her lips, lifts her eyebrows once to say, *Our little secret*, then dashes off. I'm left alone, cowering in the corner of a hedge maze, itchy leaves pricking at my neck. I wonder if Yoona has shot anyone yet. It's kind of funny that she just let me go. Clearly, I don't come off as much of a threat.

As I peek out of the dead end and keep moving, I realize that

I'm sick of staring at these close green walls. I hop up and down, trying to peek over the tops of the hedges, but I'm too short to get any kind of view.

I'm trying to find my way back to the flag station when my vest lights up and starts blinking. I can hear a distant alert ringing through the air. Someone must have found the flag. Slowly, I make my way toward the noise. As I get closer, I hear laughter, yelling, and the sound of laser gunfire. The alert sound is headed away from me—though at this point, I'm so thoroughly lost that I don't know if it's getting closer to or farther from the entrance.

Suddenly, the alert stops. Whoever had the flag has been shot down, resetting the flag to somewhere else in the maze.

I keep on moving through the hedgerows, occasionally stopping to listen for footsteps. Once, I do happen across Chris; he immediately shoots me in the chest, which makes my vest light up and vibrate. Before I can so much as shoot him a glare, he disappears around the bend, and I'm alone again.

Eventually, I come to what appears to be the outermost hedge. Beyond the thick branches and leaves, I can hear the sound of cars. I open up my phone, and my map shows that I am on the edge of the green square symbolizing this park. My feet are sore from walking, and I sit down, resigned to wait for the end. The sun is coming up, and soon it's going to be baking hot. Since I'm not going to win this challenge anyways, I might as well avoid being sweaty.

To pass the time, I scroll through old photos on my phone. As I launch further and further into the past, I think back to earlier versions of myself—sophomore Sabine, freshman Sabine, Sabine in middle school. When I see a photo of myself with one arm tossed around Em's shoulder, both of us wearing button-down shirts and untied bow ties, I stop.

I remember this picture. It was spirit week of our freshman year, during that brief period when we still tried to be a part of things at our high school. The bow ties were my idea; I recall telling Em that we were going to shock everyone and totally nail the theme of "geek chic." At the time, I really thought that that day, those bow ties, might finally mark our stunning burst onto the social scene. Once we got to school, of course, we were the same old Sabine and Em, only with untied bow ties dangling from our collars ("Told you we should have gotten clip-ons," Em said; it was impossible to tie the damn things). We ended up ditching the pep rally to ride our bikes to the river.

I smile. In the moment when that photo was taken, I know that I was trying desperately to become someone else, some better and more interesting version of myself. It should be a painful memory, and if I were in a different mood, it probably would be. But here, sitting at the edge of this interminable hedge maze, I feel nostalgia, even fondness, for the girl in the photo. She seems so earnest, so pure in her desire to be liked.

When I got to the house, I was so eager to prove that I belonged. Little did I know that I would botch the season about as badly as humanly possible. Now I feel the same thing that I did back at home: a yearning to be somewhere else. A place where my life is easier, where I don't have to face these struggles, these problems that are so unfair.

To my surprise, I hear Carrie Waters's voice in my head.

Sure, there are some mean internet trolls, but for every one of them, there are ten girls who see a little part of themselves in you and want to know how you're going to make your comeback. Everyone loves a good comeback. How is it that even now, that woman has wormed her way so deeply into my brain?

I get up and start walking. The alert is ringing again, meaning that someone else has captured the flag. With any luck, the challenge will soon be over.

Up ahead, I see another flag station. I head toward it; after staring at so much nauseating green, the multicolored lights are surprisingly soothing to my eyes. I put my gun into the imprint, hear the "Ammo replenished" message once again, and then freeze. The alert on my vest is gone. The air is dead silent. And the flag station is lighting up.

A spinning golden flag appears on the screen. *Status: Present.*

Holy cannoli. Here it is. The golden ticket.

If I take it, I'll set everyone in the place against me. I have no idea how to get back to the entrance, and even if I do make it out with the flag, it won't get me anywhere. I'll just be speeding myself toward my reunion with Danny.

A car honks from beyond the hedge, shaking me out of my reverie. A thought takes hold in my mind. I don't want to win this challenge. But what if no one wins? What if I take the flag and run? I think—I have my phone, and tucked into the case are my driver's license, my debit card, and my health insurance ID. There are cameras in the hedges, but the six of us are the only people in the maze; the producers don't have time to stop me.

In other words, I'm in business. My parents would kill me for giving up all this money, but I don't care. This may not count as a hijacking, but at least I'll be wildly pulling the steering wheel so that we all crash and burn together. I'd like that.

I open up my phone, click into the rideshare app, and set my destination for the Palm Springs bus terminal. An estimate pops up: four minutes. Now I'm one button click away from getting out of here.

From around the corner, I hear footsteps coming toward me fast. I hide behind the flag station, my heart pounding. This is such bad timing.

Whoever it is, I can't let them take the flag. This could be my one chance to fight back against the producers. I am not throwing it away.

I take a deep breath, say a prayer as I grip my gun. Then I stand up.

It's Grant. When he sees me taking aim at him, he freezes.

"Hands up," I say, hoping I sound intimidating.

Grant's jaw drops. As he lifts up his hands, his mouth curves into a rueful smile.

"Well, well, well. Nicely done, Sabine. I didn't think you had it in you."

I stare blankly at him. I didn't think I had it in me, either.

"But unfortunately, you've made a classic mistake," he continues. "Amateurish, really. You've failed to protect your flanks."

From behind, I feel a laser gun pressing into my back.

"Hello, darling," Yoona says. She's so close that I can feel her breath on my neck, making my hairs stand up. "I can't help but notice that there's a flag in this station. You don't mind if I take it, do you?"

I'm not sure whether to laugh or cry. I start to lower my gun, but Yoona tells me to keep it trained on Grant.

"Listen up, kiddos. Here's how this is going to go. Sabine, you're going to shoot Grant. Then I'm going to shoot you. Then I'm going to take the flag, and we're all going to be out of this terrible hedge maze in about fifteen minutes. Are we clear?"

"Proposition for you, Sabine," Grant cuts in. "Don't shoot me. Dive onto the ground, and we both shoot at Yoona. She knocks out one of us, but the other one gets her and takes the flag. It's fifty-fifty. You have to admit, my way works better for you."

"Yoona," I whisper. "I have an idea. My phone is in my pocket. Can I show you?"

"Be my guest," she whispers back. "But no sudden movements."

With one hand, I keep my gun trained on Grant, and with the other, I reach into my pocket.

"I'm calling a car. I'll take the flag, and I'll run away. I won't come back."

"You're leaving?"

"Yes."

And even though I haven't had the time to think this through, saying it out loud makes me feel more sure.

"I can't do this anymore. I don't want to go on another date with Danny. I don't want to have my first kiss be fake. And I don't want to stay in that house, with Carrie watching my every move. Sooner or later, she'll find out what I know."

I can't see Yoona's face, so I can only guess at her reaction. I try to reach my mind out across the air, call upon her spirits like I did last night.

"Are you sure?" She whispers the words so flatly that they're more statement than question. In front of me, I can see Grant inching his hand toward his gun.

"Yes," I whisper back.

She lets out a long sigh. Slowly, the point of her gun lifts off of my back.

"Be quick," she says.

I call the car. Yoona pulls me out of the way and fires at Grant. His vest lights up, and his own gun refuses to fire as he presses uselessly on the trigger.

"Damn it," he says, disgusted. "Lucky shot. Thirty seconds, and I'm coming right back at you."

There's no time to lose. I place my gun in the receptacle.

"Ammo replenished. The flag is in your hands."

My vest lights up and begins to emit the alert. Grant smirks at me and mouths, *RUN*. But I don't. Instead, I climb up onto the flag station and hop awkwardly onto the top of the hedge.

"What the—"

The hedge is sharp and prickly, and I'm caught awkwardly in its many small branches. I struggle to pull myself over, grabbing fistfuls of leaves and sticks that dig painfully into my palms.

"What are you doing? That's totally against the rules!" Grant cries out from below. I ignore him. From atop the hedge, I finally get a glimpse of Yoona. Despite the thousands of tiny hedge branches pricking my skin, her face almost stops me in my tracks. Her brow is pulled tight, and her eyes are sad, sadder than I've ever seen them. Suddenly, it hits me. I'm leaving. I'll never see her again, most likely. This is goodbye.

I swing my leg over the other side and tumble down heavily onto the lawn. The hedge wall that I've just climbed looms over me, insurmountable. There's no turning back now.

I brush the branches off of my clothes, take stock of the angry red welts on my skin. My phone buzzes with a notification: *Your driver is two minutes away.* Across a stretch of dry desert earth is the road, and beyond that, the highway. Freedom.

I dash over to the road, and when the car arrives, I pull open the door and clamber into the back seat. In the rearview mirror, I see the driver's eyes bulge. This is probably the first time he's ever picked up a girl with hedge leaves in her hair, wearing a flashing, beeping vest attached to a laser gun.

"It's been a long day," I say wearily.

"You better be a good tipper," he grumbles. But then we're off.

As we pull onto the highway, the vest stops making noise and appears to go dead. I take it off, feeling the lines of sweat it's left on my shirt. When we get to the bus station, I'll trash it.

It's so surreal to me to have crossed that invisible line, to now be in a loose, fugitive state simply by virtue of having walked in one direction instead of another. This plan was so flimsy, so hastily constructed, and yet it's working.

After a short ride, we get to the bus station. It's quiet, with only a few vacationers waiting forlornly with their suitcases. At the ticket desk, I buy a one-way ticket to LA; from there, I'll take the overnight bus to Iowa City. It'll be a long ride, but I'll get through it. I'll even get to see Utah and Colorado. I've heard it's beautiful there.

As the bus pulls out of Palm Springs, I think about Yoona. That wounded look on her face was unlike anything I've ever seen from her. I wonder if she was sad to see me go. We never did figure out how to be friends with each other. We were so close. If only we'd had more time.

That kernel of regret aside, I breathe a sigh of relief. I know I made the right decision. The thought of Carrie and the editors flipping out over my sudden departure is some consolation. And that shot of me, carrying the twenty-thousand-dollar flag, disappearing over the side of the hedge maze, never to be heard from again? They'll have to include it; it's the only way to explain my absence from the rest of the show. I think I may have actually pulled this off. The hard part is over, and now all that separates me from home are a few long stretches of waiting and looking out the window.

As we start to pass by the outlying suburbs, I'm struck by the beauty of California. Clouds soar across the wide sky; to the north, mountains loom over rows of houses, making them look plain and small. I wonder if Mari is from a town like this. I miss her already.

As we get into downtown LA, I realize that I'm not far from where Grant and I went on our bookstore date. I remember, with a pang, that I've left *The Bell Jar* back at the house, along with the rest of my things. I wonder what the producers will do with my stuff. Maybe Mari and Yoona will help get it back to me, or maybe the showrunners will burn it all.

It would have been nice to say a proper goodbye to everyone, to have some more closure. But that's what I gave up when I climbed over the hedge. I'll mourn the loss, and I'll move on.

At the bus stop, I shuffle out into the parking lot and blink in the sunlight. The lot is oddly empty, except for what appears to be a camera crew, getting ready to film for some TV show or another.

One of them calls out, "Action!" and I hear the snap of a clapboard.

The cameraman pans across the parking lot and then fixes the camera on me. As I shade my eyes to get a better look, I notice someone running toward me out of the corner of my eye. Am I in the shot? I whip my head around, wondering if I should get out of the way.

"Well, isn't this shocking!"

It's Carrie. She's flanked by two of the production assistants, wearing their usual polos and baseball caps. My heart leaps up into my throat. I brace myself for more words, more arguments. Even though she's found me, she can't make me go back.

But Carrie skips the talking. She lifts up her hand, and the two assistants charge at me.

"Hey, don't touch me! What the hell—"

They pull me to a car, throw me inside, and slam the door shut behind me. I wonder how they can do this in broad daylight, so brazenly. Then I realize. The cameras. They make this all seem fake. Just another Hollywood drama.

SABINE

THE CAR TAKES US OUT TO THE EDGE OF THE CITY. WE PULL UP TO a complex of office buildings, glass and steel glittering under the afternoon sun. Each building is adorned with the familiar logo of the streaming platform. We're at HQ.

After we park, two more assistants in polos escort me into one of the buildings. Inside, I have to pose for a photo, which then gets printed out onto my visitor's badge.

Sabine Zhang, Talent

I'm "talent." I guess it's better than "hostage."

Next, I'm taken to an office. I sit down on an office chair; in front of me, seated at a semicircular desk, are Carrie and a businessperson type in a suit.

"Good afternoon, Sabine," the man in the suit says. He has a salt-and-pepper beard and square-framed glasses that make him seem like an English teacher, or a friendly librarian.

"What the hell is going on?" I reply.

"There's no need to be anxious. We're going to have a brief

conversation with you, and then we're going to send you back to the house."

"Oh, sure, no need to be anxious. I've just been brought here against my will. Perfectly normal."

"It's a pity that we aren't meeting under better circumstances. But putting that aside, I hope we'll still be able to find some common ground here."

"What do you want?"

"An excellent question," the man in the suit says, smiling warmly. "Believe it or not, Sabine, what I want is exactly the same thing you want. I'm the executive producer of *Hotel California*, and I care deeply about our cast members. What I want is simply for you to recognize and attain what is in your best interests."

"That's a lie."

The man chuckles. "I like you, Sabine. I admit, when Carrie first told me about you, I didn't see the appeal. Yoona, Grant, Chris—now, those young people, I could get on board with. But Sabine Zhang? What did she bring to the table?"

"Carrie Waters is a lying snake."

Carrie smiles faintly but doesn't respond.

"Carrie Waters fought for you," the man says, still perfectly calm. "No one else on the production staff would have chosen you. But she saw something in you that no one else did. Your potential to be a star."

"It's true, Sabine," Carrie says. "I always believed in you. I'm proud of you. You don't know how proud of you I am."

"Whatever. You kidnapped me. How are you going to explain that to the police?"

"Oh, I'm sure it won't come to that," the man in the suit says. "If you'd like, I can point to the exact line in the liability release you signed that our attorneys would cite to defend our corporation in court. Or I could point to the lines that we'd use to countersue you for breaching the terms of your contract. But that would all be terribly dull, and really, it would get us nowhere. Don't you agree?"

I'm no lawyer, but there's just no way that can be true. It's not like I read the documents they made me sign—they were so long, and the print was tiny—but not even Judge Judy would let Carrie off for shoving me into a car in broad daylight. Right?

"What were you trying to prove, Sabine?" the man in the suit continues. "This season is going to be a massive hit. And you're at the center of it, getting everything you could possibly want. Fans who love you. Stories for life. Not to mention quite a significant sum of money. If you return to the house, and do as Carrie tells you, then we will pay you fifty thousand dollars."

"I don't want your money."

The producers laugh.

"I'm serious," I say. "You all think you're so smart, making this show like every other melodramatic reality show. Everyone will know it's fake."

"You think you're better than us?" Carrie asks, in a low, menacing voice. "Sabine, I'm surprised at you. Do you know why I chose you to be the center of the show? Because you judge people.

That's who you are. Add up all the algorithms we used to design this cast, and they don't even compare to the way you instantly put everyone in the house into a box. Yourself included."

"Recall the reasons you joined this show," the suit man adds. "*Hotel California* meant something to you, yes? It showed you a diverse community that you found uplifting. Many reality shows don't have a single Asian cast member, let alone an all-Asian cast. Now, you have a chance to help this show reach more people than ever before. Are you going to stand in the way? Because if you are, know this—if this show fails, then the next one like it won't be coming for a long, long time."

The statement makes my blood boil. He's trying to paint himself, and the rest of the producers, as the good guys. Like, *We're doing you people a favor.*

"No one asked for your help. I wasn't sitting by the TV, praying that you and your internet pals would come and bless my show with your money machine. It was way better before you guys showed up. That Olympics shit was borderline racist, by the way."

The man's face is infuriatingly calm. I'm desperate to find something smart and piercing and adultlike enough to get a reaction out of him, even the littlest crack in his facade. "Of course you're trying to buy me; you think everything in the world is for sale. You think that just because you give out prizes, we're all supposed to bow down and kiss your—"

"In any case, this part of the conversation is a mere formality," the man says sharply. "Let us move on to the potential actions we can take against you. We have hours and hours of footage of you. We have the ability to leak stories about you, and the media influence to make them appear to be true. We even have the contacts and the resources to interfere in your college application process. Although believe me when I say how disappointed I will feel if I am forced to ruin such a promising future."

Finally, he stops smiling. For the first time, he fixes me with a cold, hard stare. "Don't try to fight us. You will lose."

My throat constricts in horror. This man was polite at first, but I can feel the menace in his heart, the terrible violence that he's holding at bay. Against these people, with their lawyers and money and connections, I'm just a kid. That's what I've always been, from the moment I sent in my audition videos. They don't care that I jumped over a hedge maze. Even if I did make it home, I'd still be within easy reach.

"Why are you doing all of this?" I ask. "Why force me to do what you want? Why not just let us live our lives? This is supposed to be a *reality* show."

The man looks at me with pity.

"Sabine. You are familiar with your own life. Do you think it is worthy of being televised? The moments when you almost fight with the person you hate, but you bite your tongue? When you like someone and don't have the courage to say so? Of course not. Like all people, you censor yourself. You avoid situations that will cause you to experience true feelings. We have simply helped you get to those moments, shown you the height of who you can become. On TV, there's no such thing as reality, Sabine. There's only a premise, and whatever shows up on camera."

"But you made people hate me!"

"People don't love or hate you. Your job isn't to win over the audience. It's to keep the audience watching. This is a TV show, after all. And on the show, you're not a person. You're a participant. No, better yet—a star. So play your part. You'll thank us in the end."

He nods at me, then stands up and walks out of the room. Carrie and I are alone now, just like at my confessionals.

I listen numbly as Carrie tells me how the final week is going to play out. Make up with Danny. Tell him you're finally ready to open your heart. Another date, a first kiss. With the others, do as you like. Hell, make up with Yoona, if that's what you want. While she speaks, I can hardly look at her. All I can think about is what she said about me. *You judge people. That's who you are.*

I know it's pointless to resist. When she's done laying out the plan, I nod and tell her I'll do it. The polo shirts come back into the room to escort me out. Before I go, Carrie walks around the desk and puts a hand on my shoulder.

"Thank you, Sabine. You don't know what a pleasure it's been."

In her eyes, I see no triumph, no satisfaction, no resentment. I see only warmth, and genuine gratitude. It's that final look that frightens me most of all.

YOONA

LISTEN, I'M SURE SABINE WAS TRYING HER BEST. I CAN'T IMAGINE she has much experience taking on conniving *b* words like Carrie Waters, so I wouldn't have expected perfection. But getting cornered, and then jumping into a hedge and running away? All I can say is, that's not how I would have done it.

So on the morning after the challenges, when I wake up to see her back in the girls' room, asleep in her own bed, I'm not surprised. She was never going to get away that easily.

For a moment there, though, I thought I might never see her again. It was when she was climbing over the hedge, and she looked back at me one last time. Our eyes met. I thought, *So you really are leaving.* I thought, *So you're giving up on us.*

After the séance, even though it was late, and even though we didn't finish, I felt like we'd finally gotten over the hump. We still had work to do, but I knew it was only a matter of time. We were finally going to be friends, and we'd feel that much closer because we'd *earned* it. I guess that's my problem. With Danny, with

Sabine—I think I'm in control, but before I know it I've caught feelings, ones that demand to be returned. This is how you get hurt.

But now we're back together again. And I'm not giving up on us.

The funny thing is, after all that's happened, I want to be friends with Sabine now, more than ever. I understand why she did what she did. I know what it feels like when the world forms an idea about you, and you have to fight to prove that it isn't true.

I go downstairs, eat breakfast, and come back up. Sabine is still asleep. I tiptoe up beside her, close enough that I can see her eyes twitching, her mouth hanging slightly open. When I bend down to get closer, she lets out a grumpy grunt, and I have to stifle a laugh.

When I woke up in the living room on the morning after the séance, I was disoriented at first. After a few moments, I remembered that I'd been camped out on the couch, waiting up for Sabine. There was a blanket pulled over me, and I realized that she must have done it on her way upstairs. That was a nice thought.

Now the situation is reversed. I pull up Sabine's blanket and rest it gently over her shoulders. On my way out of the room, I stop at the door for one last look. And I think to myself, *You're not done with me yet.*

Everyone else is hanging by the pool, and even though it's sunny, I decide, for once, to join them (after whipping out the sunglasses and slathering on the SPF 100, of course). We order smoothies, which arrive just as the air gets hot. Sabine doesn't come down to join us until well past noon. There's a defeated look in her eyes, like she's a recaptured prisoner. I try to catch her eye, but she won't look at me.

"Are you okay? What happened to you?" Mari asks her.

"I got dehydrated in the maze," Sabine replies. "I was still disoriented when the producers came to get me, so they took me to a clinic for an IV. And then I slept it off for a while, so I didn't get back until really late."

"Poor thing," Mari says, wrapping her up in a hug.

Grant and I share a look discreetly. The producers told everyone a version of Sabine's story already, so Grant and I are the only ones who know what she really did. And I'm the only one who understands why she did it.

"Have a smoothie," I call out to her. "I hope you like strawberry-banana."

When she takes the smoothie from my outstretched hand, I grab her by the wrist and pull her into the pool chair beside me.

"So you're back," I say.

"I'm back," she replies, staring down at her smoothie. She's really leaning into the mopey thing. I respect her right to wallow, but I'm also dying to know what she was thinking when she tried to escape. And, of course, to give her just a *little* shit for it.

"Unfinished business?" I ask.

"I thought if I left, it would be better for everyone. It seemed like the easiest way."

"Oh?"

"But it didn't work."

"It didn't work," I repeat, letting a hint of irony into my voice. "Guess you'll have to finish things the hard way."

Sabine looks at me, eyes full of confusion. The typical Sabine expression. You'd never guess that a face so innocent would mask any kind of deviousness. Maybe that's how I let her get the better of me. For the record, I still think she just got lucky.

"Sabine! Come dip your feet!"

It's Danny. He's sitting by the edge of the pool, grinning and patting the spot next to him. He *would* choose this timing. He raises an eyebrow at me, as if daring me to speak up.

"Sounds urgent," I concede. "You better go."

Sabine glances between Danny and me, looking lost. I lean over and give her a playful shove. "Go," I say.

She gets up slowly, like she's been dreading this.

"We'll talk later?" she whispers.

She really is sad. No worries—I'll cheer her up. *You may have taken some L's, Sabine, but lucky for you, now you've got me on your side.*

I put on my sunglasses and lean back in my chair. "Obviously," I say.

Yoona:

What happened after the hedge maze?

Tell me as much as u can

But don't text back right away

They're prob watching us extra close

I reel off the texts, then sit back and sip my smoothie. Meanwhile, Sabine has to endure a full hour of getting teased and flirted at by Danny. She puts on a brave face, but I can see the strain in her smiles, the way her laughs are delayed because she has to force them out.

A while later, Sabine finally responds. She describes her escape, her capture at the bus station, her sketchy trip to see the executive producers.

Yoona:

See this is what happens when u go it alone

Sabine:

I'm sorry

I just wanted this all to end

I'm so ashamed of what I did to you

Yoona:

How about u make it up to me then?

Sabine:

Tell me how I can do that, and I'll do it

Maybe I could get her to bake me a cake or something. She totally would. If only she weren't so clearly at rock bottom, I'd probably try to have a little more fun with her.

Yoona:

It's fine

Consider us made up

U + me = friends

Sabine:

. . . That's it?

Yoona:

Hm?

Oh right duh

CONGRATS are in order

This is a rare privilege and I'm sure it's v overwhelming for u

Sabine:

But what about everything I did?

Yoona:

Forgiven

💧 under the 🌉

I prob deserved it haha

Sabine:

But I'm pathetic

I was so insecure that I was willing to take you down to protect myself

I'm like, empty on the inside

She really wants to draw this out. I don't want to rush her or anything, but there's only so much self-flagellation you can do before it's time to move on.

Yoona:

You're not pathetic

It's like u said, ur adaptable, and u don't back down, and ur also very funny

That's what makes u stand out

Not going out with Danny or whatever

As I type out these texts, I feel lit from within by a new feeling of power. The power of having the upper hand in a situation, of knowing that you're in the right, and yet using it to draw someone closer, instead of pushing them away.

Sabine:

That's so nice of you

I don't know what to say to that

Yoona:

Yeah I'm nice like that

Actually, there is one thing that u can do to make things up to me

Sabine:

Anything

Yoona:

No more running away

We're getting back at Carrie and we're doing it together

However it ends, we go out guns blazing

Sabine:

OMG

But how? They have all of the power

Yoona:

Not all of it

U said it yourself that we decide what ends up on tape

We just have to give them something so good that they have no choice but to use it

Sabine:

They've already decided what's going to happen

I go on one last date with Danny, confess my feelings, and we end up together in the big season finale

Yoona:

Booo-riiing

What is this the bachelor?!?!

We need to give them something better

Sabine:

What's better than romance?

Yoona:

MURDER

jk jk

Here's my thing

Sabine, u r the star of the show, no doubt about it

But making Danny the co-main? Out of everyone else?

> I'm getting a serious case of second-lead
> syndrome

It's just like that movie, *Maine Pyar Kiya*. There are the two love interests, and Seema, the bitchy third wheel. The story goes that the couple falls in love, and the third wheel gets what she deserves. But what happens if the third wheel is a way better character than the male lead, who can't stop showing off his pecs? Wouldn't it be way more fun to see the mechanic's daughter ditch his ass and go riding motorcycles with Seema instead?

Sabine:

> So you're saying I end up with the second lead?

> Grant??

Yoona:

> . . . ru serious

> No u blockhead

> It's like this

> As far as the show is concerned, we're still
> fighting, right?

> That interrupted seance didn't exactly make
> for coherent storytelling

> U and I have unfinished business too

Sabine:

Oh wow . . .

So that's the end of the show? We end up as friends?

Yoona:

And we do it BIG

Make them forget all about Danny

Let's give them the best damn reunion they've ever seen

Sabine:

Do you really think the editors would go for that

Yoona:

Hmmm idk

It should be a good time at the very least

Besides, don't u wanna try? Aren't u curious to see if u can beat Carrie Waters at her own game?

Sabine:

I did say I would do anything . . .

Yoona:

Don't have to if u don't want to, Sabine

I forgive u anyways

My affection for u is like velcro shoes

NO STRINGS

Sabine:

LOL

Alright alright I'm in

So what's the plan?

Yoona:

Dw I gotchu

Meet me in the game room

We're going to watch a little movie called
Maine Pyar Kiya

SABINE

I STAND IN FRONT OF THE MIRROR, ALL DRESSED UP FOR THE BIG day, the last one of the season. I thought I was nervous for my previous dates, but now I feel sick like never before. I'm going up against Carrie again, and this time, I know the full scope of what she can do.

But at least I'm not alone.

There's a knock on the door, and I turn to see Yoona poking her head in.

"I just wanted to wish you good luck tonight," she says. "I always want the best for you, even if I don't always show it. I hope you get your happy ending, Sabine. You deserve it."

"Thanks," I say. "I hope so, too."

She winks at me, then closes the door. If all goes well, though, I'll be seeing her again soon.

After getting kidnapped by the executive producers, I realized that it doesn't matter how disruptively I behave. The editors have the final control; if I do something they don't like, they'll cut it, and I'll get punished for nothing.

So this time, the plan is different. Yoona and I aren't going to sabotage Carrie's ending. We're going to top it. We're going to give her and her bigwig homies the showstopper finale that they're asking for. And we're going to do it on our own terms.

I wait in the living room until Danny comes downstairs to take me away. He's got his blazer on, and this time he's even wearing a tie. As he walks closer to me, I catch the aggressive, musky scent of his cologne. This must be what going to prom feels like.

As the date gets underway, I find it surprisingly easy to act like I'm into it. Maybe because I know it's just a game. But also shout-out to Yoona, who earlier today sent me some of her tips.

Yoona:

U have to understand how his brain works

He basically views being with u as a game where he scores points by seeming funny or cool

So think of yourself as an Olympic judge rating everything he does

So that's what I try to do.

In the car, Danny tells me this *totally rad* story about the time he and his boarding school friends split a six-pack of 'Gansetts and climbed onto the roof of the school chapel. Meh. Four-point-seven out of ten. I stifle a yawn.

At dinner, he stares at me across the table, turning up the smolder in his eyes. "You're so pretty. I can't stop looking at you." Now, this I can get on board with. A solid nine-point-one.

"You can look all you like."

As the entrées arrive, I get a text from Yoona. My phone is in my lap, and I type my reply without looking down at the screen, trying to be as surreptitious as possible.

Yoona:

How is it looking over there

U good?

Sabine:

About to kick things off

Yoona:

Good luck babe. U got this!!

Here we go.

"Danny, I want to talk about what happened at our last date. I've been thinking. About us. It was hard, because you make me feel so many things that I've never felt before. But I've come to a decision."

"What is it?" He looks smug, like he knew all along that no woman could possibly resist him.

"I'm going to tell you. But not here. I want to take you somewhere. A place where I can really show you how I feel."

Danny frowns. No one told him that I was going to suggest another location. He opens his mouth, hesitates, then closes it again. Meanwhile, the producers are probably watching a live stream of this right now, with the polo shirts standing by.

"I know it's not fair of me to make you wait even longer," I continue. "But I really want it to be special. In the right setting, we'll be filled with a sense of life's grandeur. This is an important moment, and I know that I'm going to want to watch it over and over again. So I want it to look right."

Finally, Danny breaks out into a smile. It's almost like he's wearing an earpiece and the producers just gave him a "Go." "That sounds great," he says.

"Cool! Our driver is"—I pick my phone up from my lap—"six minutes away."

I get up and march outside before anyone can stop me. Danny follows, looking happy but a little confused. As we wait on the sidewalk, I'm feeling a little exposed—the goons could be around the corner, or even parachute in for an aerial attack—but only the cameraman follows us, still filming. Maybe I'm acting too quickly for the producers to respond, like Yoona predicted. Or maybe they're playing along, lulled into a false sense of security. Whatever the case, we make it into the car.

"Where are we going?" Danny asks.

"Shh. It's a surprise."

Now this is the part that's going to take timing, and some good old-fashioned luck. In my mind, I go back over the words of Yoona's text.

Yoona:

We'll both surprise our dates with a change of scenery

Meet u at Rendezvous Point Alpha. AKA Griffith Observatory

The most romantic spot in the city. I've watched *La La Land*, so even I know that. I'm surprised that Danny didn't think of it himself. Taking a girl there is a move straight out of his playbook.

When we get there, I gasp. The view really is incredible. It's just getting to twilight, and the lights of Los Angeles are twinkling to life. The glowing lines of the boulevards reach out and kiss the horizon. In the distance, the downtown skyline looms facelessly over the landscape like a steel Stonehenge. From up here, you can see LA in its full, improbable scope. A metropolis, teeming with life, in the middle of the desert. A miracle.

"So what's up?" Danny asks me.

Now to stall. Cross my fingers and hope Yoona and Grant make it in time.

"Let's enjoy the view for a while. Really immerse ourselves in it. It's intoxicating, isn't it?"

"Yeah. It's cool," he replies. I can sense his impatience, but for the moment, he obediently leans over the white stone banister and looks outward. "Intoxicating for sure."

I need to check in with Yoona, but I can't be on my phone too much or the producers will get suspicious. The most I dare do is pull Danny in for a series of selfies, then pretend to pick through and delete the ones I don't like.

"Oh no, we blinked in this one," I say as I open up my messages.

Yoona:

> We're running a little late! sry babe the traffic!!!
> LA amirite!!

Ugh. We can*not* be foiled by traffic. I fire off one last text, then put my phone away for the night.

Sabine:

> I'm going dark. Text when you're here so I know when to start.

Meanwhile, I can tell Danny is getting antsy. He starts his own confession, probably to prompt me.

"One of my goals for coming on this show was to discover a different side of myself. I know I'm not the most sweet or sensitive guy. I can come off like a bit of a douche. I'm not proud of it, but it's how the world made me. But the thing is, being around you made me want more. For the first time, I wanted to be someone better, so I could be good enough for you."

Well, this is at least smoother than the absurdly fake compliments he gave me at the French restaurant. Carrie must have prepped him. She deserves credit.

He stops and looks at me expectantly. My phone is maddeningly still. "Um, can you say a bit more about your goals?"

A flash of frustration wrinkles Danny's brow, and I feel a prickle of fear, thinking back to the way our last date ended. At this point, I'm sure that Yoona and Grant are never gonna show. Even the cameraman, normally so stoic, looks impatient.

"No, I'm sorry," I say. "I'm just scared. I'm trying to work up the courage. I'm not a very brave person, like you are. But I want to be."

His expression softens. "You don't have to be brave with me. I'll never judge you. I'll always be on your side."

I feel my phone vibrating in my back pocket. Yoona is here, thank the Lord. I smile a huge smile, and Danny, thinking it's because he nailed his lines, smiles back.

"Okay, I'm ready!" I declare.

Danny gets his smug look again and cedes the floor to my confession. Here goes. I've only practiced my speech in my head, since rehearsing it out loud would have been too risky in the house. The timing needs to be perfect.

"Last time, at dinner, I was scared. I wanted you to like me, but when I realized you actually did, I froze. I wasn't ready, so I pushed you away. That wasn't fair to you. I'm sorry."

I take a deep breath that I hope is appropriately melodramatic. "I wish I'd gotten it right the first time. Since then, I've had to do a lot of thinking. I feel silly for taking so long, but the good thing is, now I'm sure."

Pause. Danny is grinning. I wonder what Corina Bowdoin will think of all this.

"I really like you, Danny," I begin. Out of the corner of my eye, I spot Yoona at last, sprinting up the stairs and turning the corner toward us. Grant is following behind her, whirling his head around in confusion. I have to fight not to laugh.

"But the thing is, I'm not sure if our relationship can carry."

Danny's eyes glaze over as his brain malfunctions in real time. "Carry? You mean like carry on after the show?"

"I think we have a lot of things going for us. But in the foundation, there are some holes. And when you have holes in your foundation, you just can't . . . carry waters."

That's Yoona's cue. Just in time, she stops short behind Danny, panting a little. Poor girl. She said she hates exercise. Grant catches up, and the two of them sidle up behind Danny like Daphne and Scooby-Doo about to unmask a criminal.

"Sorry, buddy," she says, patting Danny on the back. "You did your best. Hell, I was rooting for you guys. But sometimes, she's just not that into you."

Danny's jaw drops open. So, for that matter, does Grant's.

Although in Grant's case, I can't blame him. This is the second time in a matter of days that Yoona and I have pulled some weirdo stunt at his expense. The cameraman is riveted. As for the producers, I hope they're at least amused and curious enough to let this go on. Now for the final part of our plan. The new ending that Yoona has scripted for us.

Yoona takes a step toward me and reaches out her hands. I touch my fingertips to hers. Séance, round two.

"All along, there was something missing," I say. "I had a sickness of the heart, and I thought it was because of a boy. But even when I found my chance at love, something wasn't right. And that's when I realized. The missing piece was you."

"I've been waiting to hear you say that," Yoona says, beaming. She's even tearing up. Damn, she's good. Either she's taught herself how to cry on command, or there's some part of her that isn't really acting.

"I want the two of us to make things right," I continue. "Until that happens, I won't have a happy ending."

Danny and Grant have both melted into the background; they seem to be far, far away.

"Let's not push each other away anymore," Yoona replies. "Even if we fight, or hurt each other again, let's take a chance on friendship. We're not so different, you and I. We both have darkness in our souls, but we're both battling to see the light."

We hug it out, and by this time, I'm full-on crying, too. Even though we're following a plan, there's a vein of pure emotion in my heart that feels real. Our cheeks are pressed together, and I take a full inhale of her scent. Her body feels unexpectedly delicate in my arms. But her own grip is strong and comforting. I like it.

"Thank you," I say.

Yoona pulls back, smiling through the tears. She puts a hand out toward Grant, and he hands her a white baseball cap. Written across the panels, in black Sharpie, is the word *Friend*.

"It's a rule of friendship, Sabine," she says, placing the hat on my head. "No sorry, no thank you."

I do my head tilt, as cute and charming as I can make it. I'm not sure if I'm quite pulling it off like Bhagyashree, the actress in *Maine Pyar Kiya*, but only the hard-core fans will be checking that part anyways.

We've done it. I brought the gasoline, and Yoona brought the match. Now to sit back and watch it all burn. Grant shrugs and turns to take pictures of the view. Danny is shaking his head like he can't believe it, but I like to think that deep down, he enjoyed the Bollywood reference.

And even as the camera rolls, and Carrie and her goons no doubt close in, I feel content. Whatever happens next, at least we went down swinging. And most important, we did it together.

SABINE

IN THE DAYS AFTER THE INCIDENT AT THE OBSERVATORY, IT becomes clear to us that no matter how badly Yoona and I messed up the arc of the show, we will not be kidnapped again. At first, life in the house continues as if nothing out of the ordinary has happened. We order food, play video games, and hang by the pool.

On our penultimate day, Carrie shows up at the house. I expect her to be livid, but she appears to be completely calm. She tells us that we're having a clip show to cap off the season. We all gather in the game room to watch the footage that she's selected.

At first, Carrie lets us give our unfiltered comments. We rewatch the opening scene, each of us entering the living room, and comment on what first impressions we made, how nervous we all were. But when we get to my first confrontation with Yoona, Carrie rejects my quip about being ready to throw down.

"No. Say that you knew, all along, that she was going to come around. That it was going to take work, but it would be worth it in the end."

She pauses the clips and waits for me to do as I'm told. It's a bit awkward, but I don't see the harm, so I go ahead and comply.

As the clip show progresses, Carrie keeps feeding us quotes.

After our confrontation at dinner, Carries tells Yoona to say, "I respect her for standing up to me. There's more to her than I thought. I'll give her that."

After my first big dinner with Danny, when I refused to kiss him, Carrie tells me to say, "I like him, but something feels off. I have this guilt, and I'm not sure where it comes from. I need to figure that out before I can be with someone else."

Gradually, my hopes rise: the producers are going along with the ending we created. These quotes are a way to massage the storyline, building up to our big make-up sesh. We're going to be okay. Hopefully, this means I can still go to college.

Of all the clips that we watch, the one that stands out to me is from a confessional with Yoona, her very first one.

"Listen, I know how I come off. I'm loud and aggressive, and I even look a little scary. I'm a lot to handle. When people see me, they make certain assumptions. But I'm hoping that since we're all stuck together, they'll eventually see past that. I want people to see the real me."

During the height of my conflict with Yoona, I would have snorted at this quote. Now that I know what it means to her, I feel a pang. I was scared of her back then. I'm not scared of her anymore. When I look at her, I feel like I'm looking at an old friend.

We may have met just a little over five weeks ago, but we've been through so much that it feels like five years.

When we're done with the clip show, Carrie thanks us all for our hard work.

"This is going to be the biggest season in the history of the show. I'm so proud of each and every one of you. What we've done here is truly remarkable. The fans of this show will remember this season forever."

At the end of her speech, she looks at me, eyes shining, like I'm her favorite child, the one who made her proudest of all. Like everything that happened was just a great and terrible game, and Yoona and I took one round off of her, earning a tip of the cap. Carrie may not have gotten her pitch-perfect ending, but in the end, she still got what she wanted. A chill runs down my spine. She and I are the same, she said. We both want more. I didn't go all the way down the road she was leading me on; I managed to turn back before we reached the end. But I went far enough to understand that in a way, she was right.

After our final dinner in the house, Chris and Mari gather us all in the living room to make an announcement.

"Chris and I have a song we'd like to perform for you," Mari says. "It was inspired by the time we've spent here together. It was bright and vivid as we lived through it, but as it recedes into the past, the feelings will fade. We'll have our memories, of course, and we'll treasure them, but they won't tell the real story of what happened here."

I consider pointing out that we'll also have eight hour-long episodes of a TV show to help jog our memories, but I decide to keep my mouth shut.

"Forgetting is a part of life," Mari continues. "And that's okay, but it's also sad. So this song is an acknowledgment of that sadness. It's our way of saying, 'We can't hold on to this moment forever, so while we're in it, let's not hold back.'

"Before we begin, I'd like us all to close our eyes and breathe together. Let us inhabit this moment as fully as we can, filling our hearts with the vibrating potential of *the thing that has not yet ended*."

Mari leads us as we breathe in . . . and out . . . in . . . and out . . .

I think about how in a couple of days, I'll be back home in Moline, and my life in this house, with these people, will be over as I know it. I'm not sad, per se; this sojourn away from the familiar has always felt temporary. But I do get the sense that once I'm back to my normal life, a part of me will ache for the highs and lows of the Hotel California.

Chris has a guitar; he begins to strum out soft, plaintive chords. Mari starts to sing.

Breathless days spent living the lie
Breathless nights spent chasing the high
You said you wished that you could disappear
I said baby, anywhere but here
We shot out of the night down Rodeo Drive
I'll do anything that makes me feel alive

It's not a regular song, with a chorus and verses and a bridge. Instead, Chris is playing chords and seemingly switching whenever he wants. Then Mari follows with her lyrics, cycling through these sad couplets according to her mood. Eventually, Chris plays a minor chord that takes the song in a new direction, and Mari starts to sing, *I'm still here, I'm still here, I'm still here.* Chris keeps playing faster and faster, and Mari goes along until she's just chanting *Here, here, here, here, here.* Finally, Chris slams down three final chords, and the song ends. When he looks up from the guitar, he's crying.

At first I find it kind of funny, but before I know it the rest of us are crying, too. The song is over. All of this is coming to an end.

It's strange to think that while Yoona and I were battling it out, Chris and Mari were living on their own separate track. I've long since filed them away in my mind as a completed storyline, immune to the drama and uncertainty that afflicted the rest of us. Aside from the brief views into Mari's sensuous interior world that I got from asking for her advice, I've kept myself at a distance from the two of them. But they were still moving forward, writing songs, figuring out how to deal with the fact that our group is breaking apart. I wonder about all the things about the two of them that I've missed.

It's too late to make up for lost time with those two. But there's someone else I need to talk to, so that I don't have to leave with the burden of words left unsaid.

YOONA

AFTER CHRIS AND MARI SING THEIR SONG, SABINE TAPS ME ON
the shoulder.

"Hey. Can we talk?"

I raise an eyebrow. "Alone?"

"In the game room," she says. "For old times' sake."

I shrug. "Why not?"

The two of us head downstairs. I sprawl out onto the couch,
and Sabine sits on the floor in front of me.

"Our last memory of being in the house together," I say. "Make
it count. I'll give you a hug at the end either way, but you'll know
whether or not you've earned it."

Sabine takes a deep breath. "I thought that being on this show
would help me discover a better side of myself. But I feel like all I
discovered is that I'm a bad person. I never thought that was possible, because I was on the outside anyways, so no one noticed the
things I did. But this whole time, I've been judging people. Like
there's a hierarchy, and all I want to do is get up to the top."

"It's not your fault. You didn't think like that on purpose; Carrie made you do it. It's like you said: she had the data and algorithms on you. She knew exactly what to say."

"It wasn't all Carrie. There's a reason she chose me. The whole time I was trying to take you down, I never thought, *What if I'm hurting her?* Doesn't that show that inside myself, I'm missing some important piece?"

"But you fixed it," I say. "If you're going to try to rake yourself over like this, you have to give yourself some credit, too. It's only fair."

Sabine shakes her head. "I wish we'd spent less time fighting and more time being friends. Now we're finally on the same page, and the time's up."

"That's life. It comes at you super fast, and you don't get a do-over."

"That's why I feel so bad!" Sabine throws up her hands. I laugh. She looks at me, eyes wide, but after a moment she starts to laugh, too.

"It's not funny, though!" she protests.

"It's not," I say, still chuckling. "But you're getting so stressed out, and the thing is, we won. In the end, you didn't really hurt anybody. In a way, all of this brought us together. Look at us now! Would we even be friends if we hadn't tried to destroy each other's reputations on TV first?

"Sabine, you're not allowed to remember this summer as a series of embarrassing mistakes. We had a lot of fun together. The person you feel bad about is me, and I happen to really like you. If you still think there's something missing, you'll find it. I believe in you."

"You're incredible, Yoona," Sabine says. "The whole time I was trying to fight with you, you were trying to be nice. You should hate me, but you don't."

"Yeah, I'm pretty proud of myself for that." I wink. "I could have done better, too. I don't think I'm that good at being nice yet. I'm working on it."

"I see you, Yoona."

Sabine says this quietly, abruptly. I look at her; her eyes are suddenly bright, determined. Like she's been building up her courage for what she's about to say.

"People like me make assumptions about you. It seems like your life would be easy and perfect. But that's not fair. You have to deal with being judged and put in a box, too."

I smile. It's nice to have someone going easy on me for once.

"I like the way you come off. It's cool that you're so confident, and cool, and in control. I felt scared of you because I was insecure. But I still always looked up to you for that. I hope you stay that way. You shouldn't have to change yourself to get people like me to like you."

I'm worried that I might cry, so I slide off the couch and drop down to the floor beside Sabine, where she can't see.

"See? I told you. You're nice, too," I say. Sabine lets out a small laugh, but I hope she believes me.

I take a deep breath. "The thing is, though, I still *want* people to like me."

It's a relief to finally say these words. I can't control how people react to me, but I can bite back the anger and admit how I feel, what I want. It's hard; it takes a leap.

But with Sabine, it doesn't feel like a leap. She understands. We see each other now.

"About that hug," I say.

"About that hug."

She pulls me in, and I squeeze tight. I let go of my inhibitions and lose myself in the warm happiness of holding on to someone else, someone I care about. *The thing that has not yet ended.* We're leaving soon, but for now, we're still right here.

SABINE

"DEEP BREATHS, SABINE. DON'T BE SCARED."

I try taking a deep breath, but my stomach still feels queasy. I'm in the back seat of Em's car, steeling myself for the day ahead. The first day of my senior year of high school.

"You've gotten through three years at this place already. What else can they do to you?"

"I don't know. That's what I'm worried about."

Em drums her fingers on the steering wheel. "Okay, I'll be totally honest with you, sweetheart: I think you're being a little dramatic. The show isn't even out yet. I'm ninety-nine percent sure no one knows about it. Or cares."

I glare at her in the rearview mirror. "What happened to the soft and supportive approach?" I ask. "The trailer came out last night. *Hotel California* is under the 'coming soon' section of the website. My face is there. I checked this morning."

"Oh, forgive me, then. I'm sure it's the talk of the town."

After I get over my mini-meltdown, the two of us head into

the school building together. My head is on a swivel, searching the hallways for people whispering and pointing at "the girl who's going to be on TV." But I quickly find that Em is right. No one notices me. Here in Moline, I'm still just regular old Sabine; at least for now.

My first class is AP US History. I make Em walk me all the way to the door, even though she's rolling her eyes the whole time. Because of the extra time we spent in the car, I'm late, and most of the desks are already claimed. I spot an open seat near the front of the classroom and take a step toward it before I realize: it's next to Ricky Lee. My heart sinks. We're going to be the Asian section: two nerds sitting at the front of the class, where everyone can see us.

You judge people. That's who you are.

I still do this. There's a layer of ugly reflexes etched into my brain. The summer may have helped me work through a few of them, but now that I'm back at school, the whole suite of complexes is going to slowly reveal itself.

Nothing to do but reverse them, one by one.

I put my bag down at the desk next to Ricky's.

"Mind if I sit here?"

Ricky shrugs. "Sure."

"Thanks."

"You were on *Hotel California*," Ricky says as I'm taking out my notebook.

So at least someone has heard of it.

I smile tentatively. "Yeah. Did you watch it?"

"My sister told me about it. I don't really watch reality shows. It's cool that you were on TV, though. Bet that'll look good on college apps."

"That's the dream."

"Beats going to robotics camp like the rest of us chumps. How did you talk your parents into letting you do it?"

I chuckle. "It took a lot of convincing. All in all, I'm not sure I shouldn't have just gone to robotics camp. Would have been a lot less traumatizing."

Ricky grins. "Well, at least you got to rep for us Midwest Asians. Quad Cities!"

"Rep it 'til I die."

At lunch, Em and I take our usual seats at the edge of the cafeteria. Everything feels normal.

"See, I told you," Em says. "When the actual episodes start coming out, then you can worry. Lots of people will probably see that. And if they only check out the first few episodes and give up, they won't even see your big redemption moment. You'll just be the villain."

"Dude!"

Em cackles. "Relax, it's a joke. Whatever happens, just play it cool. Keep up an air of mystery. By winter break, this will all be a weird memory that you can look back on and laugh about."

"I don't think I'm going to be laughing. Unless it's the way you laugh at your middle school yearbook photos. Forced and hollow, masking tragedy."

"You had a couple of rough moments on TV. So what? If anyone gives you shit about it, you can clap right back. No one else here is innocent, as far as I'm concerned. Look at the football team, for example."

"What did they do?"

"Well, think of all the pointless physical violence they're inflicting on each other, just for their own entertainment. Barbaric!"

"I don't think that's the same."

I look around at the cafeteria, studying the different groups of people. There's the table of theater and a cappella kids, who I've always envied for their nonthreatening, herbivorous coolness; the people who play sports, who I mentally subdivide into smart athletes and airheaded jocks; and the table of nerds, which I have always desperately feared falling into. Ricky is there, eating kimbap. I feel a faint pang as I realize that if I had gotten to know him earlier, I could have won my housemates a bunch of money.

"Carrie saw right through me from the beginning," I say. "I thought I was cast to be the innocent one from the Midwest, but she knew all of the things that my brain does. How I subconsciously fit everyone into this twisted social pyramid. And even though I think it's unfair, I still buy into it. I want to be on the top, and everyone else is either against me or . . . you know. Below me."

I have to force out the final two words, and they leave a bad taste in my mouth.

"It's that bad, huh?"

"You don't think so?"

Em rubs her chin. "I mean, that's one way of looking at it. That's what both of us are like. And yeah, it's bad, but sue us, we're not perfect. That's how we *survived* the last three years of high school. It's not like we hurt anyone. We might have thought some bad thoughts here and there, but you don't have to feel guilty about it. They're just thoughts! Thoughts are a free zone."

"I want to find a way to atone for it. Some way of saying, *Sorry, let's make up*, even if it's just for my own sake."

Em surveys the crowd, looking skeptical. "And where are you going to find that?"

I smile ruefully. "I don't know."

YOONA

"DID YOU HEAR THAT MAGGIE CHO ALREADY COMMITTED TO Princeton? For the swim team! If I'd known you could get into Princeton for the swim team, I would have made you take lessons." My mom looks at me sternly, as if to ask why I never told her about this possibility.

It's too early for this. I'm still jet-lagged from being in California. Waking up to go to church is one thing, but dragging myself onto the subway when my body still thinks it's six a.m. is another.

"Mom, if I have to play a sport to get into college, I'd rather not go. I don't even want to *apply* to Columbia. They make you pass a swim test to graduate."

"Ah, but Maggie got in for diving. You barely even have to swim. Just jump into the pool. How hard can it be?"

I shake my head. "Well, it's a little late for that."

The train rumbles to a stop at Union Square, our stop. We

324

climb the stairs out of the station and step into the middle of a farmers market.

"Better to focus on school, anyways," my mom continues. "Sports can help you get in, but they don't help you in the long run. Too much time away from studying. Plus, I bet Maggie's ears are full of water."

"I'm sure she'll be perfectly fine."

I can see the gears of her mom brain turning. Last winter, she was stink-eyeing Jessica Um for getting into Harvard. In a few months, Maggie will be ripe for her ire.

"What are you thinking about, Mom?"

"Thinking about next year. You'll be on your own."

"Worried that you'll miss me?"

"I *hope* I miss you. I won't miss you if you get kicked out and you come right back home! Remember what I told you: don't cheat, and don't sell drugs."

"Got it, thanks for the reminder."

My mom will never say, *I miss you.* Next year, when I'm gone, she'll be riding the subway by herself. Maybe she'll think about me. But if I call her, she'll keep all the emotions locked inside of her head; instead she'll share gossip to show why I still have to be vigilant, why the college could kick me out at any moment.

"Mom, what kind of person do you think I am?"

"Hm? What kind of question is that?"

"Am I bad? Not nice enough?"

My mom frowns in confusion. "Bad? I can't call you bad. You came out of me."

"But you're always warning me to stay out of trouble. Like it's *personal*. Like that time I got into a fight with Winnie Jung."

"Oh, Winnie. I remember her. Nice girl. What happened with her again?"

I remind her about the Coca-Cola hair treatment. To my surprise, she laughs.

"Oh yeah! That was funny. It was hard to keep a straight face when I was supposed to be scolding you. Poor Winnie—she really didn't like having sticky hair."

Once we're out of the market, the streets are quieter. We walk under the shadows of the trees, dodging the morning sun.

"Did you ever wish your daughter wasn't such a troublemaker?"

My mom shakes her head. "I can't wish for something like that."

"But you said I made you look bad. Like you were ashamed."

"Who said 'ashamed'? I said 'look bad.' I want to look good. I want the other church ladies to talk about how nice you are, compare you to their daughters, instead of asking things like, *Is Bae Yoona turning out okay? Does she still make trouble?*

"When I was little, I was like you. Getting in trouble, getting yelled at. Sometimes the teacher hit me. It made me so frustrated. Like I couldn't control myself. I don't want you to feel like that. So I try to help you, if I can. Maybe I push too hard. But at least it's coming from me, and not someone else."

I raise an eyebrow. My mom is never this candid. Coming from her, this admission feels downright sentimental. I steal a sidelong glance at her, looking for a nostalgic smile, maybe some wetness in her eyes. Her expression is the same as ever, though—lips pursed together, brow creased with concentration.

"But you don't listen," she adds, as if to balance things out.

I laugh. "Well, don't give up on me just yet."

"I can't give up. I only have one daughter. If I don't do it to you, who else would I do it to?"

When we get to church, I inhale the familiar woody scent of the stuffy church building. My mom and I sit in an empty pew in the middle of the room. Now that I'm back, this place seems somehow smaller than it ever has before. But I know it's the same; the change is in me. Even though I'll still be coming here every weekend for the next year, I already feel like I'm leaving this place.

After the sermon and the hymns, the whole room stands up for some good old-fashioned postchurch socializing. Maggie Cho is busy today; a line has formed in front of her, each parent dragging a kid by the hand to come and congratulate the girl who got into Princeton. I try to catch her eye, give her an ironic smile, like *There they go!* But she doesn't notice.

Meanwhile, at the back of the room, I see Jessica Um. The contrast is jarring. A year ago, she was in Maggie's position, awkwardly accepting an expensive gift from my mom. Now she's been kicked out of paradise, and she's sitting in a pew by herself. I glance around, but I don't see Mrs. Um anywhere.

My mom has a spot at the back of the congratulate-Maggie line, so I take the time to slide into a seat beside Jessica.

"Hi. How have you been? I haven't seen you in so long!"

Jessica smiles and pulls me in for a light hug. It feels like a very older-sister, college-student thing to do. I doubt she would have hugged me hello back when we were still both in high school, getting compared to each other. But now that Jessica is in college, it's like the dynamic has shifted.

"Hey, Yoona. I'm okay. My mom told me you're going to be on TV."

"Is she here?"

"She didn't want to come. She didn't want me to come, either. But I like coming to church. I used to always complain about it, but once I went off to school, I started to miss it."

At the mention of school, I have to remind myself: Don't ask about Harvard. Maybe she doesn't want to talk about it. But Jessica must read the curiosity in my face, because she adds, "I'm sure you heard what happened."

I guess she's okay with talking about it. "Yeah. Are you doing all right?"

"I'm fine. I'm working at a coffee shop, planning to take some classes at community college. If I'm lucky, Harvard might let me go back next year."

"That's good. Sounds like things will work out."

"You might not believe me, but I feel better now than I have in years. All through high school, I was afraid that something bad was going to happen to me. Even after I got in. Now the worst possible thing has happened, and it's kind of a relief."

"Because of your parents? Did they let up on you?"

"They were really mad for a while, but since they got over it they've been supportive. But it's not about them. It's about me. I needed to learn not to judge myself based on how perfect I can be. At school, I was having panic attacks before my exams. I was so worried about not getting As, about not standing out. Eventually, it becomes impossible to keep up."

"Yeah, geez. I wonder where you got that from," I say, tilting my head toward the Maggie Cho fan club.

Jessica shakes her head knowingly. "I wish we all talked more when I was still in high school. I think about us church kids a lot. We went through a lot of the same experiences, but our parents always made it into a competition. So we never got to bond over it as much as we could have. My mom used to always gossip about your mom. Sorry."

"No worries, my mom did the same thing about yours. Does. She still does. Sorry." We both laugh.

"I guess that's the way things are. Maybe when we're all graduated and living on our own, then we'll all come back together and be friends." Jessica smiles. "Thanks for checking in on me. It was nice to see you, Yoona. Good luck with everything."

After she's gone, I feel a curious sense of yearning. It's like she said, we never really got to know each other; we were primed to push each other away. But now I wish we had; I want to know how she's feeling, how she's dealing with her situation. Everyone is working through something: some set of expectations, some way of being judged. Once you know that about someone, it's impossible to write them off.

When my mom is done talking to Maggie, we get ready to leave the church.

"Do you want to stay out? We can go have ice cream, or go shopping," she says.

"No, let's go home."

"Already? It's a nice day, not too hot. We should enjoy it."

"If we go now, we can make it home by eleven. That's midnight in Korea, right?"

My mom does the calculations in her head. "Yes, that's right."

"So Appa should still be up. I want to give him a call."

My mom looks incredulous. "Call him? Why?"

"To talk to him. Ask him how he's doing, tell him about what's going on over here. Tell him I miss him. Why do you look so surprised? You're the one who's always trying to get me to say that."

"Yes, that's true." My mom frowns, like this is some sort of trick. "But what changed?"

I shrug. "You're very persistent, Umma. I guess you finally wore me down. What's with the skepticism? Shouldn't you be happy?"

"I *am* happy. All right, let's go."

On the way back to Union Square, I could swear my mom is pushing the pace, like she wants to get home before I change my mind.

What's going to happen when I call him? My mom says he'll be happy, but I doubt that he'll show it. He'll probably tell me that my Korean sounds less and less fluent, or think of some lecture off the top of his head. Even if I come in hot with the *I miss you*, or even *I love you*, I can't imagine him saying it back.

But that's okay. We may be far apart, but at least we have time. Wherever we end the call today, that's where we'll pick up next Sunday, again and again, retracing all the distance that we've traveled away from each other since he left. And that's okay.

Because if there's one thing I've learned this summer, it's that just because someone puts their guard up around you, it doesn't mean that you have to respond in kind. Behind that prickly exterior could be a person just as soft and scared as you are. And if you open your arms wide, show that you come in peace, then you might discover that there's no need to be afraid, that all along, you were on the same side.

SABINE

A FEW WEEKS INTO THE SCHOOL YEAR, I'M BACK IN MY USUAL
rhythm. I'm not worried about hurting anyone here, because I
don't get involved in drama the way I did at the house. Em and I
sit back, watch, and evaluate, and that's it. I remember what it feels
like now. Even after the show comes out, I'm not worried. A few
people ask me about it, but no one takes it too seriously. The life
that we lived on the show barely registers here.

Yoona and I make plans to catch up over video chat, but she
bails on one date with a migraine, and I bail on another for a last-
minute video call with my grandparents. After that, the school
year and college apps get busy, and it's harder and harder to find
the time.

When the episodes drop, our cast group chat lights up for
a couple days. We recount some of our favorite memories, and
already they don't feel real. Southern California is a distant play-
ground, home to colorful fantasies whose importance I can't
quite believe in now that I've left. Moline is prom queens, and

homecoming kings, and sunsets by the river. It's quieter, smaller, but more solid. It's home.

In mid-September, Em and I find ourselves under the angry glare of the afternoon sun, sitting on folding chairs in a trailer pulled by a Ford truck, sweating onto the chin rests of our violas, for that most solemn of Moline High traditions—the homecoming parade.

"Can I just say again how messed up it is that the orchestra has to be a part of this?" I whisper to Em during a break between our scratchy renditions of "Kashmir" by Led Zeppelin. "Seriously, what do string instruments have to do with football?"

"Just be thankful that they finally let us on the truck this year," Em whispers back. We both glance at the poor violins, who are on foot. Closest to me, Mindy Appel-Zeller looks like she's about to keel over from heat exhaustion. Then we pass by a group of people who I can only assume are her family, because they scream, "Mindy! Mindy! Over here! Hey, Mindy!" At the sound of her name, Mindy seems to catch a second wind, and when we start up again, she's bravely bowing out the melody as if our team's entire season depends on it. Inspirational.

Yoona and I finally made plans to video-chat again. Tonight, during the homecoming football game, we'll be reminiscing about the Palm Springs Hedge Maze. It's nice to have something to look forward to, an excuse for not being at the game with everyone else.

Directly behind us, the JV football boys are riding in the back of a monstrous military transport vehicle, wearing jerseys and full pads, throwing candy bars and bags of chips into the crowd. Ahead of us are the cheerleaders, clapping and shaking pom-poms. When we get to the first big intersection, in front of the South Asian grocery and the hair-braiding salon, the parade halts so that the cheerleaders can do a routine.

"I think they've gotten better," I say. "I've never seen them throw someone like that before."

"That, or the statutory period on the last injury lawsuit ran out," Em says dryly.

"Necessary sacrifices to appease the football gods. We're going to get a ton of touchdowns today."

"So many touchdowns."

The one good thing about Homecoming Parade is that it's short. We hit the end of the route, the truck turns into a gas station parking lot, and we're released from our parade duties after just forty-five minutes. The rest of the orchestra chatters excitedly about the game, how well our defense has been playing. As for me and Em, we escape from the scene and drive off for a homecoming tradition of our own.

We go to La Leonessa in Davenport for gigantic calzones, and after stuffing our faces, we drive down to the river to relax in the park until night falls and the Centennial Bridge is illuminated. It's been our way of greeting the new school year ever since we were freshmen. I still remember the magic of the first time:

painfully pedaling my bike because my stomach was so close to exploding, then getting to the river, seeing the bridge lights fill up the night sky.

Only this time, it's the last time. One more year to get through. We sometimes joke about leaving Moline, moving to whatever city will take us. Soon it will all come true. The two of us will have made it out, whatever that means.

"Hey, Em," I ask, as the sun begins to set, "are you glad you're from Moline?"

Em rubs her chin.

"I don't know," she says. "Growing up here kind of sucked. But I can't blame it all on the town. Most of my time here was middle school and high school, and both of those things just kind of suck."

"But don't you wonder who you would have been if you grew up somewhere different? Like, look at us now. Everyone's at homecoming, and we're here. And I'd rather be here than at homecoming, but what if instead of homecoming, the big thing at our school was something that was more for us?"

"I guess so. But we're not doing so bad over here. Would it make that much difference if we also got to be, like, cheerleaders, or quarterbacks?"

"We wouldn't have been cheerleaders or quarterbacks, though," I say. "We would have been something else, along with the rest of the people at our school. The point is, we'd be in the middle of things, instead of just watching."

"At least you got to watch with me." Em throws an arm around me and cheeses broadly. I wrap my hands around her waist and squeeze.

The sun has set, and the sky is darkening rapidly. Lights blink to life on both sides of the river, and their reflections shimmer in the water. When the bridge lights go on, setting the sky aglow, I gasp. Even though this is a familiar scene for us, each time still feels like the first time.

We don't have long to enjoy it. The park closes at sundown, and in the distance I already spot the headlights of the park staff's golf cart. They're making the rounds now, gently kicking people out.

"Take a good last look, Sabine," Em says.

So I do.

We walk back to the parking lot, climb into Em's car. The finality of this ending is dawning on me: even if we were to come back here on another night, it wouldn't feel the same. A chapter in our lives is now definitively closed.

I have my call with Yoona to look forward to, but somehow it doesn't feel right to go home just yet. I want to do something more, something special to cap off the night. And I feel strangely sure about what that something is supposed to be.

"Em, it's only seven. The homecoming football game should be starting. Wanna go?"

Em whips her head toward me, wearing a look of disdain. "Is that a trick question?"

"No, I'm being serious. Why not?"

"Why not?" Em snorts. "Same reason why I don't jump into the gibbon exhibit at the zoo. Because I don't want to suddenly find myself surrounded by screaming, feces-throwing primates."

"Come on, it's our senior year. High school's practically over. Just this one time, we can be with the rest of our class."

"Is this because of what happened on the show? You want to prove that you've changed by finally going to a football game? Sabine, I'm all for personal growth, but this is *not* what I had in mind."

"We've never been. It's our last chance. I know we gave up on this kind of thing a while ago, but what if we give it one last try?"

I put on my puppy-dog face and stare sweetly at Em. She rolls her eyes.

"When we get there, and you realize what a terrible idea this is, just remember that you *chose* this."

I send Yoona another text: Sorry, but something came up that I know I have to do. I'll make it up to you, I promise. I know that our story is not over yet, that we'll continue it eventually. But not tonight.

Em and I don't have any of our Moline High School gear on hand, so we put on our sweaty orchestra shirts. They're not even the right color—plain white, not our school's maroon—but at least they say *Moline* on the front.

When we get to the field, the stands are packed with our classmates. Em and I squint under the glare of the stadium lights until we spot an empty section in the first row of the bleachers. The roar of the crowd is intimidating, and Em shoots me a dubious look.

I know we must stick out. In a sea of our classmates, clapping and cheering and looking perfectly at home, we're adrift, searching for something to cling to. I could have been home by now, planted on my couch, alone but comfortable.

I take Em's hand and pull her into the stands. Yes, this is the first time either of us has come remotely close to a high school football game. But no one can say that we don't belong here.

Sitting in the same row as the two of us is Ricky Lee, who's alone, writing in a spiral-bound notebook.

"Are you here by yourself?" I ask, pointing to the empty seats.

"Yeah," Ricky says casually. Then, as if he's remembering that being alone is supposed to be sad, he explains, "I'm writing about the game for the school paper."

"Mind if we join you?"

"Sure. But just so you know, I'm going to be paying close attention to the game."

"Us too," Em says cheerily. "We love football!"

I've half watched enough Bears games that football isn't a totally unfamiliar phenomenon to me, but Em and I don't know the players, or the chants; we're not even totally clear on the rules. As we watch, we're not following the game so much as we are trying to follow the rest of the crowd, cheering and booing approximately when they do.

Meanwhile, Ricky seems to be *really* into football. He watches the game, gripping his knees so hard that his knuckles turn white. Although he's not cheering along with the rest of the crowd, every few seconds he lets out an esoteric plea toward the field.

"Ah, come on ref, that's PI!"

"Shift! Shift! See the safety coming across!"

"Open your eyes, Twelve, you've got your best receiver in man coverage!"

Then he opens his notebook and scribbles furiously, no doubt excoriating his classmates' inability to recognize the situations unfolding right before their eyes.

"Wow, you're really into football, Ricky," I say.

"Yeah. Even high school games. I have a serious addiction," he replies.

I scan the bleachers to look at my classmates. I'm struck by how *many* of us there are, and how rare it is to be seeing all of us at once. There are so many faces, and I know the name of just about every one.

"Oh! Sabine!" Em elbows me and points out the wave starting at the other end of the bleachers; we raise our arms up just in time to take part. On the next play, one of our players catches a long pass and tumbles into the end zone for a touchdown. The crowd goes wild. Em and I yell our heads off—"Mo-LINE! Rep it! 'Til! I! DIE!"—and exchange high fives with Ricky.

"That was actually really exciting," Em says. "I'm still only enjoying this ironically, though."

It's the second quarter, and we're down by three points. As the other team marches down the field, Ricky berates our team's coaches for the unpardonable sin of "obnoxiously sticking to cover two even though the tight end is killing us over the middle."

"You tell 'em, Ricky," Em says.

"What should we be doing instead?" I ask.

Ricky blinks, raises an eyebrow, as if he's unsure of my intentions. I worry for a second that he thinks I'm making fun of him. But then I realize, to my relief, that he's just thinking over his answer.

"Well, our linebackers are pretty slow, so I think a zone is still the right idea. I'd probably line up in cover two, but then bring the free safety in to cover the middle of the field. Cover one robber."

I don't understand a word of it, but I've heard what I needed to hear. I whisper into Em's ear, and then I count us in to start up a cheer.

"Robber! Robber! Robber!"

Em and I scream ourselves hoarse. Perhaps because we're losing, the home crowd is mostly silent, and everyone can hear us chanting. Out of the corner of my eye, I can see the people around us turning and giving us funny looks. But then Ricky stands up next to me, joins us in chanting "Robber!" and I forget about everyone else.

One of the players on our sideline spots us and gives us a puzzled look. Then he smiles, waves, and cheerfully flexes his bicep. I'm confused, until I recognize the boy looking at us. It's Robert

Wishnowski. He must think we're calling his name. Em and I dissolve into a fit of laughter.

"Think they got the message about the robbers?" I ask Ricky.

"Doubt it. These are just high school players. You can't expect them to execute adjustments on the fly like they do in the pros," Ricky says sagely, as if he isn't a high schooler himself.

On the next play, the other team throws a deep pass. The ball is tipped off of a receiver's hands and falls to one of our players for an interception. The crowd roars louder and louder as our player breaks tackles, spins away from danger, and stiff-arms the opposing quarterback. When he gets into the end zone, Ricky grabs me by the arm and starts shaking me, shouting his head off. Then he breaks off, embarrassed, and sits down to write in his notebook.

"Do you like football yet?" I ask Em.

"Not even a little bit."

"But we're winning! And it's because of the two of us!"

Em raises an eyebrow. "Because we yelled 'robber'? You think that helped?"

"Maybe not directly. But haven't you heard of the butterfly effect?"

Lauren Moody and Kiara Adams lean over from the row behind us for high fives, even though we've never spoken before. From there, it's a chain reaction: we're stretching two rows back, claiming every high five within reach.

When we sit down again, I put an arm around Em. Then I look at Ricky, frowning at his notebook, and I put an arm around him, too. I take a look around at the crowd, these people I've grown up with, who I've watched, skirted around, and occasionally judged. A surge of affection wells up out of an obscure part of my heart.

Suddenly, it's like a veil has dropped away, a veil that I've had over my eyes for half my life. Football games, cool kids, being associated with Ricky Lee—I've been afraid of these things for so long. But now, through some strange alchemy of the crowd, the touchdown, the celebration, I feel like I can actually *see* the people in front of me. Behind the labels, the assumptions, the narratives that we hold in our heads, we're all the same flesh and bones and beating hearts.

Sometimes we do each other wrong. But that doesn't mean that we're all in some rat race, some climb to the top. It doesn't mean that some of us are on the bottom, either. We're each of us travelers who find ourselves on the same path.

And though the night is dark, and the shadowy shapes around you may appear to be monsters, when you reach out, you find people who are not so different from yourself. You walk together for a while, and the journey feels a little safer. You realize that you don't have to go it alone.

Sometimes, if you're lucky, you even find a friend.

ACKNOWLEDGMENTS

FIRST AND FOREMOST, THANK YOU, DEAR READER, FOR TAKING the time to read this book.

Thank you to my agent, Stephanie Kim, for reading a very early, very different version of this book and seeing how much better it could be. Adding Yoona as a second POV was such a good idea! And this killer title was all you. I'm grateful that we get to be a part of each other's journeys in this industry. Thanks also to Veronica Grijalva—your welcome note was so unexpected and lovely, and your suggestions for the book were really helpful, too. To the rest of the team at New Leaf—Patrice Caldwell, Trinica Sampson, Victoria Hendersen, and many more—thanks for having my back from start to finish.

Thank you to my editor, Jen Ung. Your enthusiasm and positivity gave me the confidence to make big revisions, even when I wasn't sure I could pull them off. I'm really happy about all of the ways this book changed and grew while we worked on it together. You made the whole process fun. And thanks to the rest of the team at Quill Tree Books who read and worked on this book: Celina Sun, Rosemary Brosnan, Allison Weintraub, Janet Rosenberg, Shona McCarthy, James Neel, Suzanne Murphy, Jean McGinley, Lisa Calcasola, Patty Rosati, Andrea Pappenheimer, Tara Feehan, Laura Raps, and many more.

Thanks to Jacqueline Li for this beautiful cover illustration, and Kathy Lam for the design. Thanks to Stephanie Yang for providing an authenticity read. Your note was so kind!

Thanks to all of my friends who read early drafts of this book and offered feedback: Juliet Lubwama, Yani Lu, Brian Jin, Ivey Choi, Carolyn Huynh, and Bharat Chandar.

Thank you to my parents for raising me to love books.

Thanks to Leslie Teng. You're the best.

Thank you to my high school teachers: Ms. Bosch, Ms. Creney, Mr. Gardner, Mr. Aramati, Ms. Pan, Mr. Olsen, and so many more. I know I was annoying at times, but I loved being in your classrooms. Special thanks to Liz Crowell, my sophomore English teacher. On the last day of the school year, you told me that you looked forward to reading my book someday. I think about that memory all the time. Thank you for teaching me how to write.